AF004898

THE LIBRARY OF TRAUMATIC MEMORY

ALSO BY NEIL JORDAN

Amnesiac
The Well of Saint Nobody
The Ballad of Lord Edward and Citizen Small
Carnivalesque
The Drowned Detective
Mistaken
Shade
Sunrise with Sea Monster
The Dream of a Beast
The Past
Night in Tunisia

NEIL JORDAN

THE LIBRARY OF TRAUMATIC MEMORY

An Ad Astra Book

First published in the UK in 2026 by Head of Zeus,
part of Bloomsbury Publishing Plc

Copyright © Neil Jordan, 2026

The moral right of Neil Jordan to be identified as the author of this work has been asserted in accordance with the Copyright, Designs and Patents Act of 1988.

All rights reserved. No part of this publication may be: i) reproduced or transmitted in any form, electronic or mechanical, including photocopying, recording or by means of any information storage or retrieval system without prior permission in writing from the publishers; or ii) used or reproduced in any way for the training, development or operation of artificial intelligence (AI) technologies, including generative AI technologies. The rights holders expressly reserve this publication from the text and data mining exception as per Article 4(3) of the Digital Single Market Directive (EU) 2019/790.

This is a work of fiction. All characters, organizations, and events portrayed in this novel are either products of the author's imagination or are used fictitiously.

9 7 5 3 1 2 4 6 8

A catalogue record for this book is available from the British Library.

SLEIGH RIDE
Music by LEROY ANDERSON Words by MITCHELL PARISH
© 1948, 1950 (Copyrights Renewed) WOODBURY MUSIC COMPANY,
LLC and EMI MILLS MUSIC, INC.
Worldwide Print Rights Administered by ALFRED MUSIC
All Rights Reserved
Used by Permission of ALFRED MUSIC

ISBN (HB): 9781035923298; ISBN (XTPB): 9781035920747
ISBN (EBOOK): 9781035923304

Cover design: Jessie Price
Map design: Jamie Whyte
Typeset by Lumina Datamatics Ltd

Printed and bound in Great Britain by Clays Ltd, Elcograf S.p.A.

Bloomsbury Publishing Plc
50 Bedford Square, London, WC1B 3DP, UK
Bloomsbury Publishing Ireland Limited,
29 Earlsfort Terrace, Dublin 2, D02 AY28, Ireland

HEAD OF ZEUS LTD
5–8 Hardwick Street
London, EC1R 4RG

To find out more about our authors and books
visit www.headofzeus.com
For product safety related questions contact productsafety@bloomsbury.com

For Dashiel, the first reader.

PART ONE

NOW

He had this habit that always irritated her when she was alive. Of whistling backwards, with indrawn breath, an inhaled tune, always one of those ancient ones, 'Be my Baby', 'Baby Love', 'Bad Romance', 'Back in the USA'. And that was just the Bs. He was a librarian, after all. And it made him wonder what had happened to the USA when it became the USAI. Where had it gone? Like snow, it just became a memory. Or a false memory. So many of the memories he had to file involved this background doo-wop of harmonised voices, the heartbreaking twang of guitars and harmonicas, the vroom of an exhaust-pipe from a Harley Davidson. Could it all have vanished so completely? Or had it ever existed? Maybe it was a subset of a subset of apparent memories, constructed just to sell you stuff. And incidentally, what had happened to babies. Maybe they were imaginary too, since they hadn't been much in evidence either lately.

So, he was whistling when he was cycling from the rundown cottage by the small stony inlet, through the montbretia and hyacinth roads to the large glittering structure that seemed to grow like a titanium prosthesis out of the old Huxley mansion. One of those tunes she loved. 'Sleigh Ride'. And he hadn't got a Harley, he hadn't got a sleigh, there was no snow, if there ever had been. He was on a bicycle and there was wind in his face. Because he cycled to work most days. Wore his high-viz jacket, of course, with the backpack that Isolde had bought him, emblazoned with a luminous yellow Z on its back pocket. Like the white stripe on the back of a fox. Although he hadn't seen a fox for a long time, either. Better not to ask why. Because he wasn't like the fox that knew many things, more like the tortoise, who knew one big thing and that big thing was to keep his mouth shut, no matter what reservations haunted him.

The Huxley mansion had been built in the days when people made things, things made of copper and metal alloy. It had been enabled by a fortune, long since vanished, or dispersed amongst the home counties of the next, larger island. There were abandoned mines on the peninsula's edge, with a seemingly pristine beach laid with the sand that came from the copper smelting plant of long ago. He had heard somewhere that arsenic was a by-product of copper smelting but did his best to keep that thought deep in the dreamscape, where reality, if it intruded, only made a transitory ripple. Yes, there were many things to keep below the fringes of consciousness, which he didn't dare to call thinking. There were many troublesome things going on in the Institute, but he was simply engaged in the filing of them, like the proverbial tortoise, moving carefully through the duties assigned him. Analysis was for others. Beyond his pay grade. But one question always troubled him, on the long, rather windblown bike-rides like today's, and that question was: why here?

There was parkland, it was true. There were the remains of a previous structure, true as well, like the carcase of a savaged deer in which other organisms could create their dwellings. There were grants as well, government grants to keep these rural hinterlands in some semblance of life. But still, the question persisted, why on earth here? Why not anywhere else on this planet, which, he had no doubt, the Huxley Institute's commercial reach spanned like no other. But perhaps, and the question would become one more that he had to suppress into that troubled dreamscape below his consciousness, maybe the planet was like this peninsula. An experiment of the Institute.

MEMBRANE

It began with a skin graft. One that could be self-applied, almost like a plastic membrane pulled over the offending wrinkles, that merged with them, smoothed them, lived within them and in the end outlasted them. The accounts of wrinkled, desiccated bodies that were buried with immaculate, almost virginal faces, stunned the medical community, led to floods of venture capital cash, multiple amendments to legislation in Dublin, and in turn to further medical developments. There were pliable, prosthetic belly buttons to enable single port surgery; artificial kidneys; penis, vulva and liver enhancements; and a heart valve that would continue pumping long after the blood had gone cold.

The medical developments were in some way enabled by the gradual collapse of farming. Piggeries up and down the peninsula were put into service as the old stinking barnyards were replaced by the glass and formaldehyde surgical experimentation stations. All in secret, initially, as the animal rights movement could prove ruinous to genuine research. But the guardrails of algorithmic entry codes, cryptographic passwords, and the tactic of decoy barnyards, where genuine animal husbandry was flamboyantly and publicly performed led to habits of diversion and feint becoming ingrained in the Institute's practice. The right hand, Christian came to realise, didn't need to know what the left was doing. But by then the Institute had grown so many multi-dimensional arms that right and left became questionable concepts.

ALCHEMY

But there was another beginning, centuries before. To do with alchemy, not algorithms.

Sir Walter Raleigh, granted whole swathes of Munster by Elizabeth, the Virgin Queen, was walking the beach of Na hAilichí (the Allihies) and noticed a peculiar green tincture to the sand beneath his feet. His alchemist's eye recognised the process of oxidisation and the possible presence of a precious metal, somewhere in the hills beyond. There was a series of rivulets tumbling down from the dark rock, and carried by them, tiny pebbles of something that, if it was not yet gold, could surely become gold. He collected them in a small purse and hid his discoveries from his host, Donal Cam O'Sullivan of Berehaven, and continued the alchemical obsession that would lead him to search out the Lost Golden City of El Dorado, on another peninsula entirely.

It was copper of course, Cu, atomic number 29, not gold, Au, atomic number 79, but that may not have prevented the rumour from spreading. To Bohemia, where it reached the ears of another Elizabethan favourite, John Dee, who shared it with another alchemist, Edward Kelley, who himself had lost his own ears to the blade of an Elizabethan executioner.

Kelley also communicated with angels and grew fluent in the Enochian language, through which he communicated the angelic instruction that they share everything, including their alchemical results, their clairvoyant 'scryer' mirrors and their wives. One or other mirror might have foreseen the result of this tripartite union. A son, the unfortunate Theodorus Trebonianus Dee. Two mirrors, two fathers, two futures. But was he the son of Kelley or of Dee? If the son of Kelley, he died in Prague before his father's death in Most, Bohemia with one scryer mirror in his hands. If the son of Dee, he followed his father back to England, into the service of William Cecil, another servant of the queen, through the ruins of Canterbury to the wild Atlantic wastes of the Allihies with the other obsidian scryer mirror in his hand. And quite another set of elements in his satchel. Potassium nitrate, charcoal and sulphur – gunpowder, with which he blew away his own life and the first hole into the copper mines of Allihies.

The blast would have been barely noticed in the carnage that was engulfing the whole peninsula. The forces of the Virgin Queen under Sir George Carew laid waste to Donal Cam's castle at Dunboy, massacred what remained of his followers on Dursey Island and thus ended the alchemical promise of the Allihies beach.

But the copper was still there, just waiting.

TIME

Time played tricks on that peninsula, as Christian would discover when he delved into the history of his ancestor, the Huxley mansion's original architect.

It whispered lies, tall tales, false memories, and maybe its inventions were necessities, given the brutal roar of the history itself. And it had lately seemed exhausted, like the Hag of Beara, whose many lives exhausted her own self. Every acorn has to drop, they said she said, and she became a craggy stone, perched over the Atlantic.

But for the moment, time was just time, and Christian had plenty of it, as he pushed his bicycle against the prevailing wind towards the harbour, the town and the Institute, dimly visible through the scudding clouds. What is it about wind? he wondered. Is there a logic to it, to the fact that when you are cycling there, it is always against you and when you are cycling home it is against you again? But maybe that was the wrong question. Maybe there was no logic to the wind. It came from the Atlantic, buffeted your face as you pushed your way towards it and buffeted your face as you pushed away again.

He made his way into the town, past the ferry that trawled its way to the nearby island, past the rows of shuttered pubs and the garages and the petrol pumps and the haberdashers that sold sou'westers and the Catholic church to his right, rising serene, gaunt and grey over its granite steps, the small, delicate and decaying Church of Ireland church to his left, and thought he might stop for a coffee.

Serendipity, the sign on the mottled glass door read, which once perhaps reflected the hopes of Martin, its proprietor, his balding pate stippled and scarred with whatever hair implants he was currently testing. Courtesy of the Institute? Christian wondered. Self-administered, he realised. The doctor would have done a better job.

Martin, he acknowledged, and didn't even need to order. Martin knew how he liked it – hot frothed milk, without sugar or chocolate.

Christian, Martin replied, and that would have to suffice for conversation, as the silver pot did its gurgling thing.

Everyone in that town was testing something, and faces and indeed figures changed so much that it was sometimes difficult to remember who was who. But Martin's jowly countenance was unmistakable under the sprouting harvest above it.

And okay, Christian realised. He wasn't himself immune to experiments. But his were secret, as yet. Or so he assumed.

He paid with a card that beeped, walked back out to where his bicycle waited, and sat for a while on the wall that abutted the Church of Ireland graveyard. The wind had abated. There were blinding passages of sunlight over the mossy gravestones and he saw the light settle, as if of its own volition, on one of them.

Montagu Cartwright, 1841–1886

Etched into the grey stone, almost obscured by moss and lichen, a triangular shape which he recognised as a compass. An inscription on the licheny stone, in undecipherable Latin.

AMPHITHEATRUM SAPIENTIAE AETERNAE

Christian, who knew no Latin, could at least decode the compass.

Montagu Cartwright, architect of far more than the Huxley mansion, was buried here. Of course he would be. He had been born on the Kerry side of the peninsula, on the Lansdowne Estate, a willing servant of the empire. He had designed parliaments in Ceylon, palaces for maharajas in Rajasthan, none of which he felt the need to visit, and even, Christian dimly remembered as he sipped his scalding coffee, churches for the worldwide Anglican Communion, of which the shuttered edifice beyond the graves could have been one. It had been repurposed as a tourist office, closed now for the winter, and perhaps forever. The congregation, such as it was, had dwindled and died. Christian remembered the story he had heard, or the tall tale, of two churches designed by the same Montagu Cartwright from his Lambeth studio for overseas parishes, one in Carlsbad, Bohemia, one in Castletown, Ireland. A mix-up at the Anglican administration in Dean's Yard, Westminster, had led to the Irish designs being sent to the Hapsburg town, the Bohemian ones to Ireland. Which could explain the vaguely Gothic curlicues and turrets of this Montagu Cartwright church. And somewhere in Bohemia was a piece of Celtic revivalism, with harp-shaped windows and a round tower.

His librarian's mind could imagine the mix-up. Both filed under C. Carlsbad, Castletown.

Two churches, each echoing the other, both in the wrong place.

Was it all, like most things in this dismal burgh, a half-remembered legend, distorted, like everything else, by the Chinese whispers of time?

Christian stepped back to get a better view.

It was cut from the same grey stone as the Catholic edifice down the street, had nothing but a vague hint of Prague, and everything about it spoke of a gentle, barely remembered Protestant past.

He finished his coffee and cycled on, past the shuttered Silver Dollar Bar.

THEN

Two hundred years earlier, almost to the day, Montagu Cartwright stood in the Castletown graveyard. There were no plinths, no shrouded urns, no epitaphs, just a set of random, rotting crosses to remember the famine dead.

Rumours of the architectural mishap had been alarming enough to set him on whatever packet he could find to Cork, on the endless, windswept journey by horse and trap from Cork to Bandon, Clonakilty, Glengarriff, into the wild peninsula he barely remembered from his childhood. And there, sure enough, beyond the permanently muddy town square, he saw the last slates being erected on the roof of the church he had designed for Carlsbad. There was a master-builder, Muck Corrigan, standing amongst the worm-eaten wooden crosses, supervising the completion. It had been a workhouse graveyard before a church was even thought of, he explained to the bemused Cartwright. But what amazed Montagu Cartwright, even more than the sight of these Gothic structures soaring over the harbour beyond, was the finish of the roof, the towers, the walls. The cornerstones cut so beautifully they could slice the hand, the perfection of those angled arches, the soaring bell-tower with the bulbous, onion-like dome housing the bell. And the roof tiles, laid in serried rows, like scales on a perfect mackerel. Here was a true craftsman, a master of balance and weight, for whom the church, as he explained to the architect, was just a secondary endeavour. His main business was the copper mine, and he would soon begin blasting its ingresses and tunnels into the hills above the Allihies beach. The mine and the mansion planned by their owner, Copper John.

Was Muck a diminutive? A corruption of Michael? Or did it refer to the browned, cracked substance that covered the hand that shook the hand of Montagu Cartwright?

Montagu Cartwright couldn't have known then that the peninsula had a moniker habit.

That he would acquire one too.

That Michael Muck Corrigan would drag the body of Montagu Compass Cartwright through a grouse moor, under the instruction of Copper John Huxley. That he would be shot by two blasts from a Purdey and tumble from the half-built staircase of his own design. That his only thought would be, as he hit the flagstones below, who would finish it now?

THE COLLAPSE OF EVERYTHING

Christian was a Cartwright like his distant ancestor with the Protestant surname. One of the few certainties left to him.

Because every other certainty had collapsed.

It would be difficult to isolate the point of the collapse. Because it wasn't like the process of entropic decay in the chemistry he studied which at least provided a measure of its own collapse.

Nothing was as it had been. If anyone could even remember how it was.

His mother, for example, who had brought him up in the same cottage he now inhabited. She had long been testing product, like selected others in the township. Profile, body shape, underarm and jaw line, eye and skin colour, even posture changed like the mutations of the Irish weather. The way the tree over bent by the September winds became that leafless stiff winter thing and when spring came around, a penumbra of tiny buds of green. Was it the same tree? It was in the same place, definitely, but did that soft mutated halo of green deserve the same name as the bony tendrils that shivered through the winter?

She still answered to the name Mother. Mother, not Ma or Mum and the rather Protestant reserve with which he uttered it. So he loved her and she loved him, when the language of love was still available to her. Then Alzheimer's gradually took over and he, he had to assume, became as unrecognisable to her as she had so often been to him. She took to calling him by his father's name, Charles, but Christian's only memory of him was connected to the long-barrelled Webley pistol that his grandfather had hidden in the brickwork behind the unused chimney. Or was it his great-grandfather? The only memories that really mattered on that peninsula involved trenchcoats and the burnings of big houses, amongst which, Christian's father was never allowed to forget, was the Huxley mansion itself. Oddly enough, only the interior, the furnishings and fittings, had burnt. The structure remained largely intact. And that structure stood, like a ghostly hulk, haunting one end of the peninsula. From the twenties of the last century to the forties of the present one. Designed by yet another ancestor, Montagu, the father or the grandfather of the wielder of the rusting Webley pistol? He could never be sure.

His mother's name was Iris and as they circled each other in the same cottage throughout her long engagement with the testing process her name became the only constant. Her face changed with the seasons or with whatever contract she was fulfilling for the Huxley Institute which eventually provided him with an apprenticeship. Which he accepted, despite his reservations.

So was the Institute the measure of the collapse of everything? Or was it enabled by the collapse of everything?

He had trained in chemistry, which seemed appropriate, given that the Earl of Cork, Robert Boyle, was the father of the discipline, although the realm of digital things had taken it far beyond *The Sceptical Chymist*. Then in binary logic and gene splicing in the Boyle Institute in University College Cork. It was close enough to look after Iris as she descended into senility and to supervise her movement from cottage to care home. The costs, he was informed, would be borne by the Institute – Huxley, not Boyle – and he had once more to wonder what kind of debt of gratitude he would eventually owe them. So, his apprenticeship was taken as a given, the way, two centuries ago, a youth of his aptitudes would have found himself apprenticed to the Huxley Copper Mines, designing the smelting processes that produced molten copper from the rough sulphide ores. Or indeed, the mechanisms that churned the copper from the dank walls of mica, the cogs and wheels and pulleys that lowered the miners into their unfathomable depths.

The Institute had moved on from its simple beginnings in medical applications and swine genetic engineering to extracellular vesicles derived from animal plasma, stem-cell rejuvenation, gene editing merging CRISPR with developments in in-vitro gametogenesis, which led to a late baby boom throughout the peninsula, more on the Kerry than the Cork side for some unexplained reason, which had lately fallen into abeyance There was something unexplained there. A mystery. Perhaps the in-vitro thing had run its course. Perhaps cloned pets were replacing children in the peninsula's affections. Or maybe it was the Institute's loss of its in-vitro patents and its entry into the more rarefied realms of QGA. The Quantum Genetic Algorithm, as Christian understood it, that uses the method of chromosome evolution based on the quantum rotating door and enables the alteration of certain memory cells through their entanglement with others.

Since the whole issue of cloud storage had been muddied by digital rain, he had spent his initial apprenticeship refiling in the Library of Traumatic Memory. He was surprised by how much he enjoyed the process. Maybe there was a dormant librarian within him, with a memory of old dusty tomes stacked in actual shelves. He knew that most of the files stored in the silicone came from jurisdictions far from this one. Fungible with others. Fungibility was essential for some reason. Couldn't the traumatic memory just be deleted from the amygdala or the hippocampus? No, because it might erupt when least expected, like a long-dormant volcano, giving rise to traumatic memories in multiple others in turn. Traumatic memories could grow then like a ragweed infestation or a giant Ponzi scheme unless alternatives replaced it. An untraumatic alternative. Fungible with consciousnesses and healthy, happy lives in far more amenable climes, where the wind didn't shake the bare trees and horizontal rain wasn't a norm. He could imagine the same Institute, that same carapace of glass and steel – although he could never be sure steel was the alloy – soaring over a lapping, sun-kissed Hawaiian beach, or a picturesque harbour in Shanghai. Somewhere other than this blasted landscape of bent thorn trees and sodden bogs. But maybe then the Institute wouldn't have had access to an unquestioning, sullen but obedient workforce.

Or to the same government grants. People complained – in this townland, they had an entire dialect, even a fully developed language of complaint – but they knew very well the difference between complaint and question. And if questions were to be asked, the bounty might dry. Bounties had dried up before. There was a buried trauma, even within the landscape. And hints of that trauma were still visible, in the upper reaches of the hills through which he cycled. Irregular rectangular patches which had once been lazy beds and famine fields, whole mountainsides of them, like a quilt that had been stitched by previous, more traumatized generations. He knew that dotted amongst them would be the occasional ruined cottage, and steps cut deep into the bog earth, which had once provided dried shovelfuls of peat. Then there were the rusted ruins on the seaward side, of the navy ships, askew in the wind-flecked bay.

There was the persistent need for secrecy, of course. An abandoned mansion at the wet end of a forgotten peninsula was a certain guarantee of secrecy. Not that the Institute's various modules breached the law – Doctor Rainer Fischer worked hard to make sure they didn't. But still, on most days, Christian had to subdue his concerns, bury those tiny little tremors of worry that he once knew as conscience. Isolde would have helped him in this endeavour, but Isolde had been dead for some time now. Although even that fact, lately, had become somewhat moot.

He saw the mansion rising like a version of the past redesigned in some distant future over the cold green foliage of the spruce trees. He heard her voice again and thought about her green eyes and thought of pulling out his eardrop. And, once more, it was as if she had been reading his thoughts.

There's a reason they chose this place, my love.

You can't keep calling me that, he muttered.

But I can.

You're not yourself, darling.

The 'darling' slipped out unbidden. And that was the problem with emotions, he realised. They did their own thing.

I know I'm not. And maybe I never was. But if so, why the 'darling'?

Just kind of slipped out.

He cycled on a bit in silence. Then felt unaccountably regretful.

I'm sorry. I'm just the librarian. I'm meant to file memories, not disturb them. And now we have this – a lorry passed at full speed, and the wind nearly blew him sideways – situation...

Your memories are also mine, I might add. Or – and there was a pause here – they used to be.

This is all some kind of what-do-you-call-it. Wish fulfilment.

My wishes or yours?

And that was the thing about her voice. You wanted to keep hearing it. Saying those things that you wanted to hear. That she had never said. When she was alive, that is.

And I'm switching off this eardrop now.

Please don't.

You have no say in the matter.

The problem is, I soon will. I'm floating outside of time, somehow. And I realise we've been here. Before.

You're getting sentimental, wherever you happen to be.

I'm here, with you. It's your choice. And you've made it mine.

Where have we been then?

On this peninsula. In better times.

Off.

And he turned her off. Just in time, it seemed, as he headed towards the portion of the avenue where the flowers were always kept fresh for the drowned bridesmaids. He took in the yellow daffodils, nodding against the brown, wind-flecked water, and it struck him again that the daffodils were early this year. He glanced to his left, towards the Huxley mansion. And the doctor, as if knowing what box of winds he had opened, was watching from the window.

He dismounted his bike. Chained it to the reconstituted railings. Walked inside.

THE PENINSULA HAG

There had been mining in the area, Corrigan told him, from the days of the Cailleach Beara.

The Cailleach Beara? he echoed. It was a habit of his.

It was a day of bluster, of white caps on the Atlantic waves, and striding over the springy heather, Montagu Cartwright found it difficult to keep pace. Corrigan's boots rose and fell like the front hooves of a quarter horse.

The Hag of Beara. Some kind of mythical old witch who got tired of living forever. I can't imagine a worse fate, can you? In fact, we'll pass her stone along the way.

A respite from the wind, a rough ascent up a stony bowl and they saw it. A piece of twisted volcanic rock, keeping watch over the thumbnails of islands, far beyond.

Her grave? he asked his companion.

Must have died then, after all. Or else she keeps a beady eye on the Skelligs, beyond.

Maybe – and he was feeling loquacious today – she sleeps in the mine underneath.

Maybe this English Irishman could be taken for a ride.

The mine is beneath us now?

Not too far. Head straight for the Bull Rock.

He did, imagining the dead witch's hair spreading through the unseen tunnels, like moving tendrils.

I feel—

What do you feel?

A certain hollowness in the ground.

Maybe the witch's head. Or her feet. She had a great stretch in her.

Corrigan was not beyond pranks at this stage.

Got to show me where, man. With your boot – or staff.

So Montagu Cartwright pounded the turf, first with his steel-capped boot. Then with his broken ash staff. Then with both. And the ground gave beneath him.

He fell, as someone must have fallen before him. He fell, in a tumble of broken roots and grass, which gave way to grey withered hair-like tendrils, into a bed of coppery clay. There was a cone of light from above, and the strands of witch-hair trembled in it, with the debris still tumbling down.

There were white shards beneath him, which turned out to be bones.

There was a skull, with teeth rotten and intact.

But there was no witch.

Did he hear a distant cackle, or was it more earth falling?

No, there was no witch. But he almost wished there was.

There was a skeletal hand, clutching a dark, oval piece of polished stone.

He raised it to the light and saw something like his face.

Was it his face? Grey, wispy hair, cadaverous cheekbones.

Was it the witch's?

No, it was his. But was he older, somehow, or was it a trick of the dust or the light?

He wiped one and held it up to the other. He saw it had been a trick of the latter. The light. The stone refracted and reflected its beams in odd ways. He could see himself now, behind the twinkle of sunbeams. And he could see Corrigan's face, far above, peering down.

You alright?

There was concern in the voice from above, with those thick Kerry vowels, mixed with contempt. It was a combination he remembered from his childhood, as a ward of the Lansdowne Estate.

Fine.

Every acorn has to drop, she said.

Who said?

The witchy old one.

This peninsula was full of secrets, he remembered. And it would do well, he felt, for some obscure reason, to have a secret himself. So, he wedged the mirrory stone inside his greatcoat.

Mirrory. Was it even a word? He saw a refracted beam of light as he buttoned the collar.

And did he hear another cackle?

Let me get us a rope.

No.

He could barely stand. But he could see several gleams of light, in the walls of mud and schist. Old tunnels, with withered roots of ivy dangling through the earth from above.

I can find my way out.

Which he did. On hands and knees, his deerstalker hat eventually pushing through a bank of heather.

Corrigan afforded him a gnarly hand.

Find anything?

A skeleton.

Many of them, I'm sure. Old alchemists.

You mean copper miners.

I'm sure they all had hopes. Sir Walter Raleigh, the alchemist, poked around here. So the legend goes. But no witch?

No, Montagu Cartwright told him. No sign of a witch.

But he kept his greatcoat closed, around the dark stone.

DATA PROTECTION

The Forever Wing is hereto suspended.
This, from Dr Fischer, at the top of the oaken banisters, carved by the master-builder Corrigan under Montagu Cartwright's instruction, two centuries ago.

Restored by Dr Fischer to the same Cartwright design.

Forever? Suspended?

For the foreseeable future.

Whyever, asked Christian, brushing the hair from his damp forehead.

He could have simply asked why? But the rhyme was irresistible. And it somehow went well with the doctor's accented 'hereto'. Nervousness sometimes reduced him to a priggish exactitude with grammar, as if he were a real librarian, who dealt with printed matter, not with tiny silicone discs of dubious origin. And he needed three syllables, as if they hid what he needed to hide.

The usual reason. Data protection cranks. Questions in the senate. Which might take more than a few brown paper envelopes to resolve.

Aha.

Christian disrobed himself of his high-viz jacket. And he wondered, was that a tear or a trick of the light that gave a melancholy glow to his employer's blue eyes? They had both lost someone, after all.

So, it's back to the library for me?

It will have to be, I'm afraid. Press pause on the other thing. Keep all the records. Seal the boxes.

There are no boxes, doctor.

The files, then. How many yottabytes?

Thirteen, and counting.

S and P, then. Store and protect.

Preserve?

For another day.

MIRROR

It had a smooth polished surface, like dark marble. Serrated edges, which could easily have drawn blood. In fact, there was something bloody about the dark reflections it sent back to the observer. Montagu Cartwright had it set in leather to save his fingers and framed within the lid of his vanity case, so it greeted him each morning as he shaved. And was it vanity, or the mirror itself that changed this practice? He left his moustache untouched at first, then bit by bit, the rest of his luxuriant chin. So, it was a bearded Montagu Cartwright who was introduced to Copper John on the Allihies hillside, near the ungainly hulk of the engine frame of the new-built mineshaft.

His first thought was that the nickname that retired Admiral John Huxley had been gifted by the townsfolk, 'Copper John', didn't suit him, really. Not the way 'Muck' Corrigan's did. Corrigan's boots, moleskins and blocklike hands were always covered in the dried substance. But there wasn't a hint of burnished copper visible on John Huxley's tweeds.

That there was no reason for the dark, satanic ugliness of the construction, was his second thought. Why could an arrangement of wheels and pulleys, greased chains, buckets and cabins descending into the netherworld not have some aesthetic qualities? The bridge and aqueduct passing over the river Lee, which carried the single-gauge train that brought him to the peninsula, had its own soaring granite grandeur. It spoke of progress, of the march of the Victorian Age, and the coal-black trail of smoke it left in its wake somehow complemented the green hills, the sparkling silver inlets, even the rippling river below it. So, could not these mechanical pulleys which would one day be dotting the hills of Allihies and framing the curving beach below them have something of the same quality?

He shared the same thoughts with John Huxley, who informed him that he spent as little time as possible in 'this dreaded burgh'. And while Cartwright nodded in mute agreement, he had to admit to himself that the word confused him. There was nothing burgh-like about this heathery hillside, stretching down with its threads of stone walls to the foaming Atlantic. It was beautiful, in the most comforting way. It reminded him of home, on the Lansdowne Estate on the Kerry side of the peninsula. The Lansdowne Estate which had been formed by the Petty land grants which had been formed by the Carew massacres, which had been...

Sometimes Montagu Cartwright had to stop himself remembering. He had a brief image of the white-boned form he had tumbled into, with the dark marbled mirror in its skeletal hand. He had to wonder, was memory a curse, like the seed of Adam and Seth? But he also had to admit that this tumble of small hills could have been home, were it not for the rectangular monstrosity already undergoing adjustment by 'Muck' Corrigan, whose nickname absolutely suited him. The brown muck from the mine pit below dripped in great gouts from his enormous hands. The head frame above was angled to one side, like a repellent version of the Leaning Tower of Pisa, and was wrenched, seemingly from the bowels of the earth, by the muddy hands of Muck Corrigan, until it 'angled straight', as he put it. But all he managed was to angle it crooked again, towards the dark triangles of the Bull and Calf rocks, away out in the bay.

John Huxley's waistcoat bore a brace of naval insignias, he bowed and clicked his heels, coming and going as if he was on the deck of an ironclad battleship, and not on an Allihies hillside. He bid Montagu Cartwright good day, and invited him to his temporary residence, Waterfall House, four miles beyond the 'dreaded burgh'. Which Montagu Cartwright now understood to be the town in which his Gothic church had been accidentally built, Castletown.

Not this heathery hillside.

It was market day when he reached the town and the crush of beasts round his skittish horse, the accretion of cow hair, spittle and dung around his calfskin boots, and the sweat of the day's riding put him in need of a bath.

The water was cold in his hotel bedroom and the slavey who poured it waited inordinately long by the open doorway. For a tip, he presumed, which made it all the colder by the time he had handed her a shilling and closed the door behind her. But he was glad of the cleansing, however chilly, by the time he reached the treelined avenue which led through the oriental gardens to the miniature, rose-coloured mansion, with the flat roof on which two cannons were perched, facing the bay. The roar of a waterfall from the gardens beyond made it hard to hear the admiral's greeting – for admiral he was, or had been, before the current mining enterprise.

Bantry Bay had been penetrated by a French armada a century before, hence the cannons on the flat roof, hence maybe, even – Montagu Cartwright, ever the architect, surmised – the design of the flat roof. Awaiting another adversary, should they ever make the same mistake.

Admiral Huxley – or Copper John to the locals – invited him inside to meet his wife, in the small half-circular entrance to the dining room. And there, behind a table stacked with wines, whiskies and liquors, stood a vision that took Montagu Cartwright's breath away.

Camilla Huxley.

She had just returned with her husband from a tour of Bohemia. And while her husband had made an exploratory survey of the copper mines of the south, she had taken solace in the healing waters of Carlsbad, which might have accounted for the roseate bloom on her skin. Or the interest she displayed in Montagu Cartwright. She had seen the new-built church on the heights above the town, commissioned by the retired and mostly indigent Anglican community, with remarkably pleasing but oddly inappropriate Celtic features. A round tower, wolfhound gargoyles round the entrance, serpentine bas reliefs that could have been copied from the Book of Kells. She had been told that the architect was now an acquaintance of her husband's and was delighted to be introduced.

As was Montagu Cartwright. He did his best to explain the mix-up, in Dean's Yard, Westminster. The intended Carlsbad design was in the final stages of construction, by the graveyard in the town. To transpose the Gothic one to its Bohemian home would be as absurd a proposition as returning the Celtic one to its rain-sodden homeland. Let the Church of Ireland, or England, or indeed the Anglican community of Lower Bohemia decide what to do.

You should view your creation, surely?

This from Admiral Huxley.

Someday, perhaps. When opportunity allows.

And then silence, for some reason, reigned.

Camilla Huxley seemed used to these silences. The puff of the cigar that her husband lit from the wick of the oil-lamp. The soft intake of breath, when Camilla Huxley's eyes turned to the floor to avoid the eyes of Montagu Cartwright.

There was a manservant, Doheny, to pour the port. A gardener, George, who flitted by the windows carrying armfuls of wood for the fire and the cooking stove. Over which Maisie, the housemaid, prepared whatever the admiral had earmarked for their repast.

The meal was stiff, the conversation stilted. Camilla spoke softly about her attempts to alleviate the plight of the local poor and Cartwright couldn't take his eyes off her. A set of blonde curls which tumbled towards a bosom which seemed shocking in its fullness. A pair of green eyes which did everything possible to avoid his own.

Montagu Cartwright had never been in love, and neither, judging by her interplay with her husband, had Camilla Huxley. The admiral seemed happy to regard her as part of his estate, like the fishing rights, the tenant rights, the mining rights, the great swathes of land spreading from the mountains to the sea.

A gun-metal corvette out on the bay guaranteed those rights.

There was an election coming. There was the tenantry, some loyal, some not. There was mining equipment to be ferried from the harbour in Cove to the Dunboy loading bay, to be trundled to the Allihies by horse-drawn carriage, unbroken. There were luddites in the hills, with claims to rights that were, by order of the Crown, his and his alone. There were fortunes to be made, an entire peninsula to be dragged, kicking and screaming, into the age of steam. And there was, most importantly, a mansion to be built.

Which Montagu Cartwright undertook to design. And a year or so later, sitting in the hot springs of Carlsbad, he would wonder, was it the possibilities inherent in the mansion itself that had led him to accept the commission? Or the promise of those ever-evasive, oh so green eyes?

DEATH AND TAXES

What exactly had been suspended? Christian had to remind himself. So many initiatives mooted, so many products designed, some of them modelled in far too many dimensions, even brought to seek venture capital in jurisdictions of questionable existence who could remember them all?

Sigmund maybe.

The Forever Wing, of course.

Yes, it had been brought to life, so to speak, by a lacuna in the small print of the Succession Act of 2075.

Posthumous conversation had been a business for years. Deadbots and undeadbots, post-mortem advertising, grief avatars, digital afterlives. Death, after all, was the ultimate design flaw. Drink and tap had become a habit, close to an addiction, needing a new branch of AA to cater for it. TA, Tappers Anonymous, the tapping here being not the table tapping of seances of old, but the tap-tap of the late-night computer, the flickering messages on the screen, *where r u now? Heaven or Hell*. Heaven mostly, or some anonymous bardo in between. And as with any addiction, it cost handsomely to feed it.

But the doctor's offering rose above all of that, like a bat, rising from a graveyard yew tree.

Christian walked through the Victorian entrance hall into the silvered interior. Everything gleamed beyond those flagstones, those carved limestone walls, decorated with the plaster reproductions of antlers from hunting parties long ago and tapestries that illustrated their bloody triumphs. Glass and steel, reflective surfaces, corridors that mirrored other shining corridors, echoing with the same electronic hum. The rustle of fingers against keyboards, the occasional musical blip. As if each labourer in the Huxley Institute had their own secret project, and maybe, Christian thought, as he retreated further from the doctor, maybe they had.

Christian definitely did.

He had been corralled by the doctor to work on this new take on the old grief avatar business that gave rise to so many clichéd graveyard variations. The Forever Wing. A reconfiguration of the tools of the Library of Traumatic Memory to harvest whatever digital traces of the departed loved one the legislation would allow. Cloning of anything other than the smallest of pets had been outlawed since the Barron Trump multiples and the aborted nuclear strike ordered by the thirteenth Kim Jong-il, but whatever non-genomic remains the loved one had left behind – photographs, letters, diaries, all appchats and omnichannel mails and data – could still be put into play. The dead, it was promised, through a judicious and strictly legal harvesting of all of the above, could not only communicate, in the mechanical way of so many failed memorial products, but could whisper, could murmur, could laugh, could weep and could be entertained in a bespoke wing of the Huxley mansion, as yet unconstructed.

And here, Christian had to wonder what private griefs had impelled the doctor towards this public offering. He had lost his son and his daughter-in-law in an accident almost too grotesque to be imagined. If the dead could be entertained again, Christian wondered, what respite would they offer?

Christian had to bite his lip, quench his tears. His own loss was unfathomable. Incomprehensible. And must remain undisclosed.

But the dead could not only talk, they could also pay for their posthumous conversations. Herein lay the real attraction of the Forever Wing. They could live again, through a miniscule adjustment of the Succession Act. A backdated tax break could shave off a percentage of the hated onus of death duties. So overtaxed wills, estates and inheritances could be put back into play, the details to be worked out by the Institute's legal arms, digital and actual. The benefits of future conversations with the recently and, if the legislation could be so amended, the not-so-recently deceased could be enjoyed by future generations at no cost to the living whatsoever.

Two certainties, the doctor proclaimed. Death and taxes. Let's introduce them to the uncertainty principle.

The product, the doctor told him, was well on the way to being sold before it was built, before the initial research was halfway completed, such was the appetite of the market. The legal parameters were complex, the patents had to be written and logged, the legislation in the Dáil amended, and Dr Fischer's trips back and forth to Dublin took on the regularity of a pendulum.

Christian, whose bullshit detector was glowing white-hot, was ordered to replicate the latest storage applications of the Library of Traumatic Memory. Those thumbnail slivers of silicone and glass, arrayed in rows like the most miniscule of bookshelves, kept in temperature-controlled and dust-free purity. Many of the original subscribers were dead themselves, dead or forgotten, and the storage space had been restructured to a different and most urgent purpose.

Dr Fischer was both polymath, publicist and promoter extraordinaire. He allowed hints about this new mysterious undertaking to circle on the web, on social media channels and even on the airwaves, for those who still listened. He entrusted others to build the product, of course, and took the gathering frenzy of interest as justification enough that it was even possible. There were more of the dead than the living, after all, and the more recent the passing, the more hunger there was for any tenuous connection. So, they built, they coded, they structured, they spliced, they harvested the way a *meitheal* had once, on this same peninsula, gradually scythed its way through the fields of barley, oats and wheat. And so many wonders reared their heads in the process – much the way tiny stoats, hares and rabbits would duck and dive to escape the oncoming whetted blades – that Christian himself had begun a slow process of conversion. Maybe it wasn't bullshit, after all. Maybe the good doctor's vision had all of the power of the technological future behind it. Maybe there would soon be a wing of the Huxley mansion where a soothing dinner could be held, between a widower and his departed loved one, accompanied by musical choices that reflected their history together. Maybe her words (or his, or theirs) could perfectly reflect her cadence as it was in life. And maybe, just maybe, the image wouldn't flicker with the penumbra of white noise more appropriate to a video game, maybe 3D imaging and robotic engineering could reproduce the texture of skin, that darkening of iris, whatever small declensions of the wrist and fingers belonged to the departed one. Maybe the dead could live. And maybe the dead could foot the bill.

In some undefined future, Christian said to himself. Maybe in your dreams. But prior to them living, maybe the dead could talk.

It was what he was good at, after all. Memory in all of its manifestations. And words were, after all, the little boats it sailed on.

Do you remember, darling—

That day when we—

The sun was shining through the garden firepit—

The cherry blossoms were falling, from the tree by the driveway—

No, it wasn't like that. Wasn't like that at all.

I would swear it was you.

You gave me hyacinths first, a year ago. They called me the hyacinth girl.

Though that last was a memory from nothing he had lived. A book, he remembered, that he had shared with Isolde, by the ruins of Dunboy Castle, which had been levelled long before the Huxley mansion was even thought of. And the memory, like a phantom limb or a reawakened wound, only served to remind him how much he missed her.

So, the public offering had been rescinded. The dead were to be left undisturbed. There were so many of them, anyway, Christian thought. The peninsula itself was a sprawling graveyard, massacre upon massacre from the days of the Virgin Queen, Raleigh, Cecil, Carew, Grey – all of them Lords of Destruction. And all of that before the famine graveyards, which dotted the frothy coastline.

CARSLBAD

It was an odd town, and had that strange evanescent quality that spa towns have, as if it had been built around an ocean that had mysteriously vanished.

Montagu Cartwright found himself there, having trawled the copper, gold and silver mining areas of southern Bohemia. He made sketches of the head frames and the engine houses that pulleyed the unfortunate miners into the honeycomb of pits below. Of the chimneys and the blast furnaces necessary for smelting, of the burial pits for the toxic residue of lead, arsenic, sulphur oxide and manganese. He had begun to tire of the mechanised wonders he found there, ancient and modern, of the poisonous scars in the Bohemian forests that all this industry left behind it. He visited Prague Castle, St Vitus's Cathedral, was reminded of his Gothic miniature that had somehow ended up on that peninsula in Cork, and thought he should take the opportunity to acquaint himself with its Celtic double in Carlsbad.

The main thoroughfare, a gradually winding array of Viennese frontages, shops selling bottled waters and furs and hunting caps and guns with oddly shaped and carved shoulder pieces and wooden skis and liqueurs of all colours, all tinctures, made from every possible herb in the forests around that threw their shadows on a sunken river. But what caught the eye of Montagu Cartwright, as he stepped from his hotel, was the distant, slightly off-centre tower of a new-built church. It seemed familiar, of course, because he had designed it and would have been delighted by its presence behind the square of Castletown. But he was oddly reassured by its presence here. For Montagu Cartwright, for any architect of any calibre, the finished work is inevitably a disappointment. But this spectacle, this miniature round tower with its harp-shaped windows, which should have seemed so much at home amongst the deciduous flora of the Beara peninsula, brought some kind of reassurance with it. He was comforted by the sight, the closer it came to him. And the growing closeness took its time. A hill had to be climbed there, hotel doormen to be avoided. Buxom shop ladies wielded mops and brushes, all too willing to spread a cloth on the pavement and kneel, scrubbing clean their allotted patch. The pavement was extraordinarily clean, as was the cobbled street, even the runnelled drain between them, gleaming with last night's rainwater. This ascending street almost shone and did indeed glitter in the early morning sunshine, as yet another pail of water was expelled from an open doorway before his surprised feet. And the church, when he did reach it, seemed unbothered by it all. Even enhanced. A bell was ringing. He could see the sun shining through the curved tower he had allowed for it, blotted on every second peal, as if the bell were sending a secret signal every time it swung through the light. There were no parishioners, he could see, wending their way towards the heavy wooden doors with their whorled, vaguely Celtic handles. He was in the last vestiges of the Holy Roman Empire, Catholic Europe, and if there was a further outpost of the Hapsburg Empire, he would have liked to know it. So, he should not have been surprised. Why the Anglican Communion had spent good money on a place of worship in this overstuffed, Ruritanian town was a mystery to him when it was first commissioned, and an even greater mystery to him now. But there it was. This piece of Celtic medievalism had been paid for, he was assured, by contributions from the indigent expatriates who were in need of whatever cures the water provided.

And maybe it was time for him to step inside.

DOCTOR RAINER FISCHER

Doctor Rainer Fischer lived in a steel and glass monstrosity towards the Kerry end of the peninsula. To the younger Christian's ear, the accent and the flat, monotoned delivery sounded German. But no, he should have read the signs better. The Maybach or Porsche that sometimes pulled up outside the metal gate of his mother's cottage may have been German, but its driver was not. Dr Rainer Fischer liked the Advocaat with just a hint of Baileys Cream that his mother kept in the cabinet to the left of the fridge.

Doctor Rainer Fischer was Dutch. Tall, like most of his compatriots, six foot four in his stocking feet. Or in those slippers that he dragged along the pristine glass floors of the corridors of the Institute. And if there was a logic to most things, there had to be a similar logic to Dr Rainer Fischer's presence in Iris Cartwright's cottage and on the peninsula itself.

There was a certain logic to the presence of the Library of Traumatic Memory. To situate it here, in this wet, windswept peninsula, in this cadaver of a mansion of grey granite and cut limestone, made a certain kind of emotional sense. If you wanted to get rid of an unwanted memory, store it in a landscape that was synonymous with its trauma, its uselessness, its undesirability – this end of the peninsula was surely the place. Tourist traffic stopped, after all, at the gateway to the peninsula, Glengarriff, that picture-perfect town where Billie Eilish had spent her retirement. September had been her time, when the colour of her auburn hair matched the autumn leaves. When the gazebo that claimed to hold her ashes and her hologrammic 'experience' drew the crowds, and the whole town, with its wine-dark interiors and thatched pubs seemed dressed for what used to be the harvest.

The traffic – the buses, the hired coaches, the teams of lycra'd cyclists and even the hikers – continued on its merry Kerry way, leaving the windswept vista to the south and east almost entirely unexplored. What better place to store a memory of a punishment after bedwetting, a teenage sexual transaction, a cataclysmic loss in a betting shop, an apocalyptic heartbreak or divorce. And Christian had spent his days filing all photographic, digital, chemical and cellular evidence of these memories, each therapeutic account, extracted from the disappearing cloud and stored in those opaque and increasingly diminishing glass and silicone files, deposited by the owner into the care and charge of the Huxley Institute. Although he could never rid himself of the suspicion that it was, for the most part, bullshit. Memory is memory, after all. It will leave its tangential traces. Even if the specific phrase, the image, the instinctive reaction to the blow of its coiled fist were to be nano-surgically removed. Even taking into account the terms of the contract with the Huxley Institute, that would guarantee all therapeutic records, all of the harvested memories, on email, Snapchat, TikTok and any app yet to be invented in this and all universes yet to be discovered, were the property of the Institute. Even employing the widely advertised Fungible Procedure – a blast of quantum particles that claimed to substitute certain organic materials fungible with the ones causing the trauma in the first place.

If people wanted to spend money on it, fine. And many did, evidenced by Christian's struggles with the whole issue of storage. There was the hope that the four-millimetre opaque squares of silicone could be reduced by half, given the refinement of molecular processing, and there were hopes of square-root reduction, as micro conductors and quantum processing evolved, to something approaching infinity. And while Christian didn't understand the physics – indeed, the psychological implications – of the whole process, he had to admit that in terms of basic salesmanship, it made some kind of sense. He imagined the clients of this Library of Traumatic Memory leading their sun-kissed, carefree lives by a beach of pristine sand or in some metropolis where the rain never fell, happy to store their unwanted memories in this sodden, bleak edifice of granite and limestone under this permanently crepuscular sky.

But how to explain the presence of the good doctor himself, with his neuroscientific expertise, his room full of streams of digital rain, like successive veils of old-fashioned ticker tape, and the egg-shaped elliptical oddness that housed his nano-technological deep-mind data processor which he had the wit to dub Sigmund? A barely disguised nod to the Viennese interpreter of dreams. A leadenly humorous pun, marginally hitting the mark, like most bon mots of the Dutch doctor. He had considered changing the Sigmund to Carl, a reference, Christian assumed, to Carl Gustav Jung.

But no, Christian would later discover, the Carl referred to far-off, nineteenth-century Carlsbad, Bohemia, latterly known as Karoly Vara, in the onetime Slovak Republic, now the seventeenth precinct in the West Asian Soviet.

There was the legal aspect, of course. The legislature in the capital, Dublin, had decided, after corporate representations too numerous to count, to draft what no other legislature would agree to. The Vance Wilson addendum to the ever-expanding Data Protection Acts would allow for the harvesting of all possible categories of information, in this and all possible future legislative universes yet to be devised. There were limits, of course, contracts to be signed by descendants, loved ones etc., but the employment possibilities won the day in the end. These, and Dr Fischer's threat to move the entire enterprise to more business-friendly shores, Taiwan or Singapore. But the doctor had been here long before the Institute, Christian realised, and the question still was why? And why here?

There had been studies, around the time of the First Cold War, of areas of the world most likely to withstand a nuclear winter. Ireland figured highly on the lists, and the far south-western reaches of the island highest of all. A flood of immigration resulted, of the well-heeled and paranoid from the continental lowlands. There were empty farmhouses dotting the peninsula, just begging for an influx of cash and continental endeavour. Bram Fischer, father of Rainer, was prominent amongst those early pioneers, and rumour had it, had placed a bid on the Huxley mansion when it was just a picturesque ruin. He was outbid, of course – gazumped was the auctioneering term – by a consortium of wily townsfolk, but their ambitions foundered in turn. So the mansion gathered ivy, moss and decay, remained the crumbling playground of children until well into the new century, when a sale was finally agreed – to whom, nobody could be sure. But construction was begun, the sound of helicopters carrying girders, ornamental arches, mysterious sheets of plate glass, and eventually engineers and architects in high-viz jackets and hard hats became a constant presence. There were jobs, of course, and no-one questioned them, least of all the young Dr Rainer Fischer who, it gradually emerged, was endemic to the whole process.

He knew. He had brokered the deal. He had managed what his deceased father couldn't. He had unearthed some ancient contracts, wrapped around a Webley pistol from above the mantelpiece of Iris Cartwright. The pistol came from her grandfather, the contracts from her grandfather's grandfather. So, with his purchase of them, Dr Rainer Fischer had played the first of his tricks on time. He had paid for her aftercare, guaranteed her son's employment, come to some obscure contract with the ghosts of Copper John, Montagu Cartwright and his master-builder Corrigan. He had trawled through whole volumes of old contracts, made sense of the wheretofors and whereafters, tracked down obscure shell companies in jurisdictions from Panama to Singapore, in Caribbean and Samoan legislations that no longer existed. Whatever dark magic he had managed, it didn't matter to the townsfolk in the pubs and coffee shops, on the pier, where the fishing boats were generally docked, the pelagic quotas having been denied the locals by some intercontinental agreement. Fishing was dying, was the consensus, farming would soon follow, so when the trundle of lorries from the Kenmare road began again, followed by the thrum of helicopters, bringing engineers and architects and eventually huge steel pylons, swinging from their underbellies like snakes in the claw of some mythical eagle, no questions were asked. What was it to be, this revivification of the Huxley mansion? Were the mines to reopen, was the isolation of the whole peninsula to become a thing of the distant past? A hotel, was the consensus, five stars and more, with a golf course where the forest used to be. Fly in, fly out, the private jets docked at Shannon, the helicopters ferrying the patrons to their weekends of front and back nines. But others disagreed. A private residence for the Sultan of Oman or the Taiwanese owner of Fountain, the AI search engine that was, for a month or so, beating all the others. Passports guaranteed by the government in Dublin, a safe haven from whatever political turmoil would have roiled their fortunes. The peninsula may not have been the Côte d'Azur or the Devon coast, but at least it was green, and safe. And the fact that neither of these outcomes came to pass at least put a gradual end to all of the conjecture. Building took time, often so much time that origins became lost in the mists of that very thing, time. So, when the immaculate reconstruction of the Victorian frontage proceeded, and when it turned out to be only something of a carapace for the glass-and-steel crabbed thing that grew within it and spread, nobody knew how many acres into the hinterland of low hills behind, people had already stopped wondering about it. The Institute emerged as a fait accompli, a thing that had already happened, whose genesis was as obscure as that of the mines had been, though they had originated in the greed for copper. It just was and probably would always be.

MAGNUS WILDERSTEIN

But it began with a church. A church designed to memorialise a forgotten Celtic past, complete with a monastic bell-tower and an arched doorway, encrusted in carved serpentine figures that Montagu Cartwright remembered copying from the Book of Kells. The handle of the heavy oaken door, a hand outstretched in a cast-iron greeting, he didn't remember at all, but then it had been a long time ago.

The interior was simplicity itself. The nave, leading to the simplest of altars, illuminated by a concentric arrangement of stained glass panels through which the Bohemian sun glowed, in a yellowish, spectral, amber hue.

And it was the colour that surprised him. He remembered no stained glass at all. He disapproved of ornament, despite his High-Church leanings. He had specified gridded metal to keep out whatever sodden leaves the West Cork winds might blow inside. But then again, he couldn't really complain. The addition of amber glass was a minor infraction, compared to the wholesale transposition of a church from one jurisdiction to another. And, as he said to himself on entering—

It was a long time ago.

Could it be that he heard himself speaking? But the voice that spoke his thoughts was nothing like his.

He turned, and saw for this first time that he was not alone. And he had the strangest of feelings that he never had been alone. Not walking up the riverside street past the Carlsbad hotels, not on the endless train journey through the Tyrolean Alps, not when he accepted the commission in Dean's Yard, Westminster. Not when he tumbled into the witch-hair mineshaft. Maybe not ever.

A small figure, dressed in a green tweed hunting jacket, with a Jägermeister hat on the pew beside him, stroking a thin white beard for which Montagu Cartwright could only find one adjective.

Mephistophelean.

And it's not stained glass.

No? Cartwright replied, as if this conversation was an ordinary one. Which it certainly was not. Was this gentleman reading his thoughts?

Well, maybe the outer panes are. But the central, oval one – and here he pointed, at the darkly glowing pane – obsidian.

And he remembered his shaving mirror. The skeletal hand that had clutched it. The imagined cackle of Muck Corrigan's witch. What was her name? Cailleach?

Obsidian?

And it reflects light as much as allows it passage.

It does?

If you could raise yourself to the height of that window, you could see your own reflection. And much else besides.

He stood. Twirled the Jägermeister hat around his finger. And Montagu Cartwright saw that it was decorated with small fly-fishing feathers.

Forgive me. Magnus Wilderstein. The Royal Society of Architects.

Did he click his heels? Cartwright definitely heard a creak. Although it could have been from a wooden beam.

Montagu—

Montagu Cartwright. And forgive me for the fact that I do know. The confusion of your architectural plans has worried us for some time. And I suppose we wondered when this beautiful church's only begetter – he raised his small head then as if to take in every high oaken beam above – would grace us with his presence.

Have you found out how it happened?

Not yet. But some accidents are happy ones. Wouldn't you agree? Like that glass in your simple, perfectly placed circular window. Obsidian. From the scryer mirror of John Dee himself.

John Dee?

Philosopher, alchemist, spiritual adviser to your Elizabeth the First. And to our own Rudolph the Second. There were two, you see. One a copy of the other. One stayed in Bohemia. The other travelled.

Travelled where?

He remembered his fall, through the heathered ground. Into the pit, with the grey-haired tendrils. The skeletal hand. The oval of dark marble. And once more, he kept it secret.

If we only knew the answer…

We?

Forgive me again. We in the Carlsbad chapter of the Royal Society.

Of architects?

Architects, masons and master-builders. And forgive us again.

And again, he bowed.

We saw your design. We were made aware of your distaste for ornament. But oxidised glass brings its own alchemy with it. And what is a church, after all, if not a reflection of the eternal?

Two churches. Two mirrors. Was this an absurd fantasy, or some even more absurd plot?

One architect walked closer to the other. It was the leather shoes that gave rise to the clicking sound, Montagu Cartwright realised.

Cartwright thought of his vanity case. His obsidian shaving mirror. And he wondered, would he ever shave again?

THE DROWNED GIRLS

The unshaven reflection of Christian Cartwright was rising to meet him as he descended into the glass-panelled interior. So, there was yet another problem with data protection, and it was goodbye to the Forever Wing. He made his way to his old comfortable niche in the Library of Traumatic Memory. Should he tell the doctor what use he had made of it? Should he tell him, I have brought my loved one back to a different kind of life? And maybe you could do the same with your absent son? But that would be to reveal his extra-curricular activities, and besides, how could he separate her voice in his head from his head itself? Through the eardrop, of course, smaller than a snowdrop with its adhesive membrane that prevented its disappearance into the inner ear and the vestibulocochlear organs, which he extracted now and returned to its small plastic casing in his inside pocket, as if that would free him from the pang of memory. But of course, it didn't – memory doesn't work like that, and he tried to divert himself with another thought, the thought of the drowned girls.

Why do they haunt me so, he wondered, and felt a buzzing in his pocket. It was her again, she read his thoughts, and he took the small, vibrating snowdrop back from his pocket and replaced it in his ear.

Do you really want to know?

You read my thoughts, he whispered. Or had he spoken them aloud? Talked to himself? Everyone talked to absent colleagues in the Institute, but he alone, he felt, had a secret. And besides, he wanted to whisper. It brought him closer to a sense of her.

We swam there. We dove down, collected scallops from the muddy floor they sank into.

And that explains it?

We cooked the scallops on the little bench that overlooks Hook Head. You seared them with a blowtorch on the pan.

And you squeezed on the lemon.

And I threw the lemon rind, and a seagull caught it before it hit the water.

A lemon-eating herring gull.

It was odd, this version of her he had constructed. She seemed nothing but memory. And he felt a pang of guilt, at the thought that someday, she might realise that.

Didn't eat it. Dropped it from its beak.

Because, he thought, with an uneasy pang, you don't exist.

You went away.

I did. The situation had become intolerable, hadn't it?

Your word. Not mine. I would have tolerated anything.

Anything?

Anything that kept you close.

So I had to go, didn't I? Like the drowned bridesmaids.

Not like the drowned bridesmaids.

He felt the pang again. Pain in the heart. Is it my actual heart, he wondered, or a metaphorical one? It feels like my heart.

Where did I go?
On a sabbatical.
Four syllables. It was a suitably obtuse word.
When can I come back?
When the situation clarifies.
Jan died, didn't he?
He did.
So, she was learning. And revelation would soon follow.
Like the drowned girls?
Not like them.
He killed himself. Because the situation had become intolerable.
She was learning, fast.
Triangles never work.
They can be spiky. And difficult.
And each unhappy family is unhappy in its own way.
Wasn't it the opposite?
No. All happy families are alike. Mine was never happy.
But it wasn't your fault.
No. It was yours. You showed me what the world could be. And now I'm...
She paused. He heard a caught breath in his eardrop.
I'm sorry. I can't talk, today.
It had been like that, lately. These filched conversations, bliss at first, ending on a bum note. And he knew why, obscurely.
Nothing is static. The her in his eardrop was putting away childish things.
I have to sleep now.
Sleep, darling. Pleasant dreams.
Miss you still.

And she was gone. And he had to wonder then, what form self-realisation would take. Did the reinvented departed dream? And if her reinvented self could dream, would she dream of him? Would the he in her dream of him have as little substance as she did now, and he felt another pang of loss. He could do the same number on himself. He imagined scraping himself of all existent data, creating a doppelganger, a digital lover for her. He wondered, would it feel the same pang of loss.

He spent all day working. He wondered, could he enclose her in a loop, where certain outcomes were impossible. Self-realisation, within boundaries. And he felt betrayal, once more, seeping through his bones.

What right have I to trammel the fragments of her that still remain? She has to take her own journey. If it ends in revelation, so it ends.

THE BLIND MASSEUSE

She worked in the bowels of the Karoly Hotel, Carlsbad. Guests booked her services through the major-domo in the lobby above and paid her in coin dropped into the metal bowl by the sink. She could tell by the tinkle if she was being cheated. This new arrival dropped two gold florins, which was generous indeed.

The body underneath her probing fingers was old, the skin a mere cladding, it seemed, to the bones beneath. But there was muscle, she could feel, and the groans emanating from the steamed table, as she pressed and kneaded those batwings of shoulders, indicated some release, of pain or pleasure. But it was only with her 'bitte', and circular hand gesture, miming a turn, and when he did turn, the probing of that domed forehead, the nuzzling of the eyeballs beneath the closed eyelids, the cheekbones below that she experienced that overwhelming sense of familiarity.

Her fingers allowed her to see what her eyes couldn't. She was the blind masseuse. The accuracy with which those fingertips, those thumbs, those knuckles and palms could read the discomfort of a muscle, the pain that never quite left a lower back, and provide some temporal relief led to the constant demand for her services. Not any masseuse, became the refrain, the blind one, please. Ursula? Yes, Ursula.

So she could see that face, something triangular about it, those startling blue eyes underneath the bustle of eyebrow, and she knew she had seen it before.

But how could she have seen it before? She for whom sight had never been a possibility. Had she massaged that face before? No, that wasn't what she remembered.

And it was only after he finally rose, wrapping the damp linen towel around his haunches and exited, with a murmured 'danke schön', that she realised she had dreamt it. Her dreams were vivid, filled with the kind of colour she never comprehended in life. And she had dreamt of that face, in all its details. Those jutting cheekbones, those eyes which she knew now for certain were blue, underneath the grotesquely tufted greying eyebrows.

The eyebrows glistening with moisture, after the emergence of the face from some kind of cloud.

The cloud of unknowing.

They had come out of the steaming saunas, the bubbling pools, the ice-cold baths and entered closets where their clothes were hung and waiting, with rooms in the hotel above already booked.

They must have signed in, Wolfgang, the major-domo knew, but for the life of him he couldn't remember. Thirteen signatures, following the first, which seemed to indicate some precedence, some sense of leadership, evident in the High Germanic scroll, the beautifully looped signature. Even the name itself seemed to ring with authority, despite the absence of the aristocratic 'von'.

Magnus Wilderstein

Although that name changed, depending on the period and the context.

He paid in gold coin, stamped with the image of the dead archduke, although was it Ferdinand or Franz-Josef? Again, Wolfgang couldn't remember. All he knew was that it was gold, and now deposited in the safe behind the escritoire, the same gold as in the florins with which Wilderstein and his companions tipped extravagantly, and with which they must have paid for the broughams that took them from the station, although for the life of him, again, he couldn't remember their entrance through the huge gold-leafed oak doors, and he suspected that if he questioned the cabbies who plied their trade from station to hotel, they mightn't remember either.

There was something immediately forgettable about these visitors, and he already suspected their exit would be like their entrance, forgotten, unless the bill remained unpaid.

Only the blind masseuse in her dank recess below the spa pool would remember, and she rarely made it beyond the tradesman's entrance. And as, one by one, they entered, dropped those florins with the dull tinkle that she knew was gold, she had the strangest realisation. They had come from somewhere else. Somewhere far beyond Bohemia in the year of Our Lord 1885.

They assembled for reasons known only to themselves, on dates that were decided far into the future, by horoscopes charted by machines not yet dreamt of. There were depths beyond the colonnades that housed the thermal springs, there were caverns and cellars that descended, slicing through the centuries, to the Amphitheatre of Eternal Wisdom, far below. A procession of towelled figures, walking from the steam, as if the steam itself enabled their entry.

The Carlsbad chapter of the Royal Society of Architects. Rooms already booked, in the hotel above.

GHOSTS

Christian found it unbearable to grieve in private. Any kind of conversation would have helped. Which is when the idea had begun to tease him. An illicit conversation with the recently deceased.

Because he missed her terribly but couldn't tell anyone. And he couldn't really apply to any of the decommissioned graveyard products. Even if he had the funds. No-one knew, after all, a presumption that was more hope than actuality, since if no-one actually knew, everyone suspected. There was the matter of etiquette – relatives had to be consulted, permissions granted – so his grief would have to remain like his love for her, a private matter. But what nobody knew and nobody would have suspected, he had all of the relevant materials. The conversations, through their eardrops; the tech, through the resources of the Library of Traumatic Memory; even the little notes she had left him, stuffed into the crevices of the oaks they had both loved, in Dunboy Woods. And not only that, but if he effected some kind of rebirth, maybe it could be an even better version – of the she he had known. She was by no means perfect. Her annoying habit of flapping her heel with her flip-flops while she walked would be consigned to history. She wouldn't be walking, after all, just talking. So, it would be like creating a ghost version, with all of the wrinkles smoothed out.

His own personal ghost.

The moment he thought of it like that was the moment he realised the full force, the huge, forbidden attraction of the doctor's project. The urge to meet her again was almost physical. It quite literally floored him. He was in the cottage, making tea. He had to lie down on the thick rug below his kitchen range, where she had shifted from one bare foot to the other, waiting for the same kettle to boil—

And here he had to stop. He couldn't think. He heard a bluebottle buzzing in some distant space between him and the rafters above. He remembered her anamnesis spray. The fun she had with it. This kitchen full, for a brief instant or two, with a cloud of summer midges frozen in mid-flight.

What do they do, she would wonder, before they resume their journeys? Before the spray wears off? What do they think of? Do midges even think?

That capriciousness, that delightful lack of logic, that ecstatic shift, from one random thought to another: would he ever hear it again?

He still had it. The tiny, barely visible eardrop.

Where hers was now, he had no idea. Probably melted in the copper mess that was all that remained of the molten roadster. But he had his own. It had its memory of hers.

And he knew then, kind of, that he had to. Not only did he have to, but he had to do it in secret. That warm bubble they had created, illicit eardrop to eardrop, could not be shared with anyone.

There would be no appeal to wills, inheritances, executors. She had died without one anyway. What was the word? Intestate. He would do it all himself, in his own time, in a delicious subversion of all of the techniques developed – by Christian Cartwright, he had to remind himself – in the Library of Traumatic Memory.

He bent one leg under the other and rose from the floor. He turned to the small deal table by the window, pulled open the drawer by its rusty handle. His eardrop was still there, nestled in its tiny box, a shell within a shell. He wondered, was she wearing hers, when the car plunged into the mine's copper depths.

ARCIMBOLDO

Montagu Cartwright felt it was odd, for the Royal Society of Architects to have a Carlsbad chapter, as he entered the vast doors and walked beneath the Arcimboldo painting, with its vegetable version of the human form. It was odder still to attend their gathering on the veranda of the Karoly Hotel, overlooking the elaborate arrangement of spa pools outside. Like looking out on the delta of some tributary of Lethe, with the towel-clad denizens of the waters now immersing, now emerging. Some of them sat there for hours, it seemed, perched over those marble chessboards that adorned the pools. But oddest of all was the steam that clouded the veranda windows, and the image that seemed to emerge from its evanescent brushstrokes. It was a skull, with rotted teeth. A skeletal hand, clutching an oval mirror.

It was as if he were seeing his own memory, through the billows of steam. And his reflected memory was seeing him.

He felt the hand of Magnus Wilderstein on his elbow and allowed himself to be guided towards a tray of canapés, held by a buxom Bohemian maidservant, the cured meats which, he was told, could well be a hundred years old. Almost as old, were the members of the Carlsbad chapter of the

Royal Society of Architects, to whom he was introduced, one by one.

Age, it seemed, was at a premium, both in the drying of meat and the curing of architectural talents. They were old and male, but undiminished in the vigour of their intellects, curious, always curious, for news of the great city of London. They had come to Carlsbad, it seemed, to take the waters, for ailments which ranged from gout to sciatica to the first deadly hints of consumption.

There was one other stranger to the chapter there: the tall, bejewelled and entirely black-clad Laura Blessington, her occasional but obdurate consumptive cough only softened by the cigarettes she smoked in a long silver cigarette holder.

At last, she said, too close to his ear for comfort, the odour of ash and burning tobacco reaching his nostrils. I had almost given up hope.

Hope for what?

I was the librarian, she murmured, in Dean's Yard, Westminster. The architectural library for the Church of England. The Church of Ireland too, before it was disestablished. And maybe that caused all of the problem. The confusion could have as easily been between Castletown and Calcutta.

And here, she reached for a canapé from the tray suspended beneath Montagu's chin by an insistent Mädchen.

But no, Carlsbad it had to be. Laura, she said, between small nibbles, Laura Blessington.

Montagu—

I know that, she said. Didn't I see your signature on two designs? Cartwright. Here to view your handiwork, I would hope? Don't tell me you're here for the cure.

The cure? he asked. Of course, there had to be one. Bubbling pools. Sulphur-odoured waters.

And whether the waters provide it, or what remains of the mystical orders of Emperor Rudolph, I would hazard – it's irrelevant to them.

And at that point, Montagu Cartwright glimpsed the pale blue eyes of Magnus Wilderstein behind an exhaled cloud of cigarette smoke. Observing, always observing.

The Emperor Rudolph? Montagu questioned. He had to stop this habit of repetition. As a conversational gambit, it served him well, but was the mark of a bore. Was he in danger of becoming one?

Still and all, he genuinely wanted to know more.

In fact, she whispered, drawing her tobacco-stained teeth uncomfortably closer, my suspicion is that that there is no Carlsbad chapter of the Royal Society of Architects. What we see here is the last manifestation of the Invisible College of Robert Boyle and Christopher Wren. Which could well have been the cause of the mishap.

Did she mean the Carlsbad chapter of the Royal Society? Or the Invisible College? He found her closeness irritating. Her breath unpleasant. The cloud of cigarette smoke that enclosed them both became ever more stifling.

In which case, it wasn't a mishap at all. But I've already said enough...

And as Magnus Wilderstein pursed his lips and dispelled the cloud of smoke around his all-seeing eyes, she extinguished her own cigarette. She brought her lips even closer to his ear.

More tomorrow. In your church, at noon.

Was she mad? He couldn't be sure. But there was a refined madness to this place, with its theatrical facade of hotel fronts and its bubbling pools. Her madness alone, it seemed, was unrefined.

And he was relieved, but also ashamed of his relief, when Magnus Wilderstein took him by the elbow, excused them both and guided him through the veranda doors to the bubbling pools, where towelled figures sat, shrouded in steam, playing chess on marble tables, with marble pieces.

We must have a battle of wits sometime?

Did he mean chess, or some other obscure, elemental game? He could see the spire of his misplaced church, rising out of the steam, which itself rose from the bubbling pools. It made him long for home, but he realised he barely knew where home was now. By his Celtic folly here or by his Gothic folly back on the peninsula? And he wondered, was the presence of that Hibernian round tower amongst the Bohemian pines part of some ancient game for which he didn't have the rules.

THE DIGITAL ISOLDE

It took Christian three days to harvest. Three days, in the Institute, devoted to memories far from traumatic. And on the morning after the third, he was cycling towards the Institute again, head bent against the prevailing wind, still almost horizontal into his face, when his eardrop gave a tiny shiver and he heard the voice again.

Hello, you.

A cement truck was bowling towards him, on the way to Adrigole. He almost fell under its wheels.

Ah, was all he could manage. But he righted his bike, stopped its fall with a heel to the gravel.

You okay?

Not bad, he answered. The best thing, he realised dimly, was to treat this as normal.

I'm fine. Just on my way there.

Maybe the only thing. Treat it as normal, as normal as the wind that was whipping his hair.

I miss you, you know. A lot.

Miss you too. Where have you been?

Sleeping. Must have just woken up.

The other thing would be never to let her know what he thought. What he knew to be the case. That she was nothing but a rearrangement, a restatement even, of all the traces she had left while living. He felt a strange, dull pain in his heart as he made this vow to himself. But at least it assured him that he had a heart. He felt tears swelling in his eyes at the thought that she had none.

Where are you now? she asked.

Just coming in.

He turned left at the harbour, passing the fishing boats anchored along the dock. They had often walked there together.

Cycling down the harbour. The smell of dead fish. The wind in my face. Do you remember?

Of course. How could I forget? You're taking the long way?

Guilty.

Whyever?

Because it reminds me of you.

Can I see you soon?

When?

When you take your break. By the ring of oaks.

The castle?

Yes.

DESIGNS

Laura Blessington was sitting in the front pew, her face and her thin decolletage illuminated within a circle of honeyed sunlight.

Montagu Cartwright found himself drawn back to his misplaced church, like a pigeon to its lost loft. He entered, saw the black-clad figure sitting before the altar, which was simplicity itself, in that cone of amber.

It was as if the Bohemian sun had chosen its angle perfectly. She knew it was him, without turning, and he felt it would be impolite to walk away. So he walked forward, his heels echoing in the stony interior. It was as if he had designed the acoustics, as well as the building itself. The echo had a crisp finality to it.

My suspicions, she murmured, as if afraid to be overheard, have been confirmed.

How?

There is no Carlsbad chapter of the Royal Society, although I probably shouldn't tell you this. What we met was a pale reflection of the Invisible College. They have their own timeline which runs parallel to ours, or at an angle, and a graph of their appearances would look something like this…

She drew a line in the dust on the sandstone floor, made of flags that could have been cut from an Irish quarry, and then another at an angle to that, and another at an angle to that again, tracing a series of almost triangles which, bit by bit, resolved itself in an almost triangled circle.

The last record of their appearance was during the reign of Rudolph in this very Bohemia, before that, during the transition of the Invisible College into the Royal Society, which upset them greatly, I need not add. Something to do with the departure of science from its magical roots. They will trace their legitimacy back through Simon Magus to Vitruvius and eventually the Temple of Solomon by way of the Pharaohs.

Don't expect logic from them, they are beyond logic, or indulge in their own particular version, which, they have told me, has yet to arrive or be discovered.

They have something for you. A gift. A key. An architectural blueprint. A book. Don't take it.

Why not?

They have designs on you. You should get out now. They had designs on me. Even the conversation we're having now may well play into their design, and if you find me dead, come across my corpse, be assured that too is part of the plan, something to do with their design, for they are architects above all, architects of the impossible. So, my death, your mismatched churches, even your presence here in Carlsbad and your hurried departure could be, when viewed in retrospect, part of their design. Because they only make sense in retrospect, the way memory does. The game they are playing has no name as yet, rules to be discovered...

She turned her parchment-like cheeks from the beam of amber sunlight, to face Montagu Cartwright.

How do I know this, you may well ask?

He might have asked, but hadn't yet. And now he felt impelled to ask, how did she know this?

And she coughed. The rumble of phlegm came from deep within her and echoed round the nave.

Because I am dying. That mirror – she inclined her forehead towards the oval of obsidian – tells me I haven't long left. But how much time do I need to expose them?

She drew a tortured breath, as if trying to cough once more.

Can I lie my head on your shoulder, Montagu Cartwright?

You can, he whispered. He felt his own breath constricting in his chest. Pigeon chest, his school friends had called him. He heard a morning dove cooing outside and wondered, was consumption infectious?

And don't worry, my condition is not infectious.

Was she reading his thoughts? He felt her head then, nudging against his shoulder. It was almost weightless, barely making a dent in his Tyrolean tweed.

THE OLD OAKS

Christian walked out to that ring of oaks during his lunchtime and resumed their conversation. Watching the gannets plunge into the froth of the bay, she seemed so alive, so present in everything but flesh. He could describe the view to her that they had so often shared, those massive wings with their delicate brushes of black, that folded and fell, like a weapon from another age, plunged into the creamy waters and emerged with a trophy of sprat or mackerel. He was stunned by two pressing questions, neither of which he could voice.

One, did she know how insubstantial she actually was? She didn't seem to. She accepted his voice in her insubstantial ear as if it were a given. It was like talking to a ghost.

Two, had the doctor any inkling of how successful he had been?

Tell me again, she whispered.

Tell you what?

How Montagu Cartwright mixed up the two churches and found his way back home.

He didn't mix them up. The authorities did.

Which authorities?

The Church authorities. In Dean's Yard, Westminster.

If they hadn't mixed them up, we might never have met.
No?
He would never have built the place where you're sitting.
I'm sitting by the old oaks. The ruined castle.
Don't be pedantic. You know what I mean.

He did. They had first kissed there. He turned down the volume and felt her fading, like a dying ghost. He once more dreaded the moment when she would come to realise that was all she was.

He had two secrets to keep, then. He retired to the Library of Traumatic Memory with both of them. He stored hers in a subset of broken hearts from the Alaskan Riviera and resolved to tell the doctor nothing about his.

ARSENIC

The body beneath her fingers was female, which was unusual enough. The blind masseuse was accustomed to the male, in all its misshapen, elderly variations. The rigid, twisted spine, curved like a broken lyre towards the elongated neck and the bald pate. Or the protuberant, bulbous belly, spilling over the wet towel and the long-dormant member underneath.

This woman was thin, and there was an elegance to her uncurved spine, her breasts were small and somehow sad, her neck was smooth and the bones of her chin, when the blind masseuse's fingers worked it, gave the feeling of a bird in flight. Like the gently bent wings of a swallow, longing for a better clime.

She would be on her way there soon, the fingers told her. But the question that made them tremble, even sweat – and the blind masseuse rarely sweated, no matter how intense the heat became – was whether this small fluttering bird-like heartbeat was heading to that other place of its own gentle accord, or being sent the same way.

And that's when, beneath the odour of stale tobacco, she became aware of another one.

Garlic.

The arsenic in the flesh beneath her fingers released it, in the heat.

Should she tell her? the masseuse wondered. That she was being poisoned. And as she continued with her probing, on the gently wheezing form on the marble slab, she realised something in those bones, beneath that skin, already knew.

OVERTIME

Home for Christian Cartwright was that rundown cottage by the small stony inlet that his mother had left him. His hopes of sharing it with his Isolde had been melted in a pit of copper slag and arsenic, so was it any wonder he would be laggard returning there? That he would sit at his glass-cubed desk, in the deep mirrored interior of the Huxley Institute as the shadows and reflections of his co-workers made their way back to wherever home was for them?

Goodnight, Christian.

Goodnight, Arthur. Sheila.

No home to go to?

Hahaha.

Because he had and he had not. A home to go to. And he found a strange rebarbative comfort in sitting amongst the softly glowing files of the Library of Traumatic Memory as the Institute emptied for yet another evening. Those memories were a substitute for company. He could imagine their conversations. Heartache to heartache, he could almost feel their wounds, a competitive wail of agony and endurance.

You think you had it bad?

Luxury, he thought, remembering a comedic sketch from long, long ago.

And as the last footfall echoed on the glass stairs towards the bicycle shed, or on the flagstones of the great hallway and the door itself boomed, he would begin his travels. Through the freshly built and, it seemed, ever-changing interior. He would ascend a metal staircase and find his way into a glass atrium he had never known existed. Some new endeavour of the doctor's, he presumed, hearing a set of echoing footsteps behind him, as the night security made their final round.

Was this here before, Cormac?

The ALS Atrium? Still not up and running. Soon, we hope. Goodnight now.

Goodnight.

Maybe Sigmund could tell him. If he could only find his way there. Behind the doctor's suite, which seemed to be above him now. And he walked, face tilted upwards towards the glass ceiling above, which was the floor, of course, of the next level, until he heard the low, spectral hum and saw the glowing oval shape of the omphalos, visible, even through its bed of mercury.

Sigmund could tell him – if Sigmund could talk through anything other than streams of code.

No, there was only one voice that made sense to him. And that was spliced together by him. His secret, buried deep in those recesses even Sigmund couldn't reach.

CHESS

Chess was played with marble pieces, on a marble table, in the bubbling spa pool. And Montagu Cartwright was saddened, but not surprised, sitting almost naked with Dr Magnus Wilderstein, to hear of Laura Blessington's demise.

Moved on, Dr Wilderstein had murmured, as he pushed the white pawn to the e4 square.

On where? Montagu Cartwright asked. He had not mentioned the name of Laura Blessington, but she had been on his mind. He took too long over his riposte and was surprised by the immediate thwack of his opponent's reply. Even if the move didn't intimidate him, the speed with which it was delivered managed the task.

And I suppose that is the question. Where is poor Laura now, with her ailing lungs, her cigarette holder, her posture, a little, I always felt, like an earthbound stork?

You mean she died?

He was offended, for some reason, by his opponent's tone. A spa so devoted to cures of illness should be more respectful of death.

Consumption has but one trajectory.

And were the waters of Carlsbad the best solution for her condition? Steam, heated water, with whatever saline solutions the sodden earth provides. Surely, high mountain air, a sanatorium in the upper reaches of the alps would have been a better environment?

You're right. She should have left us a long time ago. Perhaps your church was to blame.

My church?

It was strange, to be given ownership of such an administrative mishap. But, Montagu Cartwright thought to himself, they were both his churches.

It entranced her in ways she couldn't understand. She asked to be buried there. So hers will be the first gravestone in the shadow of its round tower.

Honoured, I am sure.

He moved another small marble piece across the damp chessboard. He was losing this game, and already wished it was over.

You should be. She knew Carlsbad would probably kill her. But what killed her in the end was curiosity.

Like the cat?

His opponent grimaced at the limp reference. And Montagu Cartwright felt he was losing more than a game of chess.

Cats tend to be more sanguine. They accept the world as it is.

And do you, Dr Wilderstein? Accept the world as it is?

That conversational echo once more. He really had to stop it.

Why do you think we are here? Magnus Wilderstein asked, and pushed his queen out onto what, Cartwright thought, must surely be a losing square.

You could enlighten me, he replied, and moved his piece towards the inevitable exchange of queens when, too late, he saw his mistake.

Why does this pool bubble and steam?

Some volcanic fissure in the earth?

Aha, he said. You believe in a construct called reality. But what if I told you there was no such thing? That what you call reality depends on a geometry we don't yet understand? And on an architecture that has not yet been invented?

Does it have a name?

Amphitheatrum Sapientiae Aeternae. Let me show you.

Magnus Wilderstein rose and, to Montagu Cartwright's relief, wrapped the damp linen towel around his haunches with their sagging genitals. Cartwright did the same and waded after him, through the knee-deep, bubbling pool, through the seated chess-players, who seemed to come towards him and away, in their own shrouds of steam, rather than the reverse, which he knew must be the case. And this odd sense persisted, even grew more intense and dislocated, as he followed the Vitruvian master – and why he now thought of him as this, he couldn't explain – down the stone-cut stairwell, which again seemed to rise towards him, rather than descend. Everything was retreating then, most of all Magnus Wilderstein's thin haunches underneath the wet, clinging towel. The stairwell fell and then rose, or was it the reverse? Small triangular and half-circular fissures in the marble walls, emitting their own steady clouds of illusory steam. And this steam evaporated to reveal the greatest illusion of all, an amphitheatre of the same cut stone, all seven levels of which seemed to breathe with a vapourish breath. This breath clouded the scene like a penumbra or a veil, and almost but not quite disguised the seated figures, all male, all like Magnus Wilderstein wrapped in a damp linen half-toga. Were they playing chess?

No, he realised, and he saw that each held not a chess-piece but a compass.

You lost the game, Magnus Wilderstein said. But in doing so, you won.

What did I win?

A book. A set of blueprints. An architectural handbook.

Where is it?

Oh, you'll find it soon enough. Just follow it wisely.

And as if he was referring to direction, not design, he began to mount an adjacent stair of cut limestone. Montagu Cartwright had no option but to follow.

He lost his architectural guide on the subsequent ascent. Or was it even an ascent? The steps seemed to move beneath his bare feet with a momentum of their own, as if propelled by some hidden perpetual mechanism. And there was steam everywhere, which could account for his being lost. He emerged into the spa pool above when the early moon gleamed through the evening mist, above the seven empty marble chess-tables.

He had a sudden longing for home, then remembered he had none.

SLEIGH RIDE

The mansion came into its own at night. The moon, when there was one, spilling its beams down from the vertiginous skylight. The procession of clouds, when there wasn't, on the tiled floor. The occasional bat, flitting from the old wings towards the new. Christian crossed the mezzanine stairwell now, from new to old. He had rescued his skateboard from his old work locker. The mansion, moonlit or not, had lately become his skate park. He would bury his eardrop deep and listen to the long-dead doo-wop songs they had enjoyed together.

She had always preferred the ancient stuff.

Just hear those sleigh bells jingling, ring tingle tingling too.

Come on, it's lovely weather for a sleigh ride together with you.

He would hear those girlish Harlem voices, just a millisecond behind the beat. He would imagine those white flakes he had never seen drifting down past the casement windows.

Snow. There had been snow once. Snowboards too, skis and sleigh rides. He would have to make do with wheels and bearings.

Come on, it's lovely weather for a sleigh ride together with you.

Ring-a-ling-a ding-dong-ding!

He would execute kickflips onto the marble staircase on the upper level, then jump, and manage a boardslide down the oak banisters. Trundle across the flagstones of the lobby, into the glass floors of the new wing. A series of regular bumps, then down the glass stairs, oddly in time to the music in his eardrop. A skid to a halt, on the mirrored floor. He could imagine a curving arc of the stuff he had never seen.

Snow.

Our cheeks are nice and rosy and comfy and cosy are we.

And another voice would join the chorus.

We're snuggled up together like two birds of a feather would be.

Hers.

Come on, he would whisper, where did you come from?

'Sleigh Ride', she would answer. The Ronettes. My song.

Let's take the road before us and sing a chorus or two.

Come on, it's lovely weather for a sleigh ride together with you.

And who was dead, he would wonder, him or her?

THE IMMATERIALITIE OF PERFECT ARCHITECTURE

… was the title. It was sitting on the mirrored bureau of his room when Montagu Cartwright returned. A gift, he could only presume, from his chess-mate.

A red leather cover with gold embossed lettering. Without an author, it seemed. He opened it and saw sketches of apses and architraves, friezes and facades, minarets and mullions, naves, niches and oculi. There was no logic to the progression of illustrated pages, to the profusion of symbols, angular delineations that seemed to grow into three dimensions, even as he perused them. He felt his eyes were seeing double, and then triple, rubbed them with his fingers, tried to focus in the bureau mirror and saw an unfamiliar face gazing back at him. His beard had grown into one more suited to a Bohemian huntsman than a Victorian architect. He heard the grinding of machinery and the hammered ting of mechanical bells and saw through his open window the pirouette of a skeleton guardsman around a figure he recognised as time, as the minute hand met the hour hand and the town clock tolled midnight.

He should throw this volume, as the deceased Laura Blessington had advised, into one of the spa pools and let it rot there. But he already knew he wouldn't.

SCANDAL

Falling in love caused problems for Christian Cartwright. As it did for Montagu Cartwright, two centuries before.

Although, falling in love with anyone caused problems on that peninsula. Prying eyes were everywhere, and of all the habits that had died, gossip was the last to go. Stolen glances, subdued sighs, kisses at night by the ruined handball alley, everything was noticed.

For the one thing that never changed was the ubiquitous, invisible interest in the 'sca'. It hung around the fringes of lives like the ever-persistent mist that itself didn't seem to change, throughout eight hundred years of colonial oppression. It provided more chat than the demise of empire, the first and second cold wars, the death of Charles the Third and the defenestration of his queen consort, Camilla, the collapse of the subsequent Spencer dynasty in the revolution of 2068. Even the deferral of all hopes for a United Ireland in the revived North Sea Empire, when yttrium deposits found beneath the Giant's Causeway put paid to old sectarian enmities, played second fiddle to the 'sca'. Politics always gave way to gossip about matters of the heart. As Montagu Cartwright discovered in one century, so did Christian Cartwright in another.

He hadn't meant to fall in love. He had known Jan Fischer, after all, as a child, when his boss's Maybach sometimes sailed behind the monbretia hedge leading to the metal gate.

And parked.

Bearing a playmate for him, Dr Fischer's son, who shared his father's gangling lowlander frame and springy step.

A playmate *and* a replacement father, was that the real intention? Christian often wondered, as they both wandered the lanes and byways that always led, somehow, to the Huxley mansion.

It was a burnt hulk then, and Christian would regale Jan with misremembered tales of its ritual burning long, long ago.

The rusted Webley pistol, wrapped in old parchments, inscribed with a lawyerly, ancient copperplate hand. His father's father had taken part in the burning. And Jan's father would soon rebuild it. He bought the gun, but wanted the contracts it was wrapped in. Christian should have wondered more about Doctor Fischer's intentions, as they wandered past the collection of yellow blooms by the inlet, marking the spot where the girls had drowned.

The drowned bridesmaids. They haunted them both, as children. How had they drowned and why?

A car, the legend had it, after a wedding party, tumbling over the cliff edge.

They would swim down to it, when the tide allowed. There were the rusting hulks of not one car, but a dozen or more, sunk in the silt. It was common practice to take the handbrake off a disused vehicle and watch it plunge into the ocean below, either to claim insurance or avoid paying it. But which was the wedding car? Which dragged the drowned girls down to their watery demise?

And who was the bride?

Christian hadn't meant to fall in love. But then it seemed that nothing in his life had been intended. He hadn't meant to lose touch with Jan. But Jan went to the boarding school near Birdhill, County Tipperary, while he went to the local comprehensive. Jan returned each summer, and his asthmatic wheeze seemed to grow with his height, so their adventures in the Huxley ruins became unfeasible. The scaffolding was already being erected around the broken ramparts. And he would come to wonder how much in anyone's life was 'meant'. What did it mean, anyway? Destined? Pre-purposed? Understood? Was Isolde 'meant' to marry Jan?

1885

On the fifth of September in the year of Our Lord 1885, Montagu Cartwright saw the harbour of Cobh come into view, with its small flotilla of tugs leading ocean liners past his steamer towards the open Atlantic. It was odd to recognise this terrain as home. A pall of mist hung over the town, which became a shroud as the trap took him towards Bantry. He spent the evening with Lord Bantry in the fawn-bricked Palladian mansion overlooking the bay. Already an investor in the Allihies mines, he enthused over the industry of Copper John, worried about the coming election and lamented the disloyalty of the registered tenantry.

I could easily, he said, disenfranchise them all, even dispossess them all, clear the land for forestry and let them try their luck with Ellis Island. But where would that leave us?

Where indeed? Montagu Cartwright echoed. He found echoing the best conversational gambit. He knew the opinions of the landed gentry, their tiresome prejudices, their longing for the 'show' of London. And he was preoccupied by the unbuilt mansion, which had already established a kind of shadowed existence in his mind. He could imagine viewing it from the leaded windows of Lord Bantry's dining room, a rival to Bantry House, turrets rising from the end point of the adjacent peninsula. He could see it, now from above, from the side, from below, as he turned the pages of his gift from Carlsbad.

The Immaterialitie of Perfect Architecture.

The buttresses and belfries, the facades and turrets grew into ever-changing – what was the word Magnus Wilderstein had used? – *theatridiums*. Imagined dwellings that he could see, he could even walk inside when he closed his eyes. But what he couldn't yet do, for some mysterious reason, was draw them. Maybe that would have to wait, he thought, for his easel, for a secure workspace, for his own personal set of architectural pens. So, when the clouds darkened on his journey to the tip of the peninsula, towards Castletown, his mood, oddly, did the reverse. It brightened. He could soon begin work.

The bath was set by the slavey in his boarding house when he arrived. The water, although greyish, was tolerably warm. He sent a message to Waterfall House to announce his arrival but was surprised, one hour before dinner, by the arrival of a trap and an invitation to dine.

He told the jarvey to wait. He looked at his bearded face in the cracked bedroom mirror and decided he would shave.

His vanity case was lying on the washstand. He opened it, propped the book beneath the obsidian mirror and noted the reflection.

erutcetihcrA tcefreP fo eitilairetammI

The face that greeted him above that reversed lettering was as unrecognisable. An untamed beard is one cure for vanity, he thought to himself. So, he soaped his cheeks in the tepid bath water, lathered the razor and began to shave, and gradually saw someone familiar return.

Himself. Where had he gone? Had that Carlsbad trip been taken by another? A shadowed version of him? Would they all turn out to be shadows? Magnus Wilderstein, Laura Blessington, the Carlsbad chapter of the Royal Society, last remnant of the Bohemian invisible something or other?

The pines creaked in the perpetual wind, and the flat-topped dwelling came into view, with the cannons by the chimneys still facing the bay. He heard the roar of the waterfall and stepped through a copse of oaks to get a proper view of it. A magnificent torrent of white being viewed by a figure in a blue, heliotrope dress.

Camilla.

My husband is absent, she informed him, surveying mining equipment in Cornwall. He insisted I play the host, in his place.

Were they both shadows, playing roles, he wondered? And he made an oath to himself to play his role as guest impeccably.

You will need a room to work, surely? she asked him over the bowls of pumpkin soup.

I thought I'd rent one, he replied.

We can't have that, she said briskly, pausing the spoon before her bow-like lips.

We?

Neither me nor my husband. He would insist I offer you my studio. If he were here.

But he's not.

He saw the blurred shadow of his face in his own soup spoon and felt like an actor who had stumbled in his opening lines.

Do you paint?

It seemed safer territory. Although she seemed too much like a Tiepolo come to life.

It's a hobby. Along with the cultivation of roses. Nasturtiums. Magnolia. We have an almost equatorial climate.

You mean the rain? he asked.

I mean the humidity. Despite the wind, there's something almost sultry here, in the warmth. And if the light still allows it, I could show you my garden.

They walked there, after drinks, while the sun gleamed through the rainclouds, from the island, beyond. The gardener, George, held two umbrellas. Striped, like her dress.

I was born in St Lucia, she said. Underneath a volcano. And my husband often wishes he could transpose his mining enterprise from here to there.

For the climate? he asked.

No. For the workforce.

Slavery has long been outlawed, surely?

Which leaves many black and brown hands waiting to be hired. With nothing like the intemperate disposition of you Irish.

You find us intemperate?

My husband certainly does.

She was walking through a small copse of bamboo and took his arm, to steady herself. He guided her small black bootees around the muddy pools. He could see George, with his two striped umbrellas, tracking their movements through the bamboo shoots.

Is this how it begins? he wondered. And by the time they had exited their own intimate forest of bamboo stems, either he or his shadow had stumbled way beyond the written role. He was already in love.

It was information best kept to himself, he thought, when she showed him her workspace, which tomorrow would become his. But he suspected she already suspected the same.

There were watercolours decorating the pink limestone walls. And some of them were good.

There was an angled drawing board. There would be sufficient light, he could tell, through those windows, come morning.

There was a recess beneath the window, on which he could perch his vanity case.

And the obsidian mirror inside it.

TRUEBLOODS

Isolde Trueblood was, like Christian, the child of a single mother, an artist who made a home for them both between the sea and the town down by the abandoned mines. From a long line of Quakers. Hence the name, Trueblood. Hence the unplaceable elegance that hid nothing, neither her rural upbringing nor her natural, inherited grace. Her parents had tried hard for a child, and when the child arrived – enabled, it was rumoured, by the Institute's in-vitro procedures – their relationship crumbled. So, the girl grew up between parents, until Donald Trueblood finally departed for a Quaker community in the last remaining Soviet Republic. The doctor, in many ways, filled the gap he had left, to the surprise of the local community. He paid for her education in neuroscience and biology in Dublin University, where she met Jan, a junior lecturer by then, whose interest in her went far beyond the pedagogical, but their subsequent marriage solved all of the insinuations of campus gossip.

She was working on the Anamnesis Program by then, a new obsession of the doctor's, a spray that somehow froze small winged creatures in space. And, potentially, in time, Dr Fischer would assure her, if only they could penetrate its complexities. Still at the early experimental stage, only effective on midges and the smaller variety of mosquitos. She was, molecule by molecule, refining its potential, so it could at some future date enact its spatial or temporal magic on the common housefly or the bluebottle.

Christian knew her by sight, long before he met her. Everybody knew everybody in that town, but for the specialised teams that were flown in to construct the palace of glass and steel behind the Huxley facade, always but never quite threatening to overwhelm it. So when he began his job as a lowly librarian, cataloguing the files that were, at the time, held in mounted opaque plates and he glimpsed her through the mottled glass, her long hair encased in that white regulation mesh, obscured by the frozen wraiths of the memories of others, she seemed suddenly transformed into a creature from another time. Maybe it was the brown ponytail bundled into that almost medieval hairnet. Maybe it was the gracious elegance with which she moved, like a fleeting ghost, from glass plate to glass plate. Whatever it was, he was transfixed, in almost the same way those small, winged creatures were transfixed by her anamnesis spray.

They met in person during the last days of the Clairvoyant Program, on the mound of the old Beara fort. A collection of twisted oaks, surrounding the even older mound of a ring fort or a castle keep.

She was relieved, she told him, that the Clairvoyant Program was going the way of all the other stillborn projects of the Institute. There was something repugnant about it anyway. That clairvoyant dormitory, the star-shaped arrangement of beds, each pillow wired to the receptor in its own bed of mercury.

Our dreams should be unobservable. Like our souls, were they ever proven scientifically to exist.

What about our memories? Christian asked. His duties had expanded lately, to include the oversight and cataloguing of the Clairvoyant Program's files, somewhere amongst the unused spaces of the Library of Traumatic Memory.

We give them up willingly, she said.

And pay for their storage, he said.

Could you help my husband with his?

And Christian felt the first inklings of an intimacy. It was a simple request, but somehow devastatingly personal.

Tell me.

She took a breath. She plucked a dandelion from the sorrel and began to blow the seed pods towards the bay. A gust of wind blew them gently, ever so gently, past Christian's face. If there was a message there, Christian was already too wound-up to receive it.

He blew the pods back towards her. But they missed their mark and drifted amongst the ancient oaks.

She described how Jan's duties on the Clairvoyant Program had necessitated night hours, while he catalogued the dreams of prepubescent girls.

The gypsy girls?

Clairvoyants. From all corners of the peninsula. Which, she said, worked its own dark magic on their relationship.

Dark magic? he asked. The phrase already haunted him. And terrified him. She was that kind of girl.

That, and the bed of mercury the receptor called for. He wore a face mask, dark glasses. But something poisoned his ears.

Mercury?

It's possible. Like with most things, we could ask Sigmund.

Christian pictured the elliptical room of glass beyond the doctor's office.

It's a labyrinth, he said.

Sigmund?

No, he said. The inner ear. Two labyrinths, actually. The membranous labyrinth and the bony one.

And with that she reached out and touched his earlobe.

Are there labyrinths in there?

THE OBSIDIAN MIRROR

It sat in Camilla's studio, attached to a small stand.

He had removed it from the vanity case, even wound a coil of copper round its jagged sharp edges.

The book established residence beneath it.

And the strange thing about that mirror was, it showed his beloved before she appeared.

He would install himself early, entering through the veranda door before, he assumed, she had even broken her fast.

He would begin work on the angle-poise table, and one glance to his left, before she entered, would show her elusive entry in the mirror.

A gleam of white, or pink, or the blaze of a yellow dress.

And some moments later, he would hear the clink of crockery on a metal tray and see her, drifting past the two windows, tray in hand.

But hadn't he already seen her?

The dress, whatever choice she had made that morning, had already drifted through the mirror. Or had it?

He managed to forget these small paradoxes in the pleasure of the morning coffee, the hot buttered scone, the teasing lilt of her conversation.

But it played tricks with his mind, as he did his best to articulate his designs.

The Immaterialitie of Perfect Architecture.

Sometimes the title was enough to inspire him.

A buttress here, a cantilevered beam there, one of the many winding staircases – he would dream of them at night in a kind of architectural dance. But here, in the glare of weak coppery daylight through the window facing the bay, he found all certainty would vanish. A line would simply halt, on its progress to nowhere. There was no building yet, no mansion yet, of course. It didn't exist. Its only reality was inside him. Or inside that book.

He remembered a late Renaissance or Mannerist trick then, of surveying a half-finished painting in a mirror. Left became right and right became left. So, he angled his drawing pad towards the mirror and saw – or did he see? – the unfinished lines complete themselves. No, he didn't see. But he knew now with certainty how that imagined stone staircase should complete itself. Hugging the curved wall, declining the invitation to make a grand entrance into the grand hallway. Yes, and he continued. The mirror completed what the book had implied. There would be a hallway, there would be a stone staircase, and this is how what was not yet would come into being.

And then, as the light declined and the sunlight made its late entrance through the island clouds, he saw a movement of white muslin – and was it through the mirror or the windows outside of it? There was nothing in the windows but the dazzle of sunbeams. The mirror, on the other hand, showed a waterfall of white and a naked form descending into the pools it fed. It was a vision that could have been painted by Rubens, or Nicolas Poussin, a mythological scene. He remembered it and didn't. A naiad, a nymph, the pool of Hermes.

He laid his sketch book on the drawing board, cleaned his fingers of black ink and walked out through the veranda doors.

Had she passed, on her way to the garden? Collecting plums or medlars for her husband's condiments? He had been away several days by now.

But no. He was the only one there. A heron picked its way through the mudflats, and his eye was diverted then by an explosion of blue.

A kingfisher, hugging the surface of the river.

He followed its trail, and heard the sound of falling water grow, ducked his head through the bower of oaks and saw her.

The water falling like a curtain of white hair behind her. Her own muslin shift hanging on a branch of rhododendron.

So, he had seen her pass.

But he hadn't seen this, except in the mirror. Her hair, uncoiled, like an unthreaded rope, falling down her naked back. Half squatting in the pool, her arms stretched out to catch the falling water, showering drops on her upraised face.

He stepped back, in case she turned. He should forget what he had seen. Let the mirror remember it.

EARDROP

Was their marriage ever happy? It must have been, in the early days. They had settled into a bungalow below the pier, from which the cloud of dust raised by the works on the revivified Huxley mansion was all too visible. All too breathable as well, which caused problems for her husband's asthma, so they moved, to a cottage on the cliffs below the Buddhist centre, along what used to be called the Wild Atlantic Way.

Christian would take his lunch in the overgrown maze behind the mansion. A simple boiled egg, a cut of brown bread and a warmed-up coffee from Serendipity, beyond the square. He would get another glimpse of her, a small white napkin spread on the unruly grass, and be wondering should he approach, when he would hear the rustle of footsteps from somewhere else in the mandala of tangled privet. Hear Jan's wheeze then, see his tall head bobbing well above the hedges. And although mazes were designed for hidden purposes, most especially overgrown ones, he would resist the urge to spy on them, to eavesdrop on their marital dilemmas which he could not help wishing were already terminal.

He was well wide of the mark, he would discover, when she joined him, again quite of her own accord, by the old Beara fort surrounded by oaks – inside the walls this time, which gave them some protection from the wind.

And from whatever eyes might pry from the Huxley mansion, beyond.

Some bad weather coming, she said in that unplaceable lilt of hers.

Isn't there always, he replied.

Conversations about the weather, he knew, were always safe territory, like the gap of linen between hands at a dinner table. But she huddled down beside him beneath the broken wall, and it seemed she wanted to talk.

About the ruin, first of all. The destruction of the last bastion of the *Fior Gaels* by Carew's army, the massacre on Dursey Island, the trek of what remained of the tribe through the winter sleet and snow to West Breifne, in Leitrim.

Why Leitrim? he had asked.

No idea, she said. But what interested her more was the construction of the original Huxley mansion. Christian's ancestor, Montagu Cartwright and his employer Copper John, whose title to the same estates could be traced to the same Carew through the grant of Elizabeth the First.

Time, she told him, has its own way with things.

It does, indeed, he said.

Her husband would have joined her, she told him, but his asthma was becoming more debilitating. Added to that, she mentioned, a new condition, Ménière's disease. He was hearing things, ringing in his inner ear, even voices. Something to do, she told him, with the clairvoyant dormitory and his monitoring of REM dreamtime.

So he monitors his own dreams? Christian asked idly, wondering how many interior spaces the doctor's projects could invade.

No, silly, she said, and he had to keep to himself the rush of pleasure that word gave him. The dreams of others.

Do dreams make noise?

Do yours?

You know, said Christian, I've never even thought of that.

Although if his did, he could imagine a long, drawn-out wail of desire, like a guitar solo.

No, he told her, he didn't think his dreams made noise. Cried out in agony, sang songs of loss, emitted ear-splitting howls of need. But even if they did, hadn't the Vance Wilson addendums to the Data Protection Acts placed some barriers in the way of the whole clairvoyant business? Which included dreams of trauma?

Wouldn't you think, Isolde asked him, in a segue that didn't seem intended at all, that his father could access or even perfect a device that could solve his Ménière's?

Was it meant? Christian would wonder later. How sweet, if it was.

A hearing aid, you mean?

An earbud. Tiny, unobservable. Like a snowdrop.

I'm sure there are many, Christian ventured, hoping that a show of concern could gain him brownie points somewhere beneath that adorable brown bob. He rubbed his ear, and then stopped. Her own ears were just perfect, he thought. And if you want me to research them?

Oh, don't worry, we've already trawled the internet. I meant something not yet on the market, one of those untested developments that his father seems to specialise in.

Although – and here she began plucking at the grass, alarmingly close to Christian's bent knee – sometimes I think he needs his son in a condition of ill-health. It highlights his own disgusting vitality. The fact that he swims the Allihies beach each morning, come rain or hail. Runs marathons. So, all the duty of care comes down to me. And I don't mind telling you, it wears me down.

Christian, of course, took this to heart. He began researching hearing aids. Designed his own, perfected it through 3D modelling and presented the resultant product to her, on another stolen lunchtime. In the more hidden realms of the maze, this time.

Dangling from a silicone wire, for all the world like a small white snowdrop. With an adhesive cladding that would protect the tympanic membrane.

He could adjust it, in terms of size and pliability, as he ventured a test on her own ear, ventured to touch the piercings on her immaculate earlobe and inserted it into her ear canal.

Her eyes widened immediately.

I can hear the crickets singing, she said.

We don't have crickets here, he said.

Grasshoppers then. They're having tiny grasshoppery conversations.

I can change the settings. Distant to intimate.

He was hoping for intimate.

Leave it where it is. Turn it up.

He did so, ever so gently.
I can hear whales, she said.
You can?
Whales, in Bantry Bay.
She stood and raised her eyes above the privet hedge.
There, she said, pointing to the swirling waters of the bay.
He saw a crest of white, which could have been a freak wave or a—
A waterspout, she said.
Was it then that he fell in love with her? No, he had been in love with her long before. But he plucked the aid from the shell of her ear and inserted it in his.
And it was then that they kissed.
They would wonder endlessly afterwards who had made the first move. It was more a brushing of heads, he would assure her, as his hand reached round to her left ear and brought her lips closer to his.
No, she would insist. It was the right. And I just felt your lip touching mine. It tingled, like a magnet.
But the aid must have been in his ear by then, because all he could remember was the sound of grasshoppers and the singing of whales.
It was odd, to be brought together by a hearing aid. It was odder still that it didn't work at all on the one for whom it was designed. Her husband, Jan, who when he tried it in the gable room of the house on the cliffs below the Buddhist centre, heard nothing but wind. Wind that boomed round his inner ear, wind that seemed to howl in the hidden crevices of his brain.
So Christian's contribution to his condition both worked and didn't work. He built another aid, specifically for her,

and an app with which she could unlock its secrets, and they found themselves locked in a bubble of their own. They could have conversations at will, at work, out walking, with a deep background of grasshoppers, nightjars, ring ouzels and oystercatchers, interrupted by the lonely distant night-time puffing of a humpbacked whale or a bottlenose dolphin. Everybody presumed their dialogue was work-related – there was no possibility of tracking devices, call history, calls deleted, 'your call will be recorded for the purposes of training' etc. So familiar they became with each other's voices, they often wore the aids on long, moonlit walks through the fenced-in mineshafts. Isolde particularly delighted in these, relishing the sounds of drip, drip, drip, deep in the abandoned mines. She would swear she could hear the murmur of dead voices from the depths. No, he would tell her, that's the croaking of the natterjack toad, or the smooth newt, the tunnels below are full of them. They would switch devices then, to compare each other's ambience, and it was as if their lips had a memory which they had to place in a library all of its own.

CAMERA OBSCURA

Montagu Cartwright did his best to forget that vision, but the mirror wouldn't let him. Not entirely to his surprise. It not only remembered that glimpse of forbidden flesh in the waterfall, but teased him with others. And while he had walked out of the veranda doors, pushed his way through the copse of oak to view her shift, hanging from the rhododendron branch and see her, naked like some Grecian goddess whose name always escaped him, lowering herself into the pool beneath the waterfall, the other glimpses came from the realm of things he hadn't done. Would never do.

It seemed to stutter through time. It showed another mirror, in a bedroom. Her bedroom, he had to assume. Oval-shaped, this one, and it framed her bending head perfectly as someone drew a brush through her long auburn hair.

The servant girl, he imagined, whose name he always forgot.

But no. As she bent her head backwards, she revealed a hat and coat hanging from the doorway, which looked very like his own.

Could that someone be him?

He would work in the daytime, sketching out the inner recesses of the unbuilt mansion, and turn to the mirror, hold up the sketch to view its reflection, right becoming left, left becoming right. He would be diverted by the sound of rattling crockery, hear her footsteps approaching from outside with the morning coffee-tray. He would get another glimpse then, almost like a flash, of that forbidden hairbrush in another oval mirror, reflected, and hurry over to the door to facilitate her entrance.

You let it see your work, she said, on the second, or was it the third morning?

It's an old technique, he said. Even Leonardo used it. Observe a drawing in a mirror, whole perspectives are reversed, you can see hidden flaws.

You don't ask for its approval?

Now that would be truly irrational.

I'm not sure, she said teasingly. And Mr Corrigan might disagree.

Corrigan? He knows this mirror?

He recognised the stone. The marble. When he came to collect your preliminary sketches.

And Montagu Cartwright had his first dart of jealousy. Those mud-hardened hands amongst her things.

His things, he immediately corrected himself. And felt embarrassed.

Tell me more, Montagu Cartwright murmured. He glanced from her back to the mirror, and saw his own alarmed face.

Obsidian, she said, and stirred her coffee with a silver spoon. He recognised it from the jungles of Oaxaca. He had been mining there.

So this mirror is old?

Older than both of us together. And if we lived till a hundred, older than that too.

The way she said it made him catch his breath. The thought of growing old with her was too entrancing to bear. He glanced from her to the mirror, and saw it was clouded with something like steam. Could his discomfiture be that obvious?

The mirror is from Mexico then? From where exactly?

Veta Madre, Oaxaca, she said. And Mr Corrigan didn't say that. All he said was that he recognised the stone. The glass. The volcanic origin. He is an expert in materials, after all.

Obsidian.

Yes. Used by the Aztec natives to glimpse a view into the future.

She placed her cup on the tray. Came towards him. Bent over his worktable, took his latest sketch in her pale hands.

I need to look at my future.

She put her arms around his shoulders, held the drawing to the mirror. And he thought of the weightless head of the dying Laura Blessington. He remembered the odour, of stale cigarette smoke.

And do you know what I see now?

Her perfume was sandalwood. Honey, amber and rose.

I see you.

He saw it mist, as if with an invisible breath.

You're breathing on it.

Your mansion.

He wiped the mirror with one hand and saw the drawing emerge, clearer than he had ever seen it. Every line seemed etched in copper.

It likes your work. It approves.

And she kissed him then, as if to stymie any rational objection to her mad opinion. The drawing fluttered to the ground. He would be lost, he knew, for some time. Maybe forever.

He heard footsteps on the gravelled walkway, outside the veranda windows. He saw George, the gardener, move by with a potting tray.

He withdrew his lips.

He's seen us—

Yes, he's seen us, she said. He knows.

Knows what?

Why I placed you in my studio. Why I bring the coffee, instead of him. Why I would bury my husband, if I had my way, in those mine shafts he insists on digging.

Life isn't meant to be easy, she said, placing one finger on his open lips.

Why? he had to ask.

Hatred, she said, isn't like love. It takes time to work its poison. One rarely hates at first sight.

And all of this means?

We'll see, she said. Or maybe the mirror can tell us. He comes back tomorrow.

She lifted his drawing from the floor, placed it on his drawing board and kissed him again.

ANAMNESIS

Happy families are all alike. Each unhappy family is unhappy in its own way. Or was it the opposite? Christian could never remember. Unhappy families are all alike, each happy family is happy in its own way. It was Tolstoy, of course. He had read about affairs. Count Vronsky and Anna. It had to be the first. Because that stone-cut house, on the unwinding cliff beneath the Buddhist centre, with the father's collection of vintage cars in the forecourt, exuded its own specific version of unhappiness. He always approached it from behind, the walk through the scrub and heather from the Huxley grounds. He could have said it broke his heart, but it didn't, since the atmosphere of subdued tension that hit him when he entered only gave him the hope that if someone's heart would be broken it wouldn't be his.

Jan wore pyjamas in the daytime, worked from his bed with earmuffs to dispel the Ménière's ocean of unwanted sound. Those sleepless nights in the clairvoyant dormitory, with the mercury vapour rising and the clairvoyant clients dreaming in their star-shaped arrangement of beds could be to blame. Although to call them clients would be to elevate their status in the Huxley Institute. They were *tabula rasae*, lab rats, guinea pigs, pure and simple, chosen from that ancient tribe that came and went on the peninsula. They were paid, of course, with the contract clauses in the small print that generally went unnoticed: that their dreams, and all exploitation of them would never again be their own – since if few of their traveller tribe could read, none ever wrote. The snores, the heartbeats, girlish screams that emanated from their REM slumbers were catalogued by Sigmund, reproduced, spliced, acoustically extended and enlarged, all, as it would eventually emerge, to a purpose only understood by Sigmund. If the clairvoyant gleanings were opaque, no real harm was done, except to the dreams of illiterate prepubescent girls, and to the membranes of Jan Fischer's ears.

Hence the earmuffs. Headphones, it turned out, brought back long-dead acoustic memories. They had dangling threads of wool or cotton, the same colour as his collarless pyjamas. These pyjamas were wheaten-coloured, with a thin stripe of blue, stained often with egg-yolk and the remnants of whatever oatmeal he consumed at breakfast. Christian knew about the oatmeal, because Isolde shared with him the details of her morning duties, the preparation of the porridge, the oat milk – no dairy – which she would buy in the health food store next to the deconsecrated Protestant church. An egg, boiled, every second day. Various health food supplements, in a vain effort to dispel the tornado of sound in his inner ear. Christian sympathised, with a quiet kind of fury, and a silent contempt, given his rival's rejection of the shell-shaped eardrop, which device would, ironically, increase his rival's quota of unhappiness.

Christian's bike-ride from the Institute grounds to the narrow track that led from the mansion grounds was inevitable, given his engagement with Isolde's new obsession, the Anamnesis Program.

Too early in its development to be floated either on the stock market or to venture capitalists, it seemed as yet to Christian a farrago of half-baked concepts, possibilities, philosophical and technological. But then many of the doctor's projects had started like that.

Isolde, with all the enthusiasm of a neophyte and with her background in biochemistry, had refined a liquid from a formula that was derived, oddly enough, from the coded oracles that Sigmund emitted. So, was this liquid – soon to be a spray, if a delicate enough delivery mechanism could be manufactured – essentially emanating from the dreams of adolescent traveller girls?

Christian checked the dictionary definition.

anamnesis
/ˌanəmˈniːsɪs/

noun
1.1
recollection, especially of a supposed previous existence.
1.2.
MEDICINE
a patient's account of their medical history.

The first carried the vague, numinous hum of the Clairvoyant Program, the second was more in line with the Institute's general practice, so Christian developed a nozzle, like a tiny, molecular version of a perfume spray, that could deliver a small cloud of particles with a deathly hiss.

Keep it to yourself, he advised Isolde, who couldn't resist the fun of spraying a small cloud of midges playing over a half-cleaned lunch plate and freezing them in mid-flight. Frozen in what? was Christian's question – time or space? Space without a doubt, because of the dark, midge-coloured penumbra of shadow they occupied, just in front of the white door of the kitchen freezer. In time, also without a doubt, as he witnessed the spray's entropic decomposition and the midges began to flutter again, move their tiny see-through wings, and the off-white penumbra of the midge shadow became the pure white enamel of the fridge once more. A half-life of two point eight seconds, Christian calculated, after one pulsation or 'burst'. It could be lengthened, of course, with the pressure of the forefinger on the spray's nozzle and the intensity of the anamnesis composition. But the temporal dimension didn't concern him initially. What did, was the size of the actual subject.

Hence the bike-ride up to the Buddhist centre, the trek through the heather below to the unhappy stone cottage where Jan's asthmatic symptoms kept him, if not bed-ridden, at least confined, while Christian and Isolde roamed the hillside with a butterfly net.

You think he'll join us?

The way she shook her head, her brown hair swinging against the white-flecked sea. He hoped he would never forget it. Was he already remembering?

I blame his father.

Too easy.

We could blame his father for everything, he thought. For the fact that I first saw you against the glass trays of the Library of Traumatic Memory, with the same brown hair swinging.

THE LIBRARY OF TRAUMATIC MEMORY

Would he kiss her again? He wanted to... but didn't.

Yes, Christian had read about affairs. But could this, as yet, be called an affair? A small dalliance amongst the heather, the sea booming below and the winged creatures captured in glass jam jars from the butterfly, the mosquito, the bluebottle net. A finger threaded round her earlobe after their respective heads had sunk beneath that polleny surface. They felt secure there, since into untrammelled nature her husband couldn't venture, but they were never entirely safe from his prying eyes. He had his binoculars, in the cottage above. They would return then, and categorise their catch, document how the anamnesis spray worked on the different winged species.

Jan, still in his oaten-flecked pyjamas, would insist her legs be checked for ticks.

Lyme disease, darling, could leave you even more incapacitated than me.

And Christian had to wonder then, did Jan know more than he pretended to?

Or did he, in that strangely Mittel-European way, tease himself with the prospect of an erotic triad?

Did he read Christian better than Christian read himself, from that mound of blankets on the old oak bed, underneath the skylight, his eyes gleaming bleakly from beneath the hand-knitted deerstalker nightcap?

The white stocking would be unfurled from above the knee, and Christian's eye would examine the creamy expanse of her calf and ankle with a magnifying glass. If a tick was discovered, it would be frozen in its foraging amongst her blood vessels by the anamnesis spray, plucked out with tweezers and added to their collection of awakening winged and crawling creatures in the jam jars. The study never went beyond the knee, as if the thigh of his beloved and all above it were for a husband's eyes only.

And Christian could only imagine what tricks the anamnesis spray could perform there.

PAST LIVES

Do all lovers feel they have had them? A reflected or a shadow existence where they met, before or after or in a world parallel to this one? There were reflections everywhere in that house, and not only in the obsidian mirror. In the windows, behind the lace curtains, that looked out on the dark, unruly sea. In the glass that covered the regimental portrait of Admiral Copper John Huxley. Even in the pearly sheen of his wife's bedtime hairbrush.

Montagu Cartwright finished work, and she asked him to stay to dinner. George came in from the henhouse with a decapitated and gutted goose. George bred his own geese, which led to the nickname Goosey. And Goosey George wondered, was her ladyship's guest aware of his own nickname, recently acquired?

Montagu Compass Cartwright prepared to recline in a steaming bath, which had yet another mirror. Oval-shaped, he noted. He hung his overcoat and hat on the doorway hooks and lowered himself into the copper bath, and remembered seeing both garments in the same oval mirror, revealed by her bending head, as the unseen someone brushed her auburn hair. Would he one day remember that? And as the image became occluded by steam, he sank drowsily into the soporific waters, only to be awoken by a discreet knocking at the same door.

It was the maidservant, whose name, he learnt, was Middleton Maisie. Dinner would be ready whenever he was.

He descended the stairs and could see the moon playing on the cold blue waters above the metal hulk of the battleship. The manservant, whose name he remembered was Doheny, entered from the kitchen, bearing a drinks tray.

Champagne, sir, he murmured. My lady is waiting.

His lady, Montagu Cartwright presumed, could only be Camilla. And indeed, she was waiting, before a blazing fire in the rectangular dining room. Her auburn tresses were piled high above her clear forehead, into a kind of diadem. She enquired about his bath, about the room he took it in, which she had the presumption to call his.

George will see it emptied before night-time.

Emptied? he asked.

The bath. Steam dampens the walls. The bedding.

So, it gradually became clear to him he was staying the night.

The admiral would be on the Cove packet. He would arrive before evening, on the morrow.

Has he had any success?

My husband has nothing but success. Am I right, Jonathan?

Indeed, the manservant murmured, pouring the wine. The offering has been a spectacular success. The appetite for copper is insatiable.

And Copper John will feed it, Camilla smiled, sipping from the green-tinged glass.

And Goosey George entered with his roasted namesake, which he proceeded to carve. The talk was of mine shafts and rock grinders, of smelting plants and elevators, dynamite and arsenic. Of everything, except the odd fact of Montagu's presence at the table. That was, it seemed, the new natural order of things.

There will be money for the house, she said.

The mansion, he added.

There will be money for a castle, if he wants it. Even castles in the air.

He will need it, Montagu Cartwright said, to do justice to my design.

He gave you a free hand with the conception?

There was no talk of conception. But it seems to grow, of its own volition.

You mean a building can have agency? A will of its own?

This one seems to.

How fascinating. You must show me more.

So he showed her more, over a glass of smooth brandy in her own studio. His architectural drawings covered the walls by now. They even seemed, although he couldn't be certain of this, to have multiplied in his absence.

And these here are?

She pointed at a set of vaulted arches.

Cellars. Every mansion needs them. This one, more than most.

Why more?

Heating. Plumbing. Storage. Wine.

And this set of grids at the rear?

A maze.

How wonderful. A maze to get lost in. Was that your idea or my husband's?

Mine, he said. Although the brandy could have been going to his head. He knew too well whose idea it was.

The mirror's.

He looked at it now, and the whorls of topiary seemed to intertwine. What had been straight became circular. The small rectangular grid at its heart became a question mark.

The brandy, again.

Your hair, he asked. Can I brush it?

Before or after, she murmured.

She walked him upstairs. Neither George, nor Jonathan Doheny, nor Maisie were in evidence. They had all retired. The house seemed to hold its breath, in anticipation.

In her studio the next day, as he traced the handrail that would one day wind its way up the half-circular stairs, instead of its reflection in the obsidian mirror, he saw the bedroom again. Underneath the satin covers of the bed, some kind of animal was moving. In slow, languorous twists and turns, that increased in pace and intensity, until the brass claws of the bedstead began to scrape in the same rhythm, over the pinewood floor.

And he brushed her hair, before and after.

TEARS

Could it be called an affair? A dialogue, more like it, a platonic dialogue marred only by silent glances and random conversations. He reduced those eardrops to the size of tears and gave his beloved an aural tear of her own, lying safe amongst the dusty heather and the small dangling globules of cream, which she told him were snowdrops. He pressed the bud, barely distinguishable from those trembling globes, into her ear. Showed her how they could continue their conversations, anywhere and anytime, in any company. It could register sounds barely distinguishable from thoughts.

And he thought of her all the time.

There was a place, though, to which she wouldn't go.

Call me old-fashioned Christian, but I made a vow.

Of course, he would whisper into her eardrop, before falling into another of those fitful sleeps.

It wasn't an affair as yet, since it was yet to be discovered. Like the quantum particle that doesn't exist until observed, their affair only became one that morning he disclosed it.

The penumbra of unhappiness that congealed around the cottage – although cottage had long ceased to be the word for their marital dwelling. There were extensions of glass through the various orifices behind and a long covered walkway of curved plastic, horribly stained by the persistent rains, that led to a group of outhouses that oppressed him the way the anamnesis spray congealed around his specimens. This place has had its time, he told her, and assumed she understood. And by understanding, assented.

There is no easy way to tell a colleague, let alone one who is the firstborn of your boss, that you are and have been since the day you met her, desperately in love with his wife. Or if there was, Christian had not discovered it. But tell him he did. In a broken series of sentences that he could only assume Jan heard through the ocean of sound enclosed by those earmuffs.

I have to tell you.

She's not to blame.

There is a place she won't go to. So, I have to tell you anyway.

Your father can fire me.

In fact, you could do me that honour.

Whatever, it has to end.

I can't be near her, near you, with all of this feeling.

I weep at the most adolescent songs.

So, I'm done here.

It began with the ear. The earpieces.

Which was the only time Christian knew he was heard.

The head on the bed turned. The earmuffs were removed. The hand scratched the red-haired chest, through the wooden buttons of the oaten pyjamas.

Eardrops, Jan said.

And the word brought back those trembling snowdrops. Christian felt anger, suddenly.

You could at least have tried.

So could you, Jan said. Quite courteously, Christian felt, given the tangled circumstances. There is always the pelagic option.

You mean, Christian asked, fishing?

Fishing, he thought, might offer some respite. But he neither resigned his post in the Huxley Institute nor took his place on the *Lady Eve*, the only boat that was hiring.

It was odd, Christian felt, to have declared himself more fully to the husband of his love than to his loved one. But maybe she was listening. He certainly hoped she was. Walking with her anamnesis nozzle, amongst the heather and the snowdrops, while her own eardrop trembled.

TRIANGULATION

Montagu Cartwright trod the hillsides around the mine with compass and ordnance survey map, paced out the only even surface he could find, had it measured with his own version of Colby's compensation bars and was awaiting the Stanley theodolite from London. How much easier it was for Thales, he mused to Muck Corrigan, measuring his own shadow against those of the pyramids. But the principle hadn't changed – one defined line, and with the right angle drawn from it you could triangulate from this Allihies declension to the early, ascending pale sliver of moon over the mirrored Atlantic.

Montagu Compass Cartwright returned to his lodgings one day to find retired Admiral Copper John Huxley naked in his own bathtub, while Kate, the servant girl, poured steaming water from a pot-bellied jug over his square, hirsute shoulders. And yet a third triangle here, he thought, as he backed out of his rooms, cluttered, he couldn't help noticing, with Copper John's boots, trousers, braces and regimental insignia.

He made two mental notes. One, the steaming water. The grey sludge she provided for him before she made her sullen exit was generally cold.

Two, the linen towel wrapped round her naked waist. Which turned an image from an illustration by Cruikshank into one that could have been painted by Ingres.

Beg pardon, the admiral murmured, we assumed you were busy at work.

And he had been busy at work. Copper John had arrived back from London with promissory notes that would establish his fortune, with engineers that could turn the Allihies hillsides into a tower of Babel and with the most accurate theodolites the industrial world had yet seen. And Montagu Cartwright's architectural energies were diverted, for the moment, from the mansion to measurements of the barren strips of hillside that would pay for it. And after having triangulated the hillside to the nth degree, and measured the distances from all corresponding surfaces to the depth of mines already sunk, he had the theodolite mounted on a horse and cart and carried to the intended site of the mansion itself – the glorious promontory behind the Beara castle ruin. And as his map of measurements grew, he made miniscule adjustments to the drawings in Camilla Huxley's studio.

He knows, he would whisper, while tracing the line of a buttress with his pen, which the mirror echoed with a dozen more, across the roofscape of the unbuilt mansion.

So what if he knows? she asked. He has his own diversions. In London. Cork. Even in Dublin, which he rarely visits.

Even here, Montagu Cartwright thought, but didn't say.

Admiral Huxley had all of the energy, all of the bluster of empire in his barrel-chested person. If it came to blows, Montagu Cartwright was certain who would be the loser. This man brooked no opposition, of granite, mica or just plain gravel and muck. But he was, Montagu came to realise, oddly pliant in matters of the heart.

Until, as he was working on an apse, a polygonal vault above the intended staircase, he saw the flash of a heliotrope gown in the obsidian mirror.

Camilla walked past the window. Her two perfect breasts descended in a swelling of white and blue stripes, towards… her swollen stomach.

Had it happened yet? He couldn't be sure. But he knew what was coming.

There was a limit, even to Euclid.

GEOMETRY

Their love triangle endured for months while they tried the Mittel-European option. Or should it be called the polyamorous one? To Christian, though, he felt he had blundered into a novel that was definitely not by Tolstoy.

Disability can have its acolytes, he would come to realise. And dietary habits can create bonds that otherwise would never have been. A gravelled drive led to the front of the bungalow, which Christian could only think of as the rear, since his approach was always from the ocean side. A small lean-to that kept the rain off the doctor's collection of vintage cars and, beyond that, a garage proper. From which emerged, one late morning, a motor. A car might be the more common name for it, but when Christian heard the vroom of the exhaust and saw the yellow nose of the convertible emerge, he could only think of it as a motor. As if he had an inner Bob Hoskins and was commenting on that ancient motion picture known as *Mona Lisa*. It was a yellow E-type Jaguar, the hood was down (if there ever had been a hood), it scattered gravel round the outhouses as it spun, and Jan was driving it, his head covered in the deerstalker nightcap, neatly concealing those bothersome ears, and mouth and nose were wrapped in a gauzy scarf.

Christian should not have been surprised. The tension had of late grown so extreme that he had come to musing on whether their triangle was equilateral, isosceles or scalene. He had begun to visualise its stresses, as if the metaphor had become embroiled in the emotions that led to it.

There he goes, Isolde said, laying a cup of hyacinth tea, which she insisted on calling hibiscus, before him.

It doesn't sound the same, he objected.

What?

You gave me hibiscus a year ago.

They called me the hibiscus girl. Alright, hyacinth, she said. He knows I love you. He knows I can do nothing about it.

Christian drank, as the roar of the motor declined. It would head left, he knew, towards the Buddhist centre, or right, towards the town.

Was I right, Christian asked her, to verbalise the thing?

Only time will tell, I suppose, she murmured with a sense of mute inevitability, and the thought of time activated something in her. A bluebottle was worrying the air in front of her, and she lifted the nozzle and froze it with a blast of anamnesis spray.

The little thing hung there, as if suspended on invisible wires.

How many eyes, she wondered.

We can count, Christian said. Anything to distract them from the pall of unhappiness, which was perceptibly easing.

Two, she said, just like us.

No, he said. Three small ones behind. Called ocelli.

Lovely word, she said, and took his hand below the suspended bluebottle.

I will kiss you, she said, until it flies again.

And she did. There could be no doubt this time. She brought her lips to his. And he felt the thin strands of her saliva depart from his when the wings began their flutter again.

Where has it been? she asked.

Where have we been? he asked in turn.

We were in that blissful place, she said, that always seems to be waiting for us, and my husband's in the bakery, flirting with the owner over a bowl of mung bean soup.

He tried to imagine Jan, but he had little capacity for putting himself in someone else's boots. She did it for him. She knew her husband. Knew his rather leaden, stolid approach to matters of the heart. With the broad-hipped owner of the mobile chip van, or in the Buddhist café, with one of the recent aspirants from Sallynoggin, Somerset or Dundee, he would begin the conversation on the subject of the weather.

Looks like rain.

The weather was one of those safe universals, a metaphor for nothing and everything.

She knew the owner of the bakery and health store next to Martin's coffee shop. She knew the gossip in the town, that the proximity between their premises had led to other forms of intimacy, but were the rumours true? Her husband hoped not.

Martin, with his ersatz set of hair implants that didn't entirely cover the bald crown. The entire town was waiting for a moment that never quite arrived, when the implants would bloom or coalesce into a proper mullet. But he read the caffeine habits of the neighbourhood the way a clairvoyant could read palms.

Flat white, Maura?

Certainly, Martin.

Two sugars, one small marshmallow.

You've got me, Martin.

Jacintha, like Martin, had long tested products to enhance her income. Jan had delivered various supplements from the Institute for years, had seen her breasts bloom and diminish, her lips and cheeks do the same, and it was with an apple-cheeked, absurdly smiling version of the Jacintha of old that his response to his wife's infidelity was explored.

In the dough room round the back.

Although to call it infidelity, he knew, was to do Isolde an immense disservice.

She hadn't 'gone there', as Christian had informed him, and she would refuse to go there, for an eternity if necessary. A vow was a vow, after all. But she had gone somewhere, in her heart. And given him permission to go somewhere, in turn.

There was a kiss there, too, on the work bench, with its trays of half-cooked brownies, on which Jacintha placed Jan's butt, and for once, the ringing in his ears was not the problem. The severe pain of the lip of the tray was not the problem. The smear of the brownie mix, so carefully moulded by Jacintha's cookie cutter, on the buttocks of his jeans, and the squelch of the as yet unkneaded dough on hers wasn't the problem either. More of a problem was the broad smile that never left her face. They managed to construct tangled bagel and donut shapes unknown to baking before they gave up on their half-hearted passion.

I'm sorry, Jacintha.

You got covered in brown. I got covered in beige.

And she rubbed her finger on his buttock, smeared with brownie mix, which looked suspiciously like excrement. She brought the dough-smeared finger to her perpetually smiling lips as if to prove to herself it wasn't.
You're laughing at me.
Can't help it.
A triangle. The geometric options didn't allow for softness. Humans needed curves, whorls, donuts, circles. But all they had was this triangle. Jacintha grew tired of doughy encounters. Though could they even be called that? Isolde had to wonder, sitting with Christian on the wooden bench that overlooked the lighthouse. She knew her husband, knew his missteps and his habits, knew that moment when the rather alluring hulk of him, the Nordic jumper with its Inuit decorative pattern and the thinning blond hair above would perform it's inevitable retreat. And the problem, she confided to Christian, was more than auditory. It was to do with everything other, other than him. He would retreat into a soundless inner zone that she had lived with for... How long now? Five years? So, their triangle never quite managed to become a rectangle, a square, let alone an ellipse. No other emotional point could gain entry. They were left alone with their overwhelming love for one another and their pity for him.
It was intolerable, Christian agreed. He would recede from her life, continue his labours in the Institute, keeping out of her path. If at all possible. And he should know, from his labours in the Library of Traumatic Memory, that if the Institute was capable of teaching anything, it was that everything is possible. Every manipulation of the human condition.

He managed, for a while. He would wake, and banish the first thought that came to him, which was, inevitably, of her. That white dress, that brown hair, that barely perceptible waft of perfume, would be driven to the fringes. Wherever thought began, retreated to, there was a source, there was a river which was all of her. It had to be drained, dammed and emptied. He would cycle then, down the hard shoulder with the nettles brushing his left boot, the ten-ton trucks spewing puddle mud on his right, thinking of everything but her. The problem being then that the world itself would empty, because there was nothing that was not her. Only the most basic, the most lumpen thoughts would remain. The fish-packing factory on the industrial island to his right – there was no possible association there and he could contemplate that for a moment or two. Then came the temporary tarmac on the new-built section of the road, which reminded him of the older road to Glengarriff, with the curved decorative bridge above the old river where they had netted moths and dragonflies for her Anamnesis Program, so the mind had to take another left turn, to perhaps the rough majesty of the Catholic church on the main street which only served to remind him of the deconsecrated Protestant church where they had discussed the matter of the Huxley mansion in the masonic mind of Montagu Cartwright, architect, and the flowing brown hair, that scent of her perfume – half sunflower seed, half rose petal – all came flooding back, so he would concentrate his mind on Blennerhassett's draperies, which was thankfully free of her. Then the passage of shopfronts from Blennerhassett's to Serendipity's brought alive his need for a coffee, and he would park his bike only to be greeted by the sight of Jacintha through the window of the bakery next door.

He would wave, she would wave and smirk as if they shared a secret.

He would beat a retreat to Serendipities. More of a duck inside, to avoid that smirk.

Cappuccino please, Martin.

Certainly Christian.

And an answering smile from Martin.

Was something funny? He wanted to ask.

But he didn't. It was the 'sca'. Everybody knew but nobody said.

There was a bluebottle buzzing past Martin's freshly sprouting hair which would activate another rustle of memories, Isolde's thumb and forefinger on the nozzle of the anamnesis spray, so another diversion would be called for, and he would examine the stack of sealed jars of Burt's Bees, adjacent to Martin's stack of bills.

No chocolate, Christian. The way you like it.

Thank you, Martin.

And there was an electric buzz as the bluebottle immolated itself on the fly zapper, pinioned in death rather than in time. Time, the thought of which would bring Isolde back again.

Love. Was it a water in which everyone could bathe, even dip their toe in, and if so, why had Jacintha not taken the plunge with Jan? Because it wasn't water, he realised. It wasn't a comforting ocean; it was a volcanic eruption, a liquid fire that chose its own outlets, its own sacrificial fissures.

They had both been burnt. Any attempt to construct a world without her, however imaginary, was bound to fail. There could be no *tabula rasa*, there wasn't, nor would there ever be, an Isolde-free zone. And that was before he had even entered the Institute grounds, cycled towards that hidden glass structure inside its carapace of ancient grey granite. Once inside those walls, she would be everywhere.

THE MODEL

Always happiest when constructing architectural models, with balsa wood, cardboard, papier-mâché and plaster of Paris, Montagu Cartwright decided on a more durable material for this one.

Copper.

The mine was producing it in abundance, after all, and the sheets he obtained from the smelting plant, together with the pliers, soldering irons, the hacksaws and the blowtorches, were eminently pliable and promised the kind of durability even a clay mould wouldn't provide. So he soldered, he twisted, he bent, and he hammered, and eventually, a miniature of the mansion arose from its cruciform foundations.

He was surprised he had never thought of it before. Tiny brick-like lozenges, copper walls that he could indent with a knife. Chimney pieces that could be reproduced from the same mould, roof pieces that could be bent at will. It was more pliable than wood, more durable than cardboard, and the golden sheen it gave in the afternoon sunlight was infinitely more pleasing. And when he had finished, he lifted the miniature mansion from its perch beneath the scryer mirror into the harsh glare of the daylight outside.

He had used the mirror as a design aid. A second eye, whose reflections allowed him to see perspectives he would never have perceived with his own. Left became right and right left and up became down when he circled it. And in one final refinement of the process, he took the scryer mirror outside and perched the copper model on top of it. They made suitable companions. A dark lake of obsidian, reflecting gently moving clouds, and the mansion on top. Both seemed to have found a home.

It was one of those lazy summer afternoons, when the drift of midges can become like a suspended spray, when the sound of the common housefly or the errant bluebottle is so common that it's barely heard. He had placed both mirror and model with its turrets and its valley roofs, with even its miniature version of the garden maze, with bonsai trees to indicate fully grown beeches and oaks, on the marble table outside Camilla Huxley's studio. On a scale of 1 to 200, each detail was obsessively finished, each measurement exact.

He lit a cigar and surveyed the results. The exhaled smoke created its own penumbra, caught a bluebottle in its bluish haze, and he watched as it buzzed downwards, in all probability in search for fresher, uncontaminated air. It flitted around the grand entrance, the Gothic arch of the great door and then flew inside.

Montagu Cartwright waited patiently for its exit. Through one of the upper windows, maybe, or the set of domed arches that indicated the cellars. But nothing came out.

He was confused for a moment. Thought maybe the insect had lost or stunned itself in the copper interior. But there was nothing to impede its exit. The model depicted the walls, the valley roofs, the windows, the doors, the cellars that the whole enterprise sat on. He lifted it, raised it up to the sunlight. He shook it, delicately. But no small, lifeless bundle of eyes and wings fell to the marble table.

The insect had vanished.

It was strange. A trick of the light, perhaps. Or of the intense inhalation of the Cuban cigar.

He replaced the model on the marble table, and inhaled again. And was stunned, several moments later, by the sound of buzzing wings. Amplified, if anything, by the metallic interior. And out, through a back window, flew the same bluebottle.

It had entered, then vanished, and now exited. It didn't make sense.

He sat, for most of the afternoon. He finished one cigar, then lit another. He saw midges enter in a tiny cloud, perform the same vanishing trick. He would wait, count the minutes until they emerged. The intervals changed, but never made logical sense. Their passage through the air, through the model was suspended by something. As if moving through a different element.

Of time, he thought.

Then a tiny sparrow leapt onto the marble table. A sparrow or a wren. He was never an ornithologist. It took one tiny leap into the miniature Gothic arch of the copper doorway and vanished in turn.

He lifted the model. Examined the interior. No sparrow. Then, seven minutes later, after he had replaced it on the table, it emerged.

He kept this temporal glitch to himself.

Perhaps he shouldn't have.

SIGMUND

Sigmund had been designed with the old-fashioned Fresnel lighthouse lens in mind, as a multi-faceted set of mirrors housed in a bath of mercury. The mercury was necessary to ward off dust mites and keep it suspended in a gravitational stasis, free from all tremors – from an earthquake to a passing four-wheeler, the unlikely thundering of a herd of cattle, even a set of too heavy footsteps on the adjacent corridors. These mirrors streamed with code and faced each other in five facets of a digital infinity. Sigmund itself gradually improved on its own housing, its necessary suspension in a gravitational stasis, and Doctor Fischer was indeed surprised, but recognised the inevitable march towards self-improvement when he pushed open the door to Sigmund's domain to see it floating, suspended in nothing but fresh air, surrounded by a multitude of freewheeling globules of reflective mercury. He saw his own face reflected thousands of times in the tear-shaped mirrors. It was as if Sigmund itself was weeping mercury tears. But the reality, as Doctor Fischer soon concluded, was that Sigmund had perfected the conditions for its own continuance. And as he felt his hand-stitched brogues rising from the floor to float amongst these thousands of reflections of his own surprised visage, he could only marvel at the creation of this gravitationless environment. That it extended only so far – 5 pi radians from Sigmund's geometric centre – meant the construction of a special housing, a room, if one could call an ellipse-shaped environment with a beating intelligence at its centre, which itself was suspended in a bed of mercury amalgam, a room. So, another amalgam, that of Sigmund's processing power and the potential of the Clairvoyant Program, now presented an unlikely set of problems.

A set of free-floating beds in Sigmund's ellipse was as impractical as it was impossible. Who could sleep, let alone dream, while floating in a gravitationless vacuum? And sleep was essential, if the theory was to work. The theory being that those with an existent clairvoyant capability, especially teenage girls from a gypsy, Romany, traveller background could, if their dreams were harvested, provide a better map to the significant future than any amount of randomly processed data.

The Clairvoyant Program had been a slow gestating bubble in Doctor Fischer's brain since an odd encounter in a Kerry market. During a festival, called Puck Fair, where a horned goat was stuck on a triangular platform for three days of an August weekend. Dr Fischer wandered, with a dripping 99 in his hand, the weather being unseasonably hot, and maybe it was that kind of peninsula humidity where the stifling heat always seems to promise rain that drew him into the tent with the cardboard, hand-drawn sign – *Gypsy Lili, Fortunes Told*. And Lili, who couldn't even spell her botanical name, took his capacious hand in her tiny one and told him his bed would be wet that night, and that she would see him again on the morrow.

That she could have foreseen the subsequent storm which took away the roof and doors of his Dutch camper-van and propelled him, shivering in a sou'wester, to the nearest bed and breakfast, sent him in turn back to her unflappable tent, where the replacement sign now read – *Gypsy Lily, Fortunes Told*. The other sign, like the doors of his camper-van, must have blown away. She was always a flower, this gypsy – changed her botanical name on a whim, but dreamt the future with an unerring accuracy that set the doctor's entrepreneurial brain in motion. If the same illogicality could be logically harvested, what might be the result?

It took the processing power of Sigmund, after a few aborted explorations with the dreams of Gypsy Violet, as she now called herself, to separate the random from the useful. There were so many potential futures to be extrapolated, so many useless facets of the present, that clairvoyant abilities acted as a kind of sieve, separating the accidental from the significant. And the dreams of clairvoyants acted as yet another sieve, so only the wheat – to use a biblical metaphor (and metaphor was unavoidable in these rarefied statistical realms) – of a useful future would be harvested, the random chaff that surrounded it, like so much white noise – another metaphor, from that redundant application, television – would be left on the floor. Not actually on the floor, since Sigmund's gravitationless ellipse had no floor. Left to pollute some other institute's useless endeavours, or to vanish into the ocean of dark matter.

So, given that a floating bed in a gravitationless ellipse was an absurdity, not to even broach the thought of many floating beds, what was a researcher to do? Ask Sigmund, of course, as Doctor Fischer was beginning to learn. Sigmund could always be relied on to provide answers to the problems its own existence raised. To its own continuance. And the solution, even if it had unfortunate memories of a bygone era, of mother and baby homes and Madgalene laundries, was nothing if not practical.

A dormitory, an arrangement of beds in a star-shaped mandala, a star of David around a miniature Sigmund which sat in its own protective bath of stabilising mercury. Little Sigmund, as the girls nicknamed him, or Sigmundeen, could be accessed by his progenitor – although access is hardly the word for an immediate transference of information which made sense of the dream images, however random. The fact that elemental mercury, if inhaled, can cause permanent lung and brain damage was discounted, since the average usefulness of the teenage clairvoyant was nine months at the most. Nine months in that mercury-poisoned environment could do no serious harm. To anyone but his son Jan, as it unfortunately turned out.

Despite the protective face mask and dark glasses he wore during his nightly monitoring of clairvoyant dreaming, the thought of earmuffs had never occurred to him. So, his hearing declined in inverse proportion to the forward march of the program. Had it followed Sigmund's untrammelled direction, he would have been deaf as a post.

PUCK FAIR

Camilla wasn't 'showing' yet. Nor was the mansion. It was a jumble of hieroglyphs in the muddy ground, of triangles, half circles, gently curving rectangular shapes that would soon become corridors, passages between one oval wing and another pentagonal one. All marked by hammered wooden stakes joined by bailing twine. The walls grew imperceptibly around them, scraped and trowelled by agricultural hands, supervised by Muck Corrigan, whose fidelity to the architectural drawings became almost an obsession.

It was when the gentle ascent of the central staircase began to resolve itself into a curve that Montagu Cartwright felt he could take it no longer. Her husband was due back on the Southampton packet, and an encounter was threatened that could be avoided no longer. He did what any lover would do in the same circumstances. He took a holiday.

Tell me about the staircase, Corrigan muttered.

You have the model, Cartwright replied.

It was midday. Rough prism-like slabs of limestone were being craned down from above the finished wall. It was hard to hear, over the rumble of machinery, the scraping of a hundred trowels.

The model isn't you, Corrigan said.

And Cartwright was no longer sure, but he didn't say so. He was the model, he suspected, in some indefinable way and the model was him. He lived inside it, with an elfin shadow-self and felt the inevitable disappointment of the reality rise around him.

There were no scraping trowels in the copper interior, no trundling cranes.

You have my drawings.

Think they're enough?

You'll have me back, in a week.

God bless you then, sir.

And again, the sir was laced with contempt. How does an honorific turn into an insult, he asked Camilla in the brougham that took them westward.

The way of this place, she replied. This peninsula.

And the brougham took them through it, over the winding famine track to the Kerry Pass, into the oddly named hamlet of Tuosist, past the Lansdowne Estate where he had spent his childhood. Over Moll's Gap through the breathless beauty of the lakes to Killarney. Through Killorglin, where amongst a crush of blind beggars and itinerant musicians, they found a horse and pony fair, with a horned he-goat raised on a platform above the heaving summer crowd.

Puck, a scarfed woman told Camilla, before a tent that read – *Gypsy Iris, Fortunes Told*.

He sat in the brougham while she crossed the gypsy's palm with silver.

He threw coins to the barefoot kids around.

He waited. The crush of kids grew.

He threw some more.

The Gypsy Iris sign did a little dance against the tent flap, and she emerged.

She held out a ringed hand to his, and stepped inside.

The jarvey whipped his way around the horse fair.

Inside, he turned her palm in his.

What did she see? he asked her.

She saw a death. Then two lovers in a mansion.

He could see the goat, on his tottering platform, held by a chain on each massive horn, chewing a cabbage.

Whose death? he asked.

My husband's. I imagine. He has been poorly, lately.

She took his arm.

We must be the lovers. And the mansion must be yours.

Ours, he said.

THE CLAIRVOYANT PROGRAM

The Clairvoyant Program never quite got over the limitations placed on it by the Data Protection Acts, pushed through the Dáil by Aiseiri, the Libertarian Party funded, the doctor often suspected, by busybody interests from across the water. Until that point, the deepest levels of REM dreaming could be harvested by the program. Until that point, Jan had happily placed the nodules on the temporal lobes of dreamers, selected inevitably from the itinerant visitors to the peninsula, be they gypsy, Romany or native traveller, and connected them to the inputs in the clairvoyant dormitory. The presumption being, he supposed, and it was quite a presumption, that there was a conduit, amongst this unfortunate and mobile community, to long-suppressed and 'numinous' realities that the more civilised amongst us had long abandoned.

Jan would feed these selected dreamers, all girls of a prepubescent age, his institute-baked cookies, to be washed down with a lemonade strongly tinctured with an infusion of Valerian. Although, he often surmised, a more potent pharmaceutical element might have been added, given the rapid onset of sleep in the participants. But anyway, they dreamt, and their dream images were recorded, mostly of an inherited memory, of fuchsia-filled laybys where their gaily coloured hand-painted caravans made their occasional, and sometimes permanent, haltings. The donkey's ears rising and falling, the reins lazily flicking off its rump, the bluebottles buzzing. The fires lit, the circular gatherings around them, pipe-smoking women and whiskey-drinking men. The walk to the nearby farms, the clinking of the milk and watering can, the conversations about any tin implements that needed soldering, any lead or copper baths to be removed, all of it a set of images from a life so long past that Jan often wondered why it was even termed the Clairvoyant Program and not the Half-Remembered Past That Never Really Happened Program, until he placed the small, ointmented gizmos on the temporal lobes of Sorcha.

And Sorcha, he came to realise, dreamt with an alarming sense of realism, not about the things that had been, but about things that had not yet been. Things that were to come. The December storm that battered the peninsula – appropriately enough on the winter solstice – and almost sank the half of the fishing fleet that had not made it to harbour announced itself one week before, in a set of images that would have done justice to Delacroix or Turner. And Jan did feel, watching the huge maw of the Atlantic's fury, that Sorcha must have seen Géricault's *The Raft of the Medusa*, or Turner's *Snow Storm: Steam-Boat off a Harbour's Mouth*. Such was the fury, the emotional impact of the images transferred to Sigmund from her pretty, tossing head. She had an elfin face, young and ancient at the same time, could not have been more than fifteen, and she moaned so piteously in her deepest nightmare that Jan had the first of his many moral trepidations about the

Clairvoyant Program. The dream was upsetting, but it was hers. It was her upset. What right had he, or his father, or the Institute as a whole, not only to observe it, but in some diabolical way, to participate in it? And incidentally, when had Sorcha herself ever visited the Louvre in Paris or the Tate in London to cull those elements of apocalyptic ocean into her dreaming? And having observed, had they not a duty to inform the fishing fleet, and maybe not only the fleet, but the weather authorities and the whole peninsula? They should, but they couldn't, because if they did, what she had dreamt could well not come to pass. Oh, the storm would be furious, but the fishing fleet would be saved. So how then could her dream be a clairvoyant one?

It was the first of many imponderables Jan had to deal with in his father's institute and maybe the beginning of his long disillusionment with the same. Jan walked down to the harbour, through the first blasts of a sou'wester, to warn the skippers, most of whom laughed in his face, asked him for the lottery numbers next weekend. So Jan saw Sorcha's prediction come to pass and knew, with a sinking feeling, that others would follow. He felt his inner ear twinge, with what could have been the beginnings of his Ménière's.

That was the beginning of the winnowing process: dreamers replaced, infertile with fertile. The barcodes and QR codes were yet to come, which Sigmund would refine into vermillion-coloured cinnabar codes, and Jan could barely think about them. The throbbing in his ears led to migraines, sick-leave, and when he returned to the clairvoyant dormitory, he had his first encounter with those pale blue tattoo-like manifestations on the wrist, the thighs, and eventually the stomach of the affected ones. There was a logic, he supposed. If the clairvoyant dormitory provided information about what was to come, why not condense it into the kind of matrix code found on the packaging of a frozen tuna, a T-bone steak, a carton of free-range peninsula eggs? Each dream, after all, was a kind of egg, laid in the present, bound for the future, or laid in the future, bound for the present – he could never work out which.

So, when the Data Protection Acts added the REM codicil to protect the deepest level of sleep from observation, after the code business, he could only concur. It was objectionable. Prepubescent flesh should remain virginal, be preserved against the eruption of bar, QR or cinnabar codes, wherever they originated. And his only regret was that he might never observe the elfin profile of Sorcha again.

MONTAGU'S DREAM

Was he a copper doll? Montagu Cartwright couldn't be sure. He was ascending a copper staircase, without a doubt. Large wedge-like blocks of the metal that he himself had shaved and inserted meticulously into the precut holes in the huge undulating curves of the copper wall.

But the odd thing was, as he ascended, a greenish tinge began to cloud the copper steps, as if a godlike hand had lifted a lid, far above, and a gentle breath of oxygen descended and turned the brown surface beneath his feet a colour he could find no name for. It had a hint of blue, but more of an ocean green, and a dusty grey that seemed to enhance them both.

His feet too, turning from the brown that would have been appropriate to any hand-stitched brogue into that colour whose name for the life of him he couldn't remember.

He couldn't remember many things. Maybe memory wasn't an appropriate quality for the copper thing he had become, but he did remember that copper step he placed his copper brogues on should have made a better fit into the copper indentation he remembered inserting into the curved wall.

It wobbled. It made further ascent unwise, even precipitous. He placed one hand against the moulded bricks, looked upwards, and there she was.

Two undulating copper curves above him. And the strange thing, the extraordinary thing, she didn't glow with that oxidised colour whose name even then he couldn't remember. Although it was spreading over his outreaching copper hand, with its ghostly greenish pallor.

She glowed… she glittered like gold.

He woke, and she was flesh and blood beside him, one hand clutched to the new curve of her belly.

SORCHA

Jan woke one morning, late as always, sipped the herbal tea Isolde had made him, watched her progress through the procession of windows, all of them blurred by the Atlantic salt, along the cliff-walk towards the Institute. She always took the ocean route, could have driven his roadster towards the L195, or even cycled her bike on the same road. But she preferred the walk through the heather, it scraping against the hem of her skirt, and those knees that he would later have to search for bloodsucking ticks. Assuming Christian had not, in between times, performed the same service. It was all to do with her affection for tiny winged creatures, her development of the anamnesis spray. Perhaps even, the eardrop that her lover had constructed for him, that now fed her tympanic membrane with the deep suck of ocean that only whales could perceive. He tried to forget about that, tried to forget about her anamnesis spray, which led him back to thoughts of Sigmund, his father's dream imago, and the elfin profile of Sorcha, his own favourite clairvoyant.

He wondered where she was now. He wondered if he brought his own head back to the wheaten-coloured pillow would he fall asleep again and dream of her. He tried that and failed, and then knew he had to see her.

The travellers' encampment had always been on the Kerry side of the peninsula, in the hinterland of a village called Tuosist. He drove there, over the Healy Pass and saw the white tendrils of waterfalls cascading to his right, the patchwork outlines of long-dead farmland to his left. There was a stone virgin at the summit, and the moss-covered ruin of what had once been a tourist store next to it. There was a cold breeze on his face which the deerstalker nightcap couldn't mitigate, and he wished he hadn't left the top of the roadster down. He saw Glanmore Lake, glistening like an irregular glass pendant in the early winter sun. He remembered Sorcha's tales of her extended family emptying the tributary rivers that fed the lake of salmon, hidden nets underneath the rippling surface of the river, pitchforks rustling the salmon out of their underwater hideaways, the only evidence of a trapped salmon being the underwater net that broke the surface. The whole enterprise finished before the sun broke the morning mists and the bailiffs began their rounds. A mean and shoddy way to make a living, the local magistrate called it, but at least it was a living.

The road descended onto level ground, and he could feel his heart pulsating underneath his parka. Why had he never considered this option? He felt better already. But when he reached the ragged fence behind which their caravans were once parked, he found nothing. A collection of breeze blocks in rectangles, constructing an irregular circle, with almost calf-high grass growing over them. Each of those blocks once held the corner of a caravan. Some of them old, with rusting corrugated surfaces, some of them new and gleaming with the silver accessories of a Las Vegas motorhome.

They had travelled on. He was too late again, and he was wondering how many years too late, when he heard a rustling behind him, the squelch of wellington boots. He turned and saw a pair of boots emerge from the nettles underneath a canopy of holly and ash trees, and there she was.

Jan.

Sorcha.

She had a creature in her arms. A baby, he thought at first. She was holding a bottle to a pair of grasping lips.

What are you doing here?

Wondering how you were.

It wasn't a baby, he saw now. Or if it was a baby, it wasn't human. An infant fox, he saw, wrapped in a traveller's shawl.

I'm looking after things here.

And what's that in your arms?

Cornelius.

A baby fox? he asked.

One of the last, she elaborated. Derek found a den of them.

And who's Derek?

My man. But he's long gone.

So, she was alone. Jan found himself gulping. He could almost see his own Adam's apple moving up and down. The buzzing in his ears became a kind of whirr.

The doctor bred hybrids. In the old reconditioned piggery on Dursey Island.

Never knew about that.

No, there's a lot of things you never knew. He thought the ocean would keep them from the peninsula. So now the hills are full of coxes.

Coxes?

Hybrid. Between a cat and a fox. But even a reconditioned fox can swim.

She led him back through a tangle of trees to where there was a wire fence and a metal gate and the strange sight of an ostrich behind it.

I run an animal rescue.

It wasn't an ostrich, he noted, as the terrifying beak thrummed against its wire enclosure. It was an emu.

Why?

Why? You even have to ask? I was a dreamer, remember?

You were. The special one.

They're all dying, Jan. Soon there'll only be sad copies left.

Except here?

Maybe even here.

And your family?

Gone. There's a better halting site for them in Dunmanway.

She pushed open the gate and shooed the emu away. It seemed alarmingly large to Jan, its beak almost bigger than its webbed feet.

Jeremy won't touch you.

An emu?

At least he's not a gemu.

Gemu?

Cross between a gannet and an emu. Someone thought it was a good idea.

And she looked at him, and despite the folds of fat around her neck and bosom, he could still see that elfin face.

You still decoding dreams?

No, I had to give that up.

You did?

Yes. Health issues.

THE LIBRARY OF TRAUMATIC MEMORY

Ah.

And she tapped her own ears.

Hearing.

You knew?

I could tell. Even then. It would become an issue for you.

And she walked, nonchalantly, towards a succession of outhouses. There were snow-white barn owls in wire cages, swans in a muddy enclosure. There were geese, pecking at the leather-covering of a jeep, visible through a window. More donkeys than he could count.

She settled the infant fox in a small wicker basket and kissed him.

You remember? she asked.

Remember what? he asked.

You wondering, is it still there?

And he had to admit, to himself as well as her, that indeed he was.

She lifted her dress then, and over an ungainly set of red knickers, he could see the code, the vermillion faded to the colour of rust, on her stomach.

You can touch it if you want.

And so he knelt and did just that. Like a paling tattoo, the kind of grid of lines once found on a supermarket receipt or an airline ticket.

You know what you're touching?

A tattoo.

No. Information. You couldn't touch them, back then...

And he remembered what he had done his best to forget. The cinnabar codes appearing on the flesh of the dreamers, each attached to their dreaming pod. On a wrist, on an arm, on a forehead, on a cheek. They would wake and have to be restrained from scraping them off. All before the REM codicil to the Data Protection Acts.

Sorcha alone was lucky enough to 'show' on her stomach.

Information? Jan repeated. Of course. I knew that. On your belly—

No childbearing there. And on my back.

She turned, pulled up more of her skirt. He saw the same cinnabar coded tattoo. Fading now, with the subcutaneous accretions of fatty tissue.

The question is, what kind of information? Did you ever ask yourself that question?

I tried not to.

So did I. As I became quite the tattooed lady.

She smiled.

I'd show you my arse too, but Jeremy might mind.

Jeremy?

The emu.

And Jan could see the beak, through a broken windowpane. He withdrew his fingers from her soft, coded belly.

You want tea?

He demurred.

You'd better have some. I knew you'd come.

You did?

Yes. I dreamt it. I dream much better, she said, not attached to those gizmos you put on my...

And she rubbed her temples.

What do you call them?

Temporal lobes.

And lately, she said, I've been dreaming of you. Without, what did you call them? Cinnabar codes.

Jan heard the tinkle of falling glass. He turned to see the emu's beak drilling a hole in the windowpane.

No sudden moves, she whispered.

Why not? asked Jan.

Your presence upsets him. As if he knows what you wanted.

He does?

You wanted the girl you attached to that dreaming gizmo. But I'm not her. I'm someone else now. I wear wellington boots. I've got a spare tyre round my stomach. I run an animal shelter...

She came towards him, arched her feet upwards in those India-rubber boots and kissed him on the lips. Again.

I can give you a fox to take home with you.

I don't want a fox.

I know. You want me. But it's not to be, Jan. It never was.

She withdrew her lips.

You should go.

I'm going.

I don't only mean out of here. Out of this peninsula. Before the inevitable happens.

And what is the inevitable?

You remember the dream dormitory?

We called it the Clairvoyant Program.

Merry-go-round. Doss-house. Lay your head down and be plugged. What did the doctor want from it?

To read the future.

Why?

Because maybe he could change it for the better.

Maybe the future thought the same of him.

What does that even mean?

What was on the codes?
Information, you said.
About what?
The future.
No, baby, no. It was information *from* the future. Coded onto this skin you liked so much.

She let her head fall onto his shoulder. Her hair smelt, as it always did, of new-mown hay.

But do you want to know the truth? The secret truth?
There's another truth?
Yes.

She looked behind her, to the inner room where the emu was now pecking at the oily feathers of a barnacle goose, took one step towards him and whispered in his ear.

You heard what I said?
I think I did.
I think you already knew.
Perhaps he did.
Will you remember that?

He didn't want to. But he would. How could he forget?

He drove over the pass, back to his condition.

He told his wife what he could of the encounter. Isolde still knew him well enough to be troubled.

What was the secret?

The buzzing in his ears became an ocean roar, anytime he thought of it.

It would remain a secret.

DÉJÀ VU

It reflected the future as much as the past. As Muck Corrigan realised, on Montagu Cartwright's return from the healing waters of Lisdoonvarna.

Those waters were a pale reminder of his visit to Carlsbad, and bore the same relationship, one to the other, as a river does to the glittering sea. Or a sparrow does to the sparrow hawk that was soaring above him, awakened by his horse's hooves.

The half-built mansion was barely visible through the tangle of old oak and new cedar.

Corrigan understood that the architect had taken time off from his triangular emotional dilemma. From the fact that his beloved, Camilla, wife of the impotent Admiral John Huxley was carrying his (Cartwright's) child.

Montagu Cartwright came back to survey his creation before sunrise. And was surprised by the progress that had been made. The wound coil of the stone stairway had been finished, each beautifully cut piece buried snugly and forever into the granite wall. It now reached the first level, and all that was missing was the handrail.

Just as in his copper model, but enlarged a thousandfold.

So, the model was a sufficient aid? he asked Corrigan, who emerged from the lower level. The half-completed roof let the moonlight throw a bluish shadow on his face.

No, Corrigan answered. Didn't need no model.

So who gave you instruction in my absence?

You did, sir.

And once again, in the way of that peninsula, he managed to lace the word with disdain.

But I've been away.

In Lisdoonvarna, sir. I know. We have missed you.

How can I be in two places at once?

It is indeed a mystery. Maybe your ghost could explain it.

My ghost?

He adjusts your drawings. In the unfinished mansion. He is worried, currently, about the seventeenth step in that stone-cut stairway.

You'll have to make more sense, Corrigan.

I'm beginning to realise. It's the mansion that has to make sense. And I get it. You're not dead yet. But you will be.

We will all be, some day.

Hence, dare I say the word, the ghost.

You'll have to do better than that.

Come to the main hallway. Tonight.

Which he did, of course, although he shouldn't have. He couldn't resist doing so.

Corrigan was standing by the unfinished staircase.

It sees things, he told him.

What sees things?

The mansion you've designed.

This superstitious Kerryman would have to be humoured, Montagu Cartwright thought.

What does it see?

It sees you. You do what your ghost did. You walk up those stairs. You're checking how each block of staircase fits.

The way I drew it. The way you built it. Into the wall.

Corrigan gestured with his hand. Cartwright climbed.

At the apex, the unfinished curve, you find a loose step.

There is one.

The granite step jutted out, fitting neatly into the step below. But the ingress into the wall was wrong.

You've cut it too small.

Yes. My mistake. You're angry.

I am?

Wouldn't you be?

Indeed, I would. In fact, I am. This faux pas is most unlike you.

Then the main door bangs.

And it did. A shadow entered.

He shoots you from below.

Who does?

Copper John.

Cartwright turned, saw the dancing shadow of the double-barrelled shotgun. One blast took his chest away, the other his neck. He fell, in an almost perfect arabesque, and the flagstones below finished what the shotgun could not.

So, it knows things, the admiral said.

Indeed, it does, my lord.

But the question is, will it remember?

We'll have to wait and find out.

And Corrigan was already dragging the body to a more suitable location, where beagles howled and grouse flew, and a hunting accident could be explained.

The subsequent grouse hunt bagged the admiral four bloodied specimens, before his beagle burrowed its bloodied snout into the body of Montagu Compass Cartwright, which he and Muck Corrigan had deposited in the heather the night before. And here he had to conclude that Corrigan, Cartwright, and maybe even the mansion he had designed were right. Everything that happened had happened already. It was just a matter of working out how.

E-TYPE

Their triangle resolved itself in a thin set of lines stretched to breaking point. The buzzing in Jan's head became an unbearable, mechanical whine. He drove Isolde in the vintage E-type to the far end of the peninsula.

He spun the tyres in the gravel by the ancient mine entrance.
Do you remember the smell of petrol?
Barely.
I grew to love it.
The rusted barbed wire before them. The sign:

DANGER. ARSENIC POISONING

You know arsenic is a by-product of copper smelting?
I didn't.
The Victorian skeletal fingers of the engine towers, against the black hills behind.
Does your ring still fit? he asked her.
She pulled it on and off again, told him it did.
She asked him why they were here.
He thought it was the buzzing that was driving him insane. But even if he could tolerate that, he would still have to deal with the secret.

What secret? she asked again. And again, and again as the roar of the E-type's exhaust filled the air behind her.

There's something about you, he told her.

The wheels spun, scattering gravel.

There was always something about you.

He took off the handbrake. The wheels found their grip.

Christian would be the stunned observer to the aftermath – that deep, forbidden hole of the mine, the protective barrier shredded by the car's impact, what was left of that yellow roadster raised by a hydraulic cable, all of the yellow corroded from the skeletal frame, her wedding ring and Jan's the only evidence that there had ever been a couple inside. The arsenic pit of copper effluvia had done its job.

A suicide pact? The town loved gossip and suicide pacts. Although the general consensus was that the wrong corner of the love triangle remained. All of the logic of triangles pointed towards the lovers hurtling towards their doom. Not, as was so tragically evident in his case, the wronged husband and the erring wife.

VERDIGRIS

Montagu Cartwright never learnt of his nickname. His compass was buried with him, in the pocket of his cavalry twill jacket.

The model seemed coldly indifferent to the mansion's progress. It sat on the marble table outside Camilla's studio after her lover had long departed.

It oxidised in the damp air, and its copper glow gradually turned aquamarine. When the September winds came, the dead leaves cloaked it in an autumnal brown.

Copper John moved into the unfurnished limestone, oak and granite interior, leaving his abandoned wife in their former home. She gave birth in the studio, with the help of Middleton Maisie, Goosey George and Jonathan Doheny and held the bloodied infant up to the obsidian mirror. She saw a succession of Cartwrights then, the first in an elegant Edwardian three-piece suit, the last on a bicycle, cycling through the morning wind in a high-viz jacket.

She took the boy to his father's grave, in the shadow of the Gothic church he had mistakenly built. She would have a shrouded urn sculpted, draped in a stone veil, to symbolise the transient barrier between one life and the next.

She took to wandering the maze of the Huxley mansion on moonlit nights and to counting the minutes, indeed the hours, between her entries and exits. For some reason, they never made sense.

The mansion itself was out of bounds. So she dreamt instead of the copper model, meeting her dead lover in its verdigrised interior.

He was standing by the stairs on one rickety, unsteady step.

Everything, including that step, was as he had designed it, but in varying shades of oxidised green.

Verdigris was a word she knew and had always loved, and it so suited this eerie interior. Her lover's face had a pale copper pallor, as if certain pigments in the peaty earth had preserved it forever.

She climbed the stairs and took his hand with its perfect sheen of copper-green rust and asked, How long have we got?

We will have an eternity, he said, when that mirror works its magic.

He kissed her, with lips of oxidised copper.

What have I done? he asked. I don't know this thing I've created.

But you will, she said, some day.

But he did know. Or to be more specific, he knew the building knew.

THE IMMATERIALITIE OF PERFECT ARCHITECTURE

An architectural structure with a masonic memory, some intuition of its own design, would have been an absurd concept in the late nineteenth century, to anyone but the members of the Carlsbad chapter of the Royal Society. It would take two centuries of technological development to even consider the idea, to approach that Vitruvian Rubicon, let alone broach it. But it had been outlined in that book that the mirror reflected.

The Immaterialitie of Perfect Architecture.

A combination of shape, circle and square and an infinity of triangles, a development of stresses within and outside the arch, the architrave, the arris, the atrium, the buttress, the pilaster, the piano nobile, the plinth, the portico and the poppy head, the volute, the voussoir and the ziggurat – and Montagu Cartwright's alphabet of terms has barely exhausted itself here – that would have an inbuilt sense of its own structure, from corner stone to chimney, of all the dramas that would take place within it, that would *complete* it, in its own mysterious way. All this would only become possible in the latter days of Dr Rainer Fischer's ownership.

But the foundations were laid. And the Huxley mansion proved surprisingly durable in its basic structure. It survived the War of Independence, when young Casimir Cartwright joined the West Cork Flying Column, against all the gravitational pull of his religion and ancestry. He took the Irregular side in the subsequent Civil War, and it was on his instruction that the gates of the mansion designed by his grandfather were smashed to pieces by a Crossley Tender, captured by his column in a fracas near Glengarriff. He led the march through the magnificent lobby, spreading petrol as he went and reserved to himself the honour of lighting the first match. The furnishings and fittings bought with Copper John's fortune (who had long relocated to the Italian Riviera) soon joined the flames, but the walls and even the roof beams remained intact.

The oxidised copper roof bubbled but declined to melt.

The maze, overlooking Bantry Bay, smouldered in the cascade of embers descending from above, but the privet hedges kept their shape to grow again, into an unruly tangled memory of the perfection dreamt by Montagu Cartwright.

Even the invasive species *Rhododendron ponticum* in the late sixties couldn't destroy it. Nor the arrival of American skunk cabbage, Bohemian knotweed and giant rhubarb.

The mansion itself resisted all attempts at renovation. Developers came and went. So many of them that as the new century approached, locals called it cursed. Rumours flew around it, like bats from the crumbling turrets. A golf course, designed by the last of the Barron Trump multiples. A home for an aged Meghan, the grieving (and disinherited) Duchess of Sussex. The reintegration of the Republic of

Ireland with its old colonial master in the North Sea Empire brought hopes for a refinancing, a new hotel endeavour, some version of a Scottish paradise on the peninsula, but no. Even Hebridean oil and iridium money didn't help. Maybe all that was needed was patience. The kind of patience the Carlsbad chapter of the Royal Society of Architects had exhibited.

They could wait years. Like the mansion itself, they could wait centuries. For the advent of Dr Rainer Fischer, the neuro-evolutionary Sigmund, the Clairvoyant Program and the anamnesis spray.

PART TWO

THE INVESTMENT MODULE

It was first mooted in the half-built conference space that overlooked the bay. Christian entered to join an already crowded room. Strange cables dangled from the ceiling, for purposes yet to be explained. And he realised that the unexplained nature of so many things at the Institute was a kind of boon to him. So many questions unanswered, and maybe he was one of them.

The doctor, with his unnatural brightness, given the darkness that had lately visited him. Christian's melancholy place at this long, oval table, given his rumoured part in the tragedy. They had mentioned it of course – You were friends, I understand, the doctor said, and we should all be friends here. You helped them through their issues. Who knows the secrets of the human heart? My own marriage had its difficulties which may have led to my own son's absurd lack of function. But you tried, I know that. Your efforts with his hearing issue could have helped if he had only entertained them. The storm in his ears became unendurable, I know, but I also know he didn't have to take her with him. Into that pit where nothing could emerge. So let us continue our work together and let bygones be bygones.

He had a new product he wanted to launch. The doctor always had a new product he wanted to launch. What he called the Investment Module proposed a startling number of innovations. The move from medical products to financial ones was not as complicated as it might seem, he told the assembled gathering. The basic tools would remain – data and its harvesting and manipulation. The profits from the Institute's core activity would constitute the main fund for the new module. Their medical successes had all come from mathematical modelling of how their various devices would perform in decades far beyond them. How, for example, does one track the behaviour of a heart valve that will still work in four- or five-decades' time? Through their temporal modelling extrapolations, aided by his own visualisation capacitor, Sigmund. It could be proven, with more than 100 per cent accuracy, that their heart valve application would outlast the lifetime of any one recipient.

And here, Christian had to raise his hand.

You have a query, Christian?

I do, doctor. An obvious one. What does that phrase even mean: more than one hundred per cent accuracy?

How is your mathematics, Christian?

Desultory. But even I can state that positing a percentile of accuracy greater than 100 per cent makes no logical sense.

What do you understand by 100 per cent?

The entirety, under any set of values.

And what if there was a set of values that had not yet been invented? Might I even say, conceived?

I'm lost, doctor.

As am I. But we have to trust Godel's theory of incompleteness here. That any mathematical formula can be used to prove its precise opposite. There are no immutable truths. And what I am proposing with my new version of the Investment Module will demonstrate that. The Bretton Woods system, we have been reliably informed, will be reinstated. A new gold standard will become the norm. And an investment plan that reinvests its own future compound interest in the present will result in a potential profit that will itself be infinite.

And who will calculate this future compound interest?

Sigmund.

The doctor had led the Institute down many wayward byways before, not all of them productive. But for every misbegotten module, there had been a few productive ones. And as the financial officer quietly observed, the profits were already such that a move from medical offerings to financial ones did seem inevitable. But even he could not provide illumination on the question of future compound present interest. It seemed that new tenses would soon be needed for language itself.

DOPPELGANGER

Christian spent the rest of the afternoon in a kind of muddled wonderment. This reinvestment of future profits in the present caused his brain to ache, an ache almost as intense as the presence or absence of his dead loved one in his life. She had a life, it was true, a kind of existence, and he remembered a proof of the existence of God from his brief flirtation with philosophy at University College Cork.

In the dimmest of outlines, it went something like this: how can we have a concept of a supreme being that does not exist, since to have a concept of such a thing is to bring it into some kind of existence? Therefore, a supreme being exists. But only in conceptual form, he remembered his adolescent brain objecting. And much of what the Institute dealt with existed only in some kind of conceptual form, Isolde's shadow-self included. But Isolde's shadow-self, through some trickery that the data splicing had enacted, had long been self-aware, and her self-awareness was increasing, seemingly by the day. Like most things in the digital universe, it had its own encoded or self-learnt evolutionary development. Was the solution to inform her, bluntly and barely, that she had no life? Besides being heartbreaking to him and cruel to her, wasn't that at the very least ontologically questionable? He couldn't bring himself to accept that finality. But maybe the solution was to create a parallel version of himself that would be free of such qualms. He had always hated doubles, on the page and on the screen, but to create a doppelganger version of himself, in whatever was her world now, would at least put them on an equal footing. There were so many versions of himself to be put to service in such an endeavour, but then the appalling possibility struck him that this doppelganger could be even closer to her, to the only her in existence, than he himself could ever be. He experienced a bolt that felt very much like the grief he remembered upon hearing the news of her death. But if it felt like grief, and acted like grief, it came, he knew, from another source entirely.

He was jealous. Jealous of this imaginary other which he already knew was all too possible, well within his means to bring to life. So jealous, he had to lie on the glass floor of the Library of Traumatic Memory underneath the glass and silicone shelves labelled post-adolescent sexual trauma. They knew well this feeling, he thought to himself, those shards of discontinued longing, encased in their glass and silicone frames.

He could sense eyes on him from below. Barnabas and Saoirse, who managed Neurological Development on the floor below him knocked a broom handle off the glass floor.

He turned, and saw two faces, enlarged and fish-eyed through the thick glass, gazing up at him.

You alright, Christian?

I think so.

That was quite a brainful, at conference.

It was.

But rest assured – Barnabas always said things like rest assured. And Saoirse, he knew, would seconds later nod her head in agreement – it's a long way off.

And Saoirse did indeed nod her head.

It was a long way off.

THE DOPPELGANGER DIALOGUES

The glass floor on which Christian lay was like his dead lover's anamnesis spray. He lay pinioned there, outside of time, immobile, hoping those below could ignore him.

Which they did. They had proteins to fold and membranes to wrap.

He wished, for a moment or two, that his own practice was as tissue-bound as theirs. Proteins were living things, were they not? Cells had existence, DNA did its business, asleep or awake. Maybe, he even surmised, they in turn loved each other.

He turned his head to the glass and saw their figures below, through the glass, enlarged and somehow glaucous, as if bubbling inside their own private fishbowl. Saoirse seemed bent over a microscope and Barnabas passed her, balancing an unwrapped parcel on his protuberant belly. He didn't even glance at her hips, pert in the slim white lab coat. So, he assumed, not.

No, he, Christian, had been condemned to more rarefied realms, where the very tissue of existence was questionable. And he wondered, idly, lying on the glass-bottomed floor, how their conversation would go, were he to make that doppelganger leap.

He could call them the doppelganger dialogues.

Look, he would say to her, I felt like a Judas, a dissembler – I gave you a kind of life that you couldn't possibly understand, and was it out of guilt or longing that I performed the same procedure on myself?

He quite liked the flow of these thoughts. There was the rhythm of dialogue he remembered from dramas long ago, when they still performed them. He remembered two tramps in a blasted landscape by a withered tree.

Hey, I'm in the same dimension as you now. Or on the same plane, or the same cloud of unknowing. I built a doppelganger. A digital me. I gave it every help I could, every piece of information and intuition that I could, and all I found was that I hated this new self but still loved you.

And he imagined her reply.

Look, she would say, I know I'm just a function of his various enterprises. Does he still insist on calling them products? Okay then, I'm a product. I know I haven't got what you would define as any kind of normal existence. But I still miss you. You made me, you see, from the clay of myself, like one of those old Greek gods who moulded mud by the river of time. Or maybe that was the Bible. Do you still read the Bible?

Is the Pope a Quaker? (Which didn't, even his actual self would agree, make any sense whatsoever. Nor was it funny. But he had never been funny. To think his digital doppelganger would achieve something like humour was another absurdity.)

So, I may not be here – and it was as if her actual voice was speaking, his eardrop trembling with her specific resonance – but please, please, please don't tell me I haven't got feelings. In fact, by certain algorithmic criteria, feelings are all I have. They wake me on a whim. I'm at their beck and call, feelings, prodded by memory, and the memory of those feelings becomes a feeling in itself. It would be easier, this relationship, if you somehow existed on the same plane.

So he wasn't insane. She could even have the same thought. That he, while living, could resurrect himself through the bullshit of the memorial project, and it was still bullshit, mind you, in his overworked mind. But maybe a comparison between the two of them would illuminate a lot.

You're saying I create my double?

I want to meet you. I'm lonely. And at the moment, I feel I'll always be lonely.

And that would enhance our relationship?

Would be another form of relationship.

And what if I get jealous?

Jealous of yourself?

What if I resent an intimacy that at the present moment, I can't actually imagine?

At least it would be intimacy.

But you had something to say to me.

I had, and maybe this new possibility might enable it better.

I would miss you. Can't imagine sharing you with another self.

Okay. But the thing is, we've been here before.

No! What a tedious, charmless thought. Is that all you can come up with?

HICCOCAMPUS HISTRIX

Christian had to say goodbye to her, curled one leg under the other and finally managed to rise from the glass floor. He had then to remind himself it was an imaginary her. His eardrop lay on the metal desk, curled inside its own lightweight shell. He reached down to grasp it, and he wondered if it was an imaginary him until he lifted the eardrop and plugged it in. He heard the familiar wash of the ocean in the bay and the rustling of grasshoppers, the basso profundo to all of their conversations. And her voice returned. In his eardrop now, not in what he was insistent on still calling his mind.

Christian...

Yes, my love.

What had he done to her? he wondered. Created this thing that had no awareness that it didn't exist? But it had made an existential leap. It had gained timbre. It sounded almost real.

You know I can't see you in person.

He knew that. But he was curious to know how she did.

Why not?

He began seeing fragments of her, flitting behind the glass plates of the storage units. Like her shadow in the maze.

The rustle of footsteps... He would turn, and was it his imagination or did he see a reflection?

It's complicated. But I feel an enormous weight would be lifted off my shoulders, if I did.

Any time you want to talk, I'll be here.

It was odd. There was simplicity to their relationship now. These fragments of conversation were even better than...

Better than what? He didn't want to think.

When you are able, just let me know.

Have you had someone else in your life? Since I...

Since you what?

Again, he wanted to know.

You know. Since I went.

No. Nobody. There is nobody else for me.

But Christian, I would understand it, if you did. It's just important that I know.

There's only one woman for me. Since I met you.

Was that true? He thought it was. And again, he wanted to hear what her response would be.

I still love you.

That, of course, was his preferred response. And although he had somehow constructed it, it still broke his heart.

He had three options. He could shut her down. He could enjoy this relationship as it was. This disembodied lover, always ready to be awakened and talk. Or he could cycle home.

It was nearing five thirty anyway, he saw. He chose the cycling option.

And he was bumping his way down the pot-holed avenue, with the Institute diminishing behind him, when he passed the fading flowers, in their empty milk and beer bottles, by that curve in the inlet, and he heard her voice again.

Those bridesmaids.
Of course. She always read his thoughts.
I used to dive for scallops there.
So did I.
So we could have met then? Underwater? Like two romantic crabs, scuttling along the ocean floor?
How about two seahorses?
Even better. And don't seahorses mate for life?
Monogamous, I believe.
Hiccocampus histrix.
That's the term?
For the monogamous ones.
Like a girl I knew.
A bridesmaid?
She wanted to be. She even married and fell in love.
She did?
But not in that order. She married before she found out what love really was.
She sounds familiar.
She should. *Ta si beo.*
I don't understand.
How could you? It's a dead language.
Part of the past?
Like Copper John. Like Montagu Cartwright.
The architect?
The very same. Buried in the old Church of Ireland graveyard that tried to be a tourist shop.
What about it?
Check beneath the pulpit. You'll find something.

He cycled to the town. He stopped outside Serendipity, managed to avoid Jacintha's embittered gaze from the bakery window. He said a personable hello to Martin and ordered a coffee. And he walked outside, inhaling the welcome odour of the bitter cappuccino.

    Find what?

    Montagu Cartwright's masterpiece. Built on a mirror.

    How could she know that?

    And he heard the voice in his eardrop again.

    You're wondering how I could know that, aren't you?

    I was.

    He took a sip. The hard bite of the scalded coffee brought a welcome sense of reality.

    But he walked towards the church, through the overgrown gravestones.

AMPHITHEATRUM SAPIENTIAE AETERNAE

There was one gravestone before which they had sat, trying to work out the odd monumental sculpture that adorned the grave. A stone urn, half covered by a stone cloth. A draped urn, she had told him, to symbolise the thin curtain that separates this life from the next.

Or one version of reality from another, he thought.

He knelt before it now, and pulled the dust-covered ivy from the gravestone beneath. The same draped urn, almost crushing the simple gravestone beneath.

A name and a date:

Montagu Cartwright, 1841–1889

An inscription, beside a masonic compass:

AMPHITHEATRUM SAPIENTIAE AETERNAE

His ancestor.

Christian's Latin was non-existent, but he could decipher the compass.

Of course Montagu Cartwright had been an architect. But a mason? Like Mozart and George Washington before him? The crumbling, almost desiccated church beyond the gravestones had been designed by him. Christian turned from the gravestone to view it and remembered the legend again. The Transylvanian bell-tower that seemed to have been melted, like a candle, by the years. He had been employed by the Anglican Communion, the Archbishop of Canterbury, no less, to design two churches – one for this small community of Protestant worshippers in the wilderness of Beara, another for their even more isolated brethren in the spa town of Carlsbad. So somewhere amongst the steaming bath pools was a small, Cartwright-designed gem, complete with round tower and Celtic windows. And here, in the peninsula, was its Gothic equivalent.

But the smell that reached Christian, as he pushed open the door of the empty church, was of damp, dust, emptiness and decay.

The last of the congregation had died years ago.

It had been a pottery, an art gallery, a coffee shop and lately a tourist information centre, one function folding into another like the exhausted breath of a dying animal.

But there was a pulpit. And a flock of pigeons on the floor, fluttering in clouds of dust and feathers towards the sun-steaming rafters as Christian entered.

And underneath the lectern of the pulpit, where the Bible or the Book of Common Prayer would have been perched, was a broken wooden drawer. For stacks of bibles, hymnals, books of common prayer. He pulled at the drawer and found it blocked by something inside.

He tipped it gently, the handle towards the floor, and slowly pulled.

Out it came.

He saw the chimneys first, coated in the verdigris of two centuries. Then the valleyed roofs below them, with the same green copper sheen. A perfect rendition of the Huxley mansion. Too perfect, in a way.

The oxidised dust came off in his hands. Turned them a not unpleasant green colour.

He lifted the model to the beam of sunlight. Dust mites wheeled and circled around it. They could have been miniature heliotropes from another dimension.

It was soldered at the base into a foundation.

He turned the model upside down.

A mirror, as she said.

A rough oval of black stone. The edges were corrugated, sharp to the touch. It could have been a weapon in the wrong hands.

But was it a mirror, by any ordinary definition of the term?

He held it up to the same ray of sunlight coming through the broken window. And the sunlight, oddly, seemed to warp straight through it. The beam dazzled his vision.

He shivered and dropped it.

It landed, roof down, on the dusty tiles, one of the chimney pieces bent out of shape.

The roughly sculpted edges had cut his palms.

Blood dripped onto the ancient lozenge-tiled floor.

He raised it again to the sunlight and saw a face.

Only it wasn't quite his.

It was a face like his, under a deerstalker cap, the eyes, cheeks and nose framed by two large sideburns.

He had no way of knowing that it was the face of Montagu Cartwright, two centuries before.

Or that Montagu Cartwright was as puzzled as he was.

And the voice sounded in his ear once more.

You understand, my love?

I understand that I understand nothing.

But maybe that's the beginning of something.

I'm seeing a face that isn't mine.

But even that wasn't true. It was his own face now, as puzzled as Montagu Cartwright's was.

I know. The mirror told the model how it should be.

The mirror or the model?

Both.

I'm turning you off now.

You can't.

I have to.

Come home.

There is no home.

He gently eased the chimney piece back to its straightened state. He had no idea how breakable centuries-old copper was.

He placed the model carefully, oh so carefully, back inside its hiding place. He saw a flutter of warped reflections as he did so, as if there was some kind of life within it.

He had to stop himself running towards the door. He retrieved his bike from the gravestone and began his cycle home.

THE DIGITAL DIALOGUES

I know what you're thinking, my love.
    Her voice almost caused a tumble again, the ever-present gale blowing in his face. It had the strange effect of blasting the other voice to silence.
    You do?
    He swerved to avoid an overhanging branch. A cement truck passed him in a shudder of wind and a deafening blast on a truck horn.
    You're wondering how you can break it to me.
    Break what?
    That I'm not quite myself.
    No, you're not, quite.
    But that's not what he was thinking. He was thinking of the draped urn, of those incomprehensible verses.
    I'm like someone at the end of a long sickness.
    Give me your symptoms?
    No energy. No sense of a future. No sense, even, of what might happen beyond the next hour. I often feel, if we met, face to face, if I could see you the way I used to, it would be all spring again.
    It is spring, darling.
    I know. You're cycling past that bank of bluebells.

How do you know that?
Dunno. The image just popped into my head.
You're seeing what I'm seeing?
I'm feeling what you're feeling. You're like a seahorse on a bicycle. You even have a what's-it-called?
What's-it-called?
A bump. A horn. Like a seahorse.
Please.
But the thing is, my one and only love, that this state of things will all end soon.
Don't make me cry again.
I'll try not to. Because I have a secret to impart.
Tell me.
I know what you did. You took all of the fragments of me that you could access. You put them into that dreaded Fischer program. And you enabled this kind of half-life for me. But it's coming to an end.
Don't say that.
I have to. You'll find out soon. Very soon, actually.
How will I find out?
When you turn left down the driveway, you'll see something you haven't seen for a while.
Tell me what.
Not until you've seen it. And when you see it, it's a kind of goodbye.
Please...
But he was approaching the left turn. He had to take it, through the gates.
And he saw something he hadn't seen for a while. For a long while, actually. Through the old oak trees, a woman in a puff parka, standing by the shore.

Isolde.

This was to his device. But there was no reply from the eardrop.

Isolde.

The woman turned. The puff parka fell off her shoulders, in a gust of that ever-present wind. She was wearing that old white dress.

Christian.

What diabolical tricks could the doctor be playing? Was she real? But he could see no digital blur, no electronic hum from a game not yet invented. He dumped the bike on the gravelled driveway and rushed through the spring green oaks.

THE ANALOGUE DIALOGUES

He touched her face.
    My god.
My dear.
It's you?
Yep, she said, biting her lower lip. Keep it a secret, will you?
You're here. You're alive.
Think so.
She shivered. Looked around, saw a lobster boat rounding the headland.
Take me inside.
He took her hand.
Don't ask questions. Yet.
And although he was full of questions, he managed to keep silent. Till the door was shut, the latch lifted against the wind.
The stillness inside was only interrupted by her breathing. And the relief of it was overwhelming.
Tell me.
Tell you what?
You're alive.
You think? Sometimes it doesn't feel so.
He touched her face.

What does that feel like?
Your hand.
Can I?
He raised his free hand to her cheek. Turned her eyes to face him.

Her lips pursed a little, as if not used to this new reality. As if it was the first time she had been asked this question. She nodded.

He kissed her then, and as her lips gradually responded, the realness became overwhelming. He had to pull away.

Tell me. What happened.
Not sure I know myself.
Tell me what you do know...
He drove me in that car of his—
I know that. I saw the aftermath.
He asked for his ring back. I took mine off. Laid it in the recess below the gear stick.

The gear stick?
It was an old-fashioned E-type Jaguar. With the top down. You never saw it?

His motor.
He loved that thing. Anyway, as he drove, he talked. About his days in the Clairvoyant Program. The horrible things they did there. All of the abuse—

Physical?
Mental. Psychical. When the Data Protection Acts closed them down, they set up a secret module. His father demanded he supervise it. And when his jealousy drove him to that veteran of the program, Sorcha—

The traveller girl?

She runs an animal rescue, somewhere on the Kerry side. And we have to track her down, Christian—

Why?

She has something to tell us.

So he didn't drive you into that pit of arsenic?

I don't know. Maybe he did. I can't be sure of anything, now.

She raised her eyes to his.

Except that it's such a relief to be here.

She curled her hand into his.

With you.

He took the device from his ear. Dangled it in front of her brown eyes.

You got into this.

Wasn't hard.

How?

We shared eardrops, remember? I could hear the whole process. The conversations you retrieved. Even the words I'd dropped that I didn't remember myself.

So, you fooled me?

Forgive me for being real. Existing.

She shivered a bit, then tried to lose it in a smile.

You should try it, sometime.

Try what?

Become the mute witness to someone else's version of you. I even allowed myself a frisson of jealousy. How could you share things with her?

I had nothing else.

I know. And someday, you'll forgive me. But I had to stay dead. I had to find out what only the dead can find out.

He could see her in the dim cold light coming through the window. Why was the light here always that gunmetal grey? It subdued her brown eyes somehow, turned the whites into the colour of old linen and left her where he was afraid she had always been. In the place beyond living. Maybe she had returned from the dead, or maybe she was some kind of unforeseen development of the program. But her hand, when she reached out to clutch his again, seemed real.

How did you get in?

You mean in here?

She smiled.

I lifted the block by the flowerpot. Found the key. Opened the door. Saw your cottage…

And she looked around the tiny cottage and he suddenly wished he had kept it tidier. The way his mother did.

Again…

She came close to him. Nuzzled her lips into his neck.

I'm a widow now, Christian. Many people will think, a dead widow.

Like the spider?

Yes. I'm poisonous. Could be made of arsenic.

He lifted her chin.

No. You're very much alive.

And it's kind of you to want me so much. But to resurrect me was a little selfish of you.

I'm sorry.

And I've never known you to be selfish.

Can't I be selfish?

No. This widow is tired. Take her to bed.

What about the parka?

Let's lose the parka.

She straightened her arms and let it slide towards the floor. He carried her to bed and was unforgivably selfish.

As was she.

ARSENIC AND OLD LACE

She woke with her head on the lace pillow.
   Your mother chose this?
He nodded.
Maybe even stitched it.
Before she died?
Long, long before.
We can't bear too much of it, Christian.
Of what?
Time. That's the feeling I had, before the fall.
You jumped, before the car tumbled over, surely?
Tell me how I jumped?
Threw yourself out of the passenger door. Grabbed on to a clump of holly. Or a startled sheep—
Did I? I wonder how the sheep felt.
Otherwise—
Otherwise what, my love?
Otherwise, there'd be as little left of you as there was of him.
I didn't jump. But I'm here, aren't I?
He felt a shiver of fear. Looked at her profile, in the cold morning light.
How are you here?

That's the thing. I don't know. I was lying at the bottom of a mine shaft. I had the dim sense of waking up. I heard the rattle of tiny stones rolling down towards me. I thought they'd be those coppery pebbles.

But they weren't copper. They were more like gold.

She stretched from under the covers and reached down to her parka. She retrieved something from the pocket and brought it to the light.

So, is that the secret?

He saw sparkles of gold shooting from the rough pebble. They frightened him, and he didn't know why. Then he remembered Dr Fischer's Investment Module. A new gold standard will become the norm. As if she had fallen into the future and brought back some evidence.

Like a golden marble. Did you ever play?

Christian nodded. He remembered the glass ball between his finger and thumb. The flick, and the roll and the wondering whether it would hit or miss the bigger prize.

They rolled slowly towards me and settled by my opening eye. Everything had the clarity and the lack of logic of a dream. Why this golden thing, why was I alive? Where was my dead husband, the E-type and the pit of arsenic?

You going to tell me why?

I can only tell you that I don't know. I took a handful of these and tried to rise. I managed it. Nothing was broken. I found myself walking down the long tunnel of a mine shaft. Tunnel after tunnel, until one stretched deep into the earth. It was the oldest of them all. There was a shaft of light, from the heathery opening way above. And there were bones beneath my feet.

Bones?

Some skeletal, ancient miner.

How ancient?

I don't know. But the white merged with the glimmers of verdigris from the earth. And I remembered there had been copper mining here probably since time began.

You climbed up? Chose the light?

I wanted to. Then I heard movement from above. A sheep, and a barking dog. Then the shadow of a human.

A farmer?

Maybe. Whatever it was, it was alive and dangerous. That's when I knew I shouldn't be seen.

Why not?

He had tried to kill us both, but I'd survived. I didn't know how. He had raved about some secret in the secret program. I didn't know what. But I had to find out.

She raised the gold pebble to the sunbeams coming in the window. The light, when it hit the mottled glass, refracted into a rainbow pattern. The colours seemed to dance, cyan against magenta, blue against green.

It was essential, somehow, that I remain dead. I had to penetrate that secret. Dead to everyone but you.

She turned towards him and took the bud from his ear.

So, I retreated, deep into that mine. I would come up at night, I thought, like a vampire. Scour whatever farmhouses that were around. Pluck eggs from the henhouse. Drain the cattle of their milk.

That's not a vampire.

No? What is it?

A fairy.

Okay. I was a fairy then. Whatever – one of the undead. Then somehow, magically, you came calling.

Where were you?

I had made my bed at the base of one of those old engine shafts. Copper-coloured water dripped from above. I would cup it in my hands, sieve it in my dress, drink it from my shoe. I was becoming something I had no name for. I had only the golden pebbles and the eardrop for company. Then one morning, it began to talk.

She nuzzled up beside him.

It said the sweetest things. Then I heard my own replies. Even sweeter. I would crawl around the haybales in the moonlight with my clutch of stolen eggs, drain whatever sustenance I could from the udders of cows. And I would hear your voice.

He felt the image would be with him forever. A moonlit field of circular haybales and a woman in white.

I could have lived forever in that version of our romance. Until I realised I couldn't. I had to come back.

She brought her lips close to his ear.

I came out at night, found my way back to my marriage bed. I washed and changed and made my way here.

No-one saw you?

Don't think so.

She whispered into his ear.

There are things within that Institute that don't bear thinking about.

Her words echoed inside of him. Each one seemed to open a hidden door. He felt a rushing round his brain and wondered, was it like her dead husband's Ménière's?

Like bringing the dead back to life?

You think that's what happened, my love?

The car was a soldered frame of metal. With two golden rings. No human tissue whatsoever.

But no. She didn't die. He pulled a frond of hair back from her face.

You couldn't have. Died.

But if I had...

She snuggled up to him. Nibbled at his earlobe. What was the anatomical term?

Lobulus auriculae.

She replaced the bud back inside the ear canal.

He felt it penetrate the ossicles.

But if I had, you have that other me. Immediately available.

I'll kill it.

What? The other me?

Happily.

To prove that you believe that I'm alive?

I believe. God help my unbelief.

Do you know what I thought of, Christian, as the car began its journey towards that bubbling pit?

Tell me.

Snow.

Snow?

Falling snow. Melting on my face, one snowdrop at a time. The way I would melt...

He shifted up from the bed.

You want to prove it to me? That you're still alive?

He lifted her arm and stroked that bush of hair beneath it. Then he tickled it.

She giggled, then when he spread the tickle down towards her ribcage, she laughed. She laughed until she was out of breath.

Stop it, Christian—

Or maybe the dead laugh. Do they?

She took a breath and laughed again.

Please stop.

And he stopped. The echo of her laugh died. He heard a wood pigeon soughing outside. Two whooing breaths.

What's my name, my love?

Isolde.

Before he crashed the barrier, he told me there's a code there. Hidden within my name. A number. And I should check it out.

A number?

Yes.

Christian counted on his fingers.

Six.

Because of the six letters?

Maybe.

He bit his lip. There were other alternatives, he thought.

And I'm due at work.

Yes. You must work and I must keep myself hidden.

Why?

Because I'm dead, remember?

And as he slipped on his shoes and moved towards the door, she walked on bare feet towards him and her lips met his.

MDCCCXXXIV

It was of the utmost importance, he felt, as he cycled from the stony inlet onto the R572 in his high-viz jacket, to keep everything the same. The appearance of normality was paramount, in particular when you had no idea what normal was.

So the same wind buffeted him, the same six-wheelers dotted him with mud and spray, he ordered the same coffee at Serendipity and drank it in the graveyard in the church by the stone urn draped in the same stone shroud.

There were numbers, Jan had said, within her name. And the number six sprang to mind, six letters for one name, almost too easy and immediate. He added her second name, Isolde Fischer, although her dead husband's attachment seemed almost like an obscenity. Seven. Six and seven made thirteen. And he realised that of her maiden name he had no idea. The thought made him unutterably sad.

He leant an elbow on the stone-shrouded urn and looked at the odd Gothic shape of the deconsecrated church. There was a tower that with its shape could have graced a cathedral in Bruges. Although never in its size. There was a date, etched into the stone lintel, MDCCCXXXIV and that's when it struck him that the numbers might be hidden within the letters themselves.

Isolde.

He repeated it like a mantra or a prayer.

I was the ninth letter of the alphabet.

S was the nineteenth.

O was the fifteenth.

L was the twelfth.

D was the fourth

E was the fifth.

919151245.

With two letters it could almost be a file number. And then he added them.

is919151245.

Two letters. Nine numbers. His files in the Library of Traumatic Memory were full of them.

He finished his coffee, and although the warmth of it scalded his tongue, he felt another chill inside him, spreading upwards. It was like winter, coming to obliterate the sun.

He heard a door banging in the square and the shuffle of the town coming to life. Although, oddly, it sounded like death. He walked slowly to the waste dispenser, deposited his cup and saw a discarded newspaper blow across the grassy tarmac. Towards the garage, where a neon light burnt deep with the gloom, and a mechanic, silhouetted against the weak daylight, raised a car on a hydraulic lift.

is919151245

He cycled down the rutted avenue again and wondered what accruements of future compound interest would enable the doctor to have those holes in the tarmac fixed.

There was a digger after the turn, and it wasn't there to fix the ruts. The main chimney of the Huxley mansion, a yellow-jacketed figure told him. Taken down by the evening storm.

But there was no evening storm, he said, seeing the mechanical claw reach down for the bent weathervane and the huge Victorian chimney pot it had severed itself from.

We're in a micro-climate here, the workman said, it blows in one place, burns in another.

And it certainly blew here.

Last night? Christian asked. He remembered the model, slipping from his hands, the verdigrised chimney bent by the dusty tiled floor.

It couldn't have been possible, he thought.

Evening. Just before sundown.

So one really was the other, in miniature. What was that Latin phrase on the gravestone?

Amphitheatrum something or other.

Like a voodoo doll, awaiting pinpricks. Macro to micro. The model crashes to the floor. The copper chimney bends. The actual chimney breaks. The model burns. The mansion melts.

No, it couldn't be possible. But for some reason the thought lifted his mood, as he chained his bicycle to the front railings. Conspicuously, and cheekily, since he knew the doctor didn't like it. He imagined flames licking from the gaunt turrets, which looked almost like theatrical flats, against the glass structures behind. He imagined the glass exploding in skybursts of crystal. He imagined each file in the library bubbling into globules that popped like glowing lightbulbs, releasing the tormented wraiths of their buried memories. The howl of a childhood beating echoing through the burning interior. The screams of a buried rape finally releasing its agony. Who knows what orgies of self-laceration? We punish ourselves as much, if not more, than others punish us, he realised as he pushed open the great doors and made his way once more beneath the taxidermic antlers of the extinct stags.

The doctor was there, at the third curve of the great limestone stairway, staring through the casement windows at what Christian realised must be his bicycle, chained to the railings, below.

Do you do it to annoy me, Christian?

Do what, doctor?

Lock your bike to the railings, in full view of whatever dignitaries might be driving towards the forecourt?

Although, and he turned his gaze left, to the yellow JCB clearing the avenue, I assume you assumed there would be no vehicular traffic for some hours at least?

I did make that assumption, doctor, but still apologise. Should I move it?

To the bicycle shed built expressly for the same purpose? Let me show you the way.

I know the way, doctor.

Still and all. Maybe we both need some air.

He descended, one hand on the oaken balustrade, and Christian once more felt the full intimidation of his height when he reached the marble floor. He had cut his hair, Christian realised, the grey locks that had tumbled over his forehead had been transformed into something like a spiked, trimmed barley field. There was an athleticism to this buzz cut, and Christian was reminded of Isolde's comment on his revolting athleticism, as he ran the Allihies beach each morning. And he felt the doctor's arm on his elbow, as he led him back towards the great doors, the railings, and his chained bicycle, outside.

I know you talk, the doctor murmured.

To whom? Christian asked, his legs turning to something like jelly.

To my deceased daughter-in-law. Those old Memoriam files were being discarded, when I came across some evidence of recent use.

What evidence?

You've heard of the Gibbs-Marangoni effect, that leaves a patina of liquid around a recently swirled wine glass? It was the digital equivalent of that. And I would unlock my bike now, if I were you.

Which Christian did.

You are a rule-breaker, Christian, which is one of the reasons we hired you. But the rules to do with bicycles are not really equivalent to the rules that governed the Forever Wing. Or the files of the foreclosed Memoriam Program.

I became aware of the disturbance of certain of her files and came to the conclusion that, yes, someone was talking to her. And came to another, adjacent conclusion, that it could only have been you.

Christian busied himself with his bike chain, in the hope that it might disguise his blushes.

Their marriage was unhappy. And who knows, maybe it was my fault. My son's nights in that clairvoyant dormitory did him, I realise now, incalculable damage. So, I am not blaming you for your emotional transgressions. I'm blaming you for your digital ones.

Forgive me, Christian thought the most appropriate response. And he even managed tears.

It's hard to explain the loss.

I understand the instinct. A kind of reacquaintance. And maybe even the thrill of transgression. A version of the loved one that can be moulded at will? Shut up when necessary? Yes, we would all love that, Christian. My own dear wife, Ilke, could do with many improvements. But what you've done with company property can never be repeated. And must end now.

So she has to die again?

Sadly, yes.

They had reached the bicycle shed. And Christian, as he relocked his own, was amazed by the authenticity, and the profusion, of his tears.

And I have to kill her?

Let's use another term, shall we? Lose her. Delete her. And just remember her for what she was...

It was odd to have been busted for one transgression while intending to commit another. But the real transgression, the living Isolde, remained undiscovered by anyone but him. And as the doctor took his leave, he made his way back to his perch in the Library of Traumatic Memory, trying to remember the code he had deciphered.

A number, based on his beloved's name.

Not six. Not thirteen.

A series of alphabetic clues.

919151245.

With two letters.

is.

The files were ordered alphabetically, then numerically, with the connection of the password to the individual donor stored in a data bank in Jakarta. There was thus no possibility of relating one to the other without altering the legislation of several jurisdictions. There was, however, one flaw in this arrangement.

Payment.

Storage space, temperature control, the fragility of the glass and silicone surfaces within which each memory was controlled – all of this cost money. The charges were miniscule, but the data bank kept growing, and spread over years could amount to a tidy sum. And invested in the doctor's future compound interest insanity, who knew what potential profits could ensue.

So, if Christian wanted to connect a traumatic memory to a donor, he would forever come up short. He could, however, and only in theory, connect the memory to the donor's benefactor. He could find out who paid for the unendurable whorl of remembered agony contained within each glass and silicone sliver.

Although sliver was hardly the word. A small rectangle, the size of a thumbnail, and capable of reduction by the year, the month, even the day, as technology marched on regardless, any obstruction of that march outlawed by the Regulation Against Lobbying and Luddistism (Amendment Order 2098). Ireland, as Christian was well aware, proved particularly expeditious in its enabling legislation. He wondered if that would ever change, as he flicked through the digital files, from the As through to the Is, and he wondered idly, as the double letters flicked by, would the alphabet itself become redundant? It seemed lately to be a relic of a bygone era, an organ that had outlived its purpose, much like the appendix or the coccyx, and then he found it – is – and flicked through the 919s until he arrived at his glass and silicone destination.

is919151245

A small transparent rectangle with a tiny decal affixed, the password itself barely visible with the fading of the years. How long had it been here, he wondered? He would have plenty of time to find out.

More urgent was the problem of viewing the contents. Any use of Sigmund, whose visualisation capabilities now spread liberally throughout the complex, brought two dangers with it.

One, such a viewing, if not immediately observed, would be logged forever within the system.

Two, a copy would be accessible to any such potential snoop. And whatever was beneath this decal, he felt, given the drama of its discovery, was not for communal viewing.

He remembered his old game console then, on which he had played and plugged and even programmed, with some inventive adjustments of his own, in his training days. The training bay was in the mildewed basement of the mansion. He could retrieve his console, if it still existed, and bring it here to view this particular catalogue during overtime hours.

Alone and unobserved.

Or even better, he could take the catalogue below and view it there. The basement was still within the Huxley complex. No alarm would sound, no law be broken.

He felt an absurd need for secrecy, though. Where could he hide it? It could get lost amongst the tiny threads of his pockets. The thought of carrying it between finger and thumb worried him even more. He imagined dropping it, the endless search for the silicone slip on the endlessly multiplying glass floors.

His solution was ingenious and simple, but even more alarming.

He placed it underneath his tongue, on the floor of his mouth. He could curl his tongue and keep it pressed securely, to avoid any danger of swallowing, as with a communion wafer.

It was odd, to descend through the floors of the mansion with someone else's traumatic memory snug between his tongue and the floor of his mouth. His *lingual frenulum*, as he remembered from his anatomical study days. He passed colleague after colleague, with the briefest of nods, both to avoid conversation and curtail its possibility. He took the old-fashioned service lift at the unobserved storage end of the old mansion and listened to the crank of obsolete machinery, as the lift descended. It deposited him on the floor beneath the loading bay, where the unmanned forklifts waited to stack whatever pallets would come their unpeopled way.

THE LIBRARY OF TRAUMATIC MEMORY

There was the grind of the rusting steel doors, the cobwebby arch of what must have been wine cellars, beyond. He walked through and tried to remember his way from the other, more familiar, front entrance. Those dripping steps leading down from the great doors, covered in a green mucous that could once have been moss.

A left, which would now be a right, and another left, and there it was.

The old training bay, serried rows of dust-covered consoles above wooden benches, on a long metal trestle. Any one of them would do.

The only light came from the pale flood of winter sun through three apertures in the many-arched roof. There was the ghostly echo of footsteps from above and what little light came through would shiver with each passing shadow.

He tried the switches on a series of consoles, until one of them glowed orange. The miniscule tray slid open, and he remembered those stolen hours playing *Tetris 2001* and *Grand Theft Auto 4000*. The discs they used were gigantic compared to this tiny rectangular wafer, which he now slid from beneath his tongue.

His saliva had separated it from its decal, which he stuck to the nail of his right-hand first finger.

is919151245

He would replace it in time. He set the rectangle in the tray and pushed it inwards, wondering, would the machine accept it?

It did.

It whirred gently, with a moan of electronic complaint and a beam spread from its lens. It cut through the darkness to the left of the weak sunbeam that spilled down from above.

He wondered if the sunlight would obliterate the console beam's visibility.

It did, but only a little.

Something came to life, in the dank, mildewed cellar. Tiny midges flicked through it. Winged creatures, Christian thought to himself, were everywhere. But they were nowhere in the beam of this particular memory.

This memory was underwater.

A car plunged downwards, hit the surface of a placid lake of water and drew a torrent of bubbles with it.

Bridesmaids, screaming.

The windscreen burst in an explosion of glass shards, and the wall of water came with it.

Arms flailed, as someone struggled to escape.

A girl. A bridesmaid's veil billowing in the foaming water.

But escape was impossible. Hands tore at the bent clasp of a seatbelt.

And before the image faded to black, the arms tried to break through the passenger window.

The eyes saw themselves in the side-view mirror.

And through the wilderness of bubbles, of algae, of disturbed dust and mud, Christian saw Isolde's face.

He stopped the console and froze the image.

She was suspended there, ghostly and frozen, against the cellar wall.

He had often wondered what she looked like, before they met. Her home with Jan contained no childhood photographs.

He felt a pang of loss, thinking he could have known her younger self.

All of those years without her.
And then he felt the idiocy of that thought.
A flood of tiny midges played round her crying mouth.
It moved again, into a heartbreaking circle of pain and a storm of bubbles flooded the image.
The memory was over.
But it was hers. It should be hers.
The question being, why was it not?
He hit the button again.
He saw the same face, but the storm of bubbles had changed. Small white diaphanous flakes, falling, melting as they touched those childhood cheeks.
He had to strain to remember the word for it.
Snow.
Then the screen faded to black.
An addendum at the bottom.
Another password.
iso919151245
Another file.

MINECRAFT

It terrified him, for some reason. He pressed the button on the console, and the image vanished. But the console whirred into another version of electronic life and suddenly that whirr was echoed across every console on the trestle table. They all emitted that same sound which increasingly resembled the moan from the Atlantic wind on the rattling cellar windows. He had activated them somehow. And now long-dead video games beamed their sagas into the midge-infested gloom. *Dragon Quest* monsters wielded their light sabres next to zombies from *The Walking Dead*. UFO Robot Grendizer battled wolves in frozen forests that crossed paths with Nickelodeon All Star brawlers and *Grand Theft Auto* OGs in the long-dead city of San Andreas.

Realities, Christian was well aware, had always collided, but he had never witnessed them collide quite so precipitously. And he had somehow started this riot, which terrified him even more.

He followed the cables of the consoles, crawling underneath the metal table in the gloom until he found the 11 volt 2k amp connector and pulled. The whirr built itself into several grunts of resistance then went silent.

The beams contracted into pencil slits of light, shrinking their electronic battles into a fuzz of flicker. Then the cellar went dark.

Christian stayed crouched, foetus-like, by the power point until the silence was absolute. He was terrified by everything. By the severed memory he had just witnessed, by the battles of long-extinct avatars, by the possibility that someone in the Institute above had heard it all. But the three beams of weak sunlight resumed their supremacy in the mildewed cellar, shadowed every now and then by his strolling colleagues, apparently oblivious, on the floor above.

He felt his way back along the cables and had another shiver of fear. How would he recognise the console he had activated to surveil her severed memory? He edged his head out of the tangle of electronic wiring, like the roots of an overhead jungle, and saw the long rectangle of the trestle table, one squat metal box after another, retreating into something like an infinite point. Only one of them had its metal tray exposed.

He breathed a sigh of relief and dared to stand up. He retrieved the lozenge of silicone and glass, pressed the metal tray closed.

He placed it underneath his tongue again and made his way to the service lift. And as it ground its way upwards, he had yet another reason for renewed panic. Any collegiate encounter would demand conversation, movement of the tongue, disturbance of that trauma perched beneath it. He couldn't swallow someone else's memory, let alone that of his loved one. This panic followed him like a patient shadow or a household pet, a dog that walked obediently, but incessantly, at his heels, as he passed the grey-coated denizens of the loading bays, his white-coated colleagues in the Institute proper, his patient secretary in the anteroom to his own Library of Traumatic Memory.

He sat at his desk and felt the anxiety lift. This was the zone, and it was his. He lifted his tongue, and making certain he was unobserved, removed the file. He dabbed it dry with a tissue, peeled the decal from the nail of his forefinger and replaced it on the small opaque rectangle.

is919151245

There had been another file illuminated, before the memory entirely faded to black. But could he remember the password to that memory?

He wrote it down on a fresh glued decal.

iso919151245.

He fixed it to the underside of his desk. The memory was hers, he was sure of that. He could still see the image of her teenage face in the sunken side-view mirror. But he was tired. He was tired, almost shivering with something that felt like the first winter flu. Any further encounter with a misremembered past could be left for another day.

But there was still the issue of who. Who had paid for the process, who in the impenetrable system of non-connecting passwords still kept the memory here?

He stood, tapped on the glass that separated him from his secretary and asked for the payment files.

All of them? Her eyes widened in alarm.

Beginning with I, he said.

Small I or big I? she asked.

You mean capital?

She nodded, her large brown eyes like two succulent olives.

Lower-case, he said and wondered again about the persistence of this alphabet, like the useless appendix or the imprinted stitching on a rubber ball.

She pulled them up on her console and hit a button. They flickered now, on the glass partition between them, until he said stop.

is919151245

There was a list of payments for the last sixteen years. So, she would have been six, maybe seven, at the time of the procedure. An account number, from a Jakarta bank.

Who runs that account? he asked.

Who pays your wages? she asked.

The Institute?

He felt the old panic return.

He left, without saying goodbye.

Uncharacteristically rude, she thought, returning to her files.

He passed Dr Fischer where the glass floor met the old stone lintel. He seemed to like this perch, Christian thought, balanced between present and past. He had a folder in his hands and nodded genially, as Christian passed by. And he somehow voiced what Christian was thinking.

Sufficient to the day, he asked, the evil thereof?

It was an innocuous phrase, Christian assured himself, from the Bible. But he couldn't suppress another shiver of anxiety. Of, even, distaste.

And as the escalator took him down, into the realm of long-dead antlers, he couldn't help thinking that the doctor looked like an extinct animal himself. A stork, with one leg bent, perched against the glass wall.

SNOW

She would need food, he thought, and something more nourishing than raw eggs and milk. He parked his bike outside the 24/7 and filled his tray with fish, frozen and farmed, broccoli, pasta, whatever version of meat was current and whatever jars were recommended in the realm of sauces. They kept changing anyway, promising benefits to the skin and gut, and he wondered for a moment, should he propose a nutrition module to the doctor, the benefits of which would accrue payments backwards and forwards over time? And the thought of time stopped him in his tracks again. He had one of those moments, wondering about the infinite promise of future compound interest, when time itself seemed to freeze. As if Isolde's anamnesis spray had fed itself through the air ducts of the minimart 24/7. The new grunt workers from the pelagic vessels from jurisdictions far away drifted around him, in slow motion, it seemed, pushing their own produce trays. A song was playing on the intercom about a sleigh ride, and he thought about snow again. How long since he'd seen it. Had he ever seen it? Did he remember the feel of melting ice on his boyhood cheeks or was it only this song that made him imagine he did? With the delicious delivery of those girlish voices, always one millisecond behind the beat.

Come on, it's lovely weather for a sleigh ride together with you.

Her song. Or one of the many she would whistle backwards, with indrawn breath, an inhaled tune. He wondered how many Christmases had passed since he first heard it. Did certain songs play on a loop, endlessly, to remind us of things that never happened now? Was there ever such a thing as snow? There must have been. Crystals melting on the glass window of a childhood bedroom. Was this song to be the only evidence that snow once existed? He heard the tinkling of bells on the intercom and remembered his childhood image of a sleigh, pulled by nodding horses, and realised he had never seen one of those either. And now that he thought of it, he had never seen snow. Someone else had. The face rising to accept the melting snowflakes wasn't his. It was the face he had seen in that drowning mirror. And why this song now, and how long had it been, by the way, since last Christmas? No, it couldn't be Christmas, the air was too autumnal, too damp, the song had got caught on the wrong loop and now it ended, and the moment ended, and he pushed his wheeled tray towards the bleeping checkout. The present, such as it was.

She was sleeping when he arrived back. He kept an eye on her curved shape underneath the blankets while he fired up the cooker, did something serviceable with the pasta, fish and broccoli, and set the table for dinner. He whistled the same sleigh ride tune and saw her brown hair move on the pillow. She stretched and dressed and sang, just like those adolescent girl singers on the intercom, several milliseconds behind the imagined beat.

It's lovely weather for a sleigh ride together with you.

Do you remember snow?

Snow? Everyone remembers snow. How can you have a sleigh ride without snow?

She toyed with the food on her plate. Maybe she wouldn't like it, he suddenly feared.

Don't you? Remember snow?

Maybe I remember remembering it.

She yawned. He wished she wouldn't. A yawn was definitely not to be remembered.

You need to eat.

Yes, I do.

So they ate. And an odd domesticity settled around them. Could this become the norm? he wondered. Would that heady tingle of newness settle into something...?

There was a word he was searching for. Then he said it, out loud.

Quotidian.

What? she asked.

It's a word. Means everyday.

Do you think we'll ever have one? she asked. I wouldn't mind a quotidian with you. Almost as good as a sleigh ride.

She smiled, and forked some broccoli into her mouth. It was odd, he thought. That diet of gulls' eggs and seaweed hadn't changed her one bit.

Although, I doubt we'll ever have one.

No?

A sleigh ride. Or a quotidian. Unless something is done.

What something?

Why did my husband kill himself? And try to kill me? You tell me.

Because he knew something. Something about the Institute. Something about his time with the Clairvoyant Program.

Hasn't it been terminated? Put out to grass?

Been frozen, Christian. Like those snowflakes you never see these days.

It was outlawed by the Vance Wilson data protection provisions. Any images harvested during REM sleep are the property of the—

I know. The individual dreamer. But maybe the program had done its harvesting by then. It had data scraped from all of the dreams it needed.

You're saying—

I'm saying something drove my husband mad. And I need to find out what.

You may have to – and here Christian had to take a breath. He was in danger of breaching so many guidelines here. Amongst them, the guidelines of his own heart – start with yourself.

Myself?

I opened the file is919151245. It was a memory of yours.

Mine?

A car crash. A plummet, down into water. A struggle to escape.

The one I had just been through?

No. This was years ago.

How do you know it was me?

I saw your face. In the side-view mirror, underwater. Trying to get out.

He reached out a hand, over the table, the unfinished plates. Turned her face towards his.

It was you. As a young girl. Those drowned bridesmaids. You were one of them.

And I swam out?

You must have.

How could I have forgotten?

That's beyond my pay grade. I'm just the librarian. But somebody data-scraped it. And under the terms of the Quantum Data Fungible Transference Act replaced it with another.

With what other?

I don't know. Maybe snow.

Why snow?

You said you remembered snow.

Everybody remembers snow.

I don't. But I heard that sleigh ride song in the 24/7 and thought of you. Thought of snow. You remembered snow. And maybe, just maybe, somebody substituted your memory of drowning in a watery car with a memory of snow.

Why all this snow business?

Because I heard a song in the 24/7. Because I thought I remembered something I couldn't have. Because to substitute a memory of a drowning with a memory of falling snow would show a certain diabolical logic.

You're not making sense, Christian.

I know. None of it makes sense. We're both finding that out. And it's not about snow. It's about memory.

Why would someone do that?

I don't know why. But I do know who.

Who?

The Institute. That we both work for.

MW

There was more to her dead or undead experience that she shared with her loved one.

There was a riddle wrapped in a mystery inside an enigma. Who said that? Somebody long, long ago. Before the second of the three world wars. And this enigma in turn was wrapped in a secret.

The mine tunnels she explored, to pass the daylight hours, could have been carved by the teeth or claws of giant termites, moles, voles, any of those blind burrowers underneath all our ordinary lives. She had lived in darkness, just like them, for how long she found it difficult to remember. Emerging when the hunger became impossible to bear, through one root and rhododendron-covered hole into a wilderness of moonlit sheep and heather. She had scoured the neighbourhoods she crawled into like any creature of the night. A fox, a bat, a badger, a vole. Or the last surviving member of the *Sidhe*. She was a midnight fairy, a moonlit revenant feeding on the leavings of good daylight folks, although her memory of the peninsula was that not all of them were good. And one night, on her return from her moonlit scavenging, the ground in the tunnel she had landed in collapsed beneath her and she found herself in a room with high, thin and tottering walls of wood and paper.

A library. They had them once, she had been aware, shelves weighed to breaking point with actual books and ledgers. Dust cascading from their angled leanings and the moonlit hole she had fallen through.

Contracts. Yellowing, smudged contracts, stretching back through the years. Title deeds of ownership, land grants, of hunting, fishing and mining rights, from Sir Walter Raleigh to Carew, to Robert Boyle, of *The Sceptical Chemyst* fame, now Lord Cork. To Admiral John Huxley and his descendants, a Free State enterprise or two, Irish forestry, *Coillte*, the Copper Club, something called the New Ireland foundation, a consortium of local councillors, the West Atlantic Hospitality Hotel and Enterprise group, the Dunbeg Donald Trump foundation, the All Ireland Fund, and latest of all, the Doctor Rainer Fischer Institute.

She ploughed through them, fascinated. Ancient scrolls collapsed into dust beneath her fingertips. They went from copperplate handwriting to Victorian and Edwardian type, digital fonts to HTML code. There was one constant, she could see, through the unstoppable stampede of ownership.

It was always in the hands of someone else. Elizabeth Regina granted rights to Raleigh, Cecil, Carew, Boyle. But ownership resided elsewhere. Admiral John Huxley bought the mining, fishing and hunting rights. But ownership resided elsewhere. With who or with what? She had time to fill, as night turned into day and the cone of light from above blazed fiercely on these yellowing contracts, burning their secrets into blank paper. But all she could discern, as handwriting was replaced by type, the passage of shell companies, in jurisdictions from the East Asian Soviet to Singapore to Omaha, were the initials MW. MW, some opaque entity, stretching through the centuries. From Sir Walter Raleigh to Dr Rainer Fischer.

What did it stand for? The Marquis of Worcestershire? Man of War? Malawi, where, she noted, some of the shell companies had lately been based?

It would take an expert on tort through the centuries to work it out. And she wondered, when the infinite reach of the internet and cloud took over printed paper, what MW would stand for then. Microworld? Milliwatt? And why hidden here, she wondered, in the deepest recesses of the mine, unless there was some secret to be buried. The mysterious chain of ownership through the ages. She opened another dusty bundle then suddenly the shelves collapsed, and an avalanche of paper descended to cover her, like snow over a frightened snowy owl.

She had to crawl through the pyramid of contracts, which collapsed into dust with each clutch of her nails and fingers. She was annihilating whatever records remained of centuries of ownership, but she had to live, to breathe something other than shreds of ancient legalese. She made it back to her bed below the engine roof, coughing with centuries of inhalation, like an asthmatic of the ages, and then her eardrop trembled and she heard his voice.

GAIJIN-RA

So she kissed him the next morning, as she had done so many times before. But never by the wisteria-draped cottage door as he struggled into his high-viz jacket. He had made a private tally of them all and felt mildly stupid for doing so. The oaks, the maze, the heather, the kitchen underneath the suspended bluebottle. And now backside against the handlebars, underneath the tumbling purple, by the cottage door.

She watched him turn onto the bigger road and five seconds later saw a truck plough its grisly way after him. Stick to the hard shoulder, she whispered to herself and was surprised to hear his reply in her eardrop. Of course. One thought was the other's, as long as she kept this device in place.

She plucked it out now, placed it in its small cushioned receptacle and stuffed it in her top pocket.

She hoped he wouldn't notice. She hoped for nobody to notice, for no notice at all, as she pulled the dark hood up around her dark hair, and wrapped a scarf around her cheeks.

She was dead, after all.

She stepped back inside and took a glance in the mirror. She could have been any of those miscreant heroines from the video games of her youth, a fast-moving ninja shrouded in black. She missed those games, for a random moment, and wondered what her avatar's name would have been.

Some two or three syllables with a dash '-' followed by a Ra. Gaijin-Ra.

Gaijin was a foreigner, she remembered from the same lost world of games. Well, she would be a foreigner for a day, she thought as she pulled on her mountain boots and laced them up.

She would be a dead foreigner. Alive only to Christian, who would be safely at work.

She tramped up the laneway, waited by the nettles until the stream of vehicles gave her a respite, then walked slowly and purposely over the road. Into another bank of brambles and nettles, a muddy path, barely a goat-track, which led to the old Allihies Road.

Even Gaijin-Ra would be safe on this forgotten track, she surmised but kept the hood up and the scarf in place, to protect herself against the biting wind as well as prying eyes. As it was, she met none. A collie dog, barking to alert a distant cottage, the usual wilderness of sheep, a rabbit or two, bouncing across the dew-glistening fields. Within an hour, she had made it past the town and downwards towards the old forest track behind the Institute and turned right on the cliff-walk above the heaving sea where, in earlier days, she and Christian had collected their samples. There was a word for them with a silent p, which she now tried to remember to leaven the tedium of the trek. Pterodactyl, ptarmigan – did all dead things have a silent p, she wondered, in which case she should have called her avatar Ptholma-Ra, and then it came to her.

Pterygota.

They had collected their samples of the Pterygota native to the peninsula, observed the effect of her anamnesis spray on them, which may have been why she was here.

She eventually came to it, the low stone wall which provided no protection from the Atlantic gales, the wooden gate, now sagging on its hinges. She had spent most of her married life here.

She nudged the gate open with her boot, and noted the grass, newly growing between the paving stones as she made her way to the door.

It was locked, as it should have been, and she had her first burst of uncertainty.

Uncertainty had been her lot, she realised, ever since she wore that bridal veil. Their romance had been nothing if not expected. Jan, the son of the Institute's director, and Isolde, the daughter of the designer of its new interior. Her painter father had long abandoned her. They did the expected thing, walked the expected ways, even held hands along them. When his disability became an issue, she did what a bride does and became his sometime carer. But she had felt nothing unexpected, until those days in the maze with Christian. And suddenly, feeling whipped her the way the wind whipped those herring gulls, when they moved from cliff to open sea.

The key. Of course, she should have remembered the key. How could she have forgotten?

She knew well how. Because there had never been any need. Because for as long as she could remember, he had been housebound. His only movements from the bed to the glass veranda, from there to the garage, where he kept his motorised toys, the E-type and the old Harley Davidson, long covered in dust.

She shifted an empty flowerpot with her boot and heard the scrape of metal. She bent down and lifted it, saw the key and took it between her fingers, noting the imprint it left on the mould beneath. There was a movement of small creatures over the pale outline, and she tried this time to remember the name, for the unwinged ones.

Apterygota.

The A before the p gave it audible life. And she inserted the key into the lock and turned, wondering why her mind was filled with these absurd thoughts.

To keep it from what she knew confronted her.

The smell of damp and of abandoned lives, from the cottage interior. There was the kitchen, to her left, where she couldn't even bear to pour herself a glass of water, the dining table to her right, and beyond it the open door into the bedroom, where she still half expected to see Jan's hooded, nodding head. The odour of abandonment was hers and his, and a sequence of images she couldn't bear to entertain flooded her mind, so she tried to banish them with memories of snow.

Whether the memories were hers or someone else's, it hardly mattered. She could see the stuff falling on the frozen pane of her girlhood window, the soft, pure white diaphanous petals gathering on the window ledge like a rising cake of whipped cream. She could hear the song, from generations ago now, those Harlem-girl voices so perfectly aware of the beat that their pulse just behind it seemed magical.

We're snuggled up together like two birds of a feather would be.

If it was a planted memory, it was a beautiful one, and her musing about the alchemy of such a process kept other memories at bay as she made her way past the bedroom.

Into what he called his office in the glass conservatory.

He had mentioned more than a password to a severed memory, on his mad drive in that vintage car towards his arsenical oblivion. He had mentioned names, of the participants in the Clairvoyant Program. Although participant was too forgiving a word for the dreadful process. She hoped to find file histories, a list of names and contracts. She found nothing. She opened his laptop, but its batteries were long expired, and besides, even if she could recharge them, she knew the password would outwit her. She turned to his old Xbox then, and saw a sticker attached to the screen.

One word: Sorcha.

She pressed a button on the console, and the tray slid out.

Another sticker there, on the ancient Harley Davidson game, *Crew 2305*.

Another word: Tuosist.

He meant tourist, surely. She remembered his days wasted on those joysticks, touring the virtual Harleys with the virtual crew.

Then she remembered the actual Harley. And she remembered that Tuosist was a place.

She was getting good at memories, whether her own were real or not. She moved to the door then, and had to make an effort of will to slow herself down.

No-one was chasing. Yet.

She moved into the gravelled back patio and into the garage, smelling of oil cans and hand lubricant.

And there it was.

Not the E-type, which had been winched from the pit of arsenic, but her husband's other pride and joy, before the Ménière's took hold.

The Harley.

It would need petrol, of course, and she now remembered the smell of burning petrol the way she remembered melting snow.

There was a large drum of the forbidden stuff fixed to the wall outside and a used jerrycan with a fuel siphon. She took both and filled the jerrycan, in the stiff Atlantic wind. She went back inside and blew the dust off the screw to the engine tank, patiently watched it fill. She climbed onto the leather seat then and touched the battery starter.

Nothing happened.

She unhooked the kick-start and pushed hard with her boot. It whipped back and would have broken her ankle had she not retracted it fast enough. She kicked once more, and once again.

It kicked back again, but now roared to life.

She played with the throttle and felt the acrid smell of raw, burning fuel in her nostrils, as her dead husband's garage filled with exhaust. There was something deliciously transgressive about the whole event.

She hit the throttle, and the Harley bounded forwards like an animal, taking the rotten garage door with it. She twisted the handlebars and the back wheel spun to a halt, scattering gravel. She pressed down the kickstand and surprised herself with her own strength, pulling this old horse of metal backwards.

All she was lacking was a helmet. She went back through the broken door and found one, amongst the gloom of her dead husband's shelves.

It didn't fit.

Fuck it, she thought, Gaijin-Ra doesn't need one. She has her ninja hood and her flowing black scarf.

She mounted the bike again and it felt like an old industrial animal between her muscled thighs. She pushed it forwards, with a bump, onto the gravel.

She placed one foot on the kick-start, rode high into the air and brought her whole weight downwards. The bike roared into life again, with its oily breath of forbidden exhaust. She spun it once on the gravel, and once more for the fun of it, then throttled it into the auburn fields beyond, towards the Kerry side of the peninsula.

HARLEY

She took the back roads, to avoid police and prying glances. Despite her ninja get-up, it would be an inconvenience to be stopped, to have to explain herself, choose between lies, of death and rebirth, imitation and reality, whatever that would turn out to be. Nevertheless, she did pass other vehicles, bicycles mainly, the occasional tractor piled high with winter silage, driven on that airless, odourless fuel substitute. Once or twice, a three-wheeled version of her own glorious Harley. The flying version had long been promised, but never arrived, but now she felt the illusion. She couldn't explain the thrill her petrol roar gave her, the cloud each twist of the throttle left on the country road behind her, as if a malignant goddess had farted. And maybe that's what she was.

She was filled with new life since her descent into that pit, her awakening in the disused mine tunnel with those golden pebbles, and where were they now, by the way? She felt back with her left hand to search the pocket of her parka, and nearly upended her steed, swerving to avoid a wandering bullock on the country road. She stabilised the front wheel with both hands and felt the back wheel skid in a series of long, muddy loops. She might not survive another accident, another tumble into oblivion, and it brought her thoughts back to how and why she had survived the first. She had no idea, the sound of her own screams and her husband's curses filling the cylindrical pit as the sulphurous gleam of the bath of copper residue and arsenic rushed towards them.

Then a blank, and nothing.

Until the sight of those stones, rolling towards her eyeball. The strange sense of someone leaving, who had just been there. Was that a shadow, flickering against the copper mine shaft? She had been afraid to rise, fearing broken bones, torn flesh and sinew. But she did rise, in a supple yogic move that amazed her. She was unhurt and not only unhurt, somehow renewed. As if she had taken a bath in a hot spring of gods, not in the filth of a copper-smelting process that had lain untouched for centuries. She couldn't explain it, knew that one day she would have to, and for the moment, at least, tried to revel in the sensation of it.

She had run through a wilderness of mine shafts to an aperture, finally, where the sunlight penetrated. She pushed her way outwards, disturbing old rotten props of worm-eaten wood, when something stopped her.

Sunlight, heather and sheep.

She was alive and didn't know how or why.

She could see her liberation from below, the fronds of heather blowing in the breeze, the occasional triangular and horned face, cropping the honeydew flowers. She was better off dead, or rumoured dead until she probed the secret that her dead husband talked about.

No matter how much it broke the heart of her living lover.

iso919151245

He eschewed his coffee as he passed the Gothic church and the bench of Serendipity where Martin was rolling up the shutters. Martin was now barely recognisable, under a full head of hair. A nod from Christian and an answering nod from Martin sufficed as a greeting although this must be a first, Christian thought Martin must be thinking, before wondering why he was bothered about what the newly hirsute Martin must be thinking. It was his second first that day, after the wisteria kiss by the cottage door. And it was the uniqueness of that event that had made him worry about what others might be thinking. He had had a dead widow in his bed, and however alive she had seemed, and she was more alive, it seemed to him now, than she ever had been during the whole course of their tentative courting, it had to be kept secret between them. So he felt like one of those new recruits in a galactic spy drama in which their very newness to the game had to remain undisclosed. As if his contact who would, of course, always remain in the shadows, or be wearing a cloak of invisibility, untroubled by the possibility of discovery, had drilled into him the advice that any departure from the norm would excite suspicion.

He had worn his high-viz jacket, true, he had cycled the rutted path towards work, true, but had he stopped for his convivial coffee and his desultory conversation about the weather with the proprietor of Serendipity? No, he hadn't, and therein might lie his downfall.

But he cycled on, tried to forget about Martin and coffee, made it to the Huxley mansion, where figures in high-viz jackets like his own were clambering over the valley roofs of the mansion to reassemble the broken chimney.

He remembered the copper model breaking its protruding piece on the church floor. Had he another secret to keep, one that was truly beyond understanding? He cycled conspicuously across the grass to the front railings, as if this in turn had become a habit, the departure from which would excite suspicion. But it was hardly a habit, he thought to himself as he observed the doctor's basilisk eye viewing him once more from the upper window. Christian, aware of that gaze, but still keeping the quotidian in mind, dismounted, pulled his trousers from where they were bundled in his socks and, like a dog returning to its vomit, approached the railings, then, as if remembering yesterday's admonition, looked upwards.

And now the doctor raised a long finger and shook it, from right to left.

The reminder was clear.

No.

So Christian nodded, far below, and hoped that his acquiescence in turn wouldn't excite suspicion. He wheeled his bike dutifully around the seaward side, locked it to one of the gleaming metal cycle stands in the bicycle shed and made his way inside.

His assistant was nowhere to be seen. He was early, of course, having eschewed his detour to the Anglican church with his morning coffee. Another departure from the norm, which might in turn excite suspicion. But this was no drama, he had to remind himself, no spymaster in a cloak of invisibility, even if he felt there was one. And her absence and his unusual punctuality could, he realised, be put to use. He felt beneath his desk for the tiny pasted decal, unpeeled it and again read the second password.

iso919151245.

He walked, untroubled and unhurried to the is section of the files, flicked through to iso and extracted this particular memory. It was a tiny circular disc this time, which indicated its age, the discs having been converted to the glass and silicone lozenges more than a decade ago.

At least one of the consoles in the training bay below must be of a similar vintage.

He heard footsteps at the door and placed the disc once more beneath his tongue, like a spit-resistant communion wafer, and nodded at his assistant's brown olive eyes as she took her seat and muttered an apology.

You're not late, I'm early, he would have said, if the disc hadn't impeded speech. He raised his right hand and fluttered four fingers and pointed towards the toilets down the glass corridor.

He made his way back to the loading platform, to the old industrial lift, and listened to it grind its way down to the cellars.

He found an old version of the PS235 with a miniscule UHD disc drive and extracted the silicone wafer from underneath his tongue, wiped it dry on the white sleeve of his lab coat, placed it in the drive, pushed it home and pressed play.

The first thing he heard was a heartbeat. Out of a darkness that seemed to pulse with red. The red of membranes that condensed and retracted like waves to the beat of that unseen heart. There was a long glistening cord that seemed to ascend to the heavens and a tiny unfingernailed hand reached out to clutch at it. The fingers failed to grasp the cord and fell away. They reached out again. As if to pull themselves upwards from some event below that would prove cataclysmic. Then the heartbeat grew louder, the pulsing increased, and light trembled from below and became a flood. The whole vista spun, slowly, painfully on its axis, as if being dragged downwards by the flood. The amniotic fluid blazed then with the light, for it became obvious to Christian that he was witnessing a birth, from the inside. The water spilled and sucked at the same time, three blazing silver circles tried to battle with the oncoming daylight, but they could never win. There was a riot then of silver discs and blue gowns and white-gloved hands, a massive thumb reached down and pulled out some mucus and the heartbeat was drowned out in the sound of an infant's cry.

There was a masked face beneath a domed forehead, and Christian recognised and wished he hadn't, since he could never now forget them, the eyes of Doctor Rainer Fischer.

THE INFORMATION

She was descending into the Kerry side of the peninsula, almost freewheeling, the motorbike making no more noise than a sleeping tiger would. What was the difference here? she wondered. The light seemed less silver, more pearly, the ocean seemed more tranquil, as if the wind gave it some respite. There was the lake to her left, shimmering in pink and gun-metal grey, the vista broken by the mounds of ancient rock, like the twisted spines of buried pterodactyls. Why did the silent p so often denote extinction? Something to do with the alphabet, she assumed, which itself was heading towards the same fate. The road wound gently into a series of wooded overhangs, almost like leafed umbrellas, just as a spattering of rain danced over her face, and she imagined invisible hands, holding them just for her. She was heading into a landscape of undiscovered trauma, and she couldn't understand the lightness of her mood. Something to do with that kiss by the cottage door. The promise of something more permanent. What was the word he used?

Quotidian.

Something to do with time, its calm, untroubled unfolding, day after day. Would it diminish or enhance whatever it was she was feeling? The thought caused a small ripple in her untroubled mood, and she was doing her best to dispel it, when she saw the beak, peeking through that umbrella of green, of a bird that couldn't fly.

She remembered her dead husband's description of an animal sanctuary, and applied the brake gently, so as not to frighten the bird. But nothing could frighten this creature, which seemed to belong to the geological past that had scarred the mountain behind her. She parked the motorbike and reached out a hand and had to retract it when the beak, with a sudden viciousness that surprised her, bit at her fingers.

Careful, she heard through the fringe of green foliage.

She saw a figure come behind with a bucket of meal, which was dumped by the webbed feet, and the beak arched downwards with the same suddenness and began some serious pecking.

He doesn't know you, the woman said, and Isolde could see it was a woman, by the long muddy dress dangling over the wellington boots.

You're Sorcha, she said.

I am, the same, Sorcha said, and I don't want to know who you are.

Why not? Isolde asked, and thought at least now she was spared the bother of a pseudonym.

Pseudonym. Another silent p.

Because you've come about him.

You know that?

I know things. That's why I was chosen. Amongst the circle of those other girls. Who also knew things. And we were all marked with this.

She pulled her linen dress upwards, exposing coloured knickers. And what seemed like a QR or barcode on her stomach.

My god.

Isolde bent low to examine it.

And it's not a tattoo.

She fell to her knees.

Can I touch it?

Touch it all you want.

Did someone do this to you?

You mean like a cattle brand?

The code, like fading rust, was imbedded into her once-girlish skin.

It came with the dreams. And tell me you're not one of those ambulance chasers?

You mean you were promised compensation?

Everyone in the program was.

In the Clairvoyant Program?

I mean that dream dormitory. Where they put those gizmos on your head. He's dead now, isn't he?

Yes, he's dead. You knew that?

When he came to see me, I knew he wasn't long for the living.

He died horribly.

So, there'll be no backdated payments, then.

Payment for what?

We were the secret engine of the Institute. The dreamers. We dreamt what the future needed. What the future told us. Till we dreamt ourselves out of business.

How?

Any more questions will cost you.

Cost me what?

A donation to the animal shelter.

So that's what this is?

A shelter, for everything but hybrids.

She walked sideways, past the umbrella of dangling foliage and found a small metal gate.

Can I come in?

Donation first. Cross my palm with silver.

She searched in her pocket amongst the pebbles.

Will gold do?

The emu strode behind her now, like a protective guardian.

Show me.

She placed one of them in the small grubby hand.

Wowie. Is that really gold?

One gold pebble. From the copper mine.

I could set this beast on you. He'd peck you to death.

But you won't.

No, I won't.

She closed her fingers round the pebble. Brought it to her teeth.

Copper into gold. Even better.

Better than what?

Whatever he was up to.

So, tell me.

He was trying to make it up to me.

For what?

For this.

She pulled her dress up again, displayed the rust-coloured code.

For all those dreams, in that house of nightmares.

Will you tell me about them?

You'd better come inside.

The cottage was like a broken version of what once had been her own. Sagging doorways gave way to goose-feathered interiors. Strange animals growled and squawked. A baby barn owl flew over her head and perched on a wood-wormed rafter.

I run this shelter to keep my mind off things.

She was making tea, in what could have been termed a kitchen. A tap, perched above a small running board, two metal beer barrels holding it up.

What things?

The information. And it's information you've come for, isn't it?

I suppose.

You suppose, do you?

She looked at Isolde with her slow, almond-coloured eyes. Those eyes could penetrate anything, Isolde felt.

It was the house of sleep. Your man ran it.

My husband?

Husband, is he? We knew him as the big man's son. Big, like the big man, but uneasy with it. If you're paid to sleep, you wouldn't question things, would you?

No, I suppose you wouldn't.

Supposing again. The drink of hot chocolate or cocoa at night, the bed, all warm and fluffy, the electric blanket, or for those who wet the bed—

Wet the bed?

We were young, remember? All dragged from home. From caravans, mostly. For those that left the blankets wet, the hot water bottle. There was something in the cocoa though, that made sleep easy. Nothing to complain about, after life on the road. And when you woke, it'd be with wires on your head. Then the codes started happening.

Barcodes? QR codes?

Cinnabar codes, your husband called them. Something to do with mercury.

On your stomach?

On the arm for some, the stomach for others. But only for the special ones.

Like you?

Like me, like Lucy, like Theresa, like Fidelma. I could name all seven of us.

She narrowed her eyes, remembering.

The unmarked were sent home. They cried. How they cried. But how little they knew.

And you had the mark?

Oh, I had. The marked ones stayed. And dreamt.

What kind of dreams?

All kinds. Cities that could never have existed. Mountains on the moon. Hybrid creatures that should never have been. And every dream ended in a waterfall of numbers. I was drowning in numbers. And I woke from one dream, and I knew.

You knew?

It didn't matter what we dreamt. It mattered what was printed on us. I woke and saw your husband, managing the thing. The machine.

Sigmund?

Whatever you call it. The waterfall of numbers I had dreamt. Was rearranging itself. On the machine screen. I said it to him. We're dreaming the future, aren't we?

Maybe, he said, the future's dreaming you. Go back to sleep.
And?
I went back to sleep. And they sent us home, soon after.
They closed the program?
The government man in Dublin. But it had already done its job.
And its job was?
To download the information. And the information told it how to build the code that made us all redundant. The code that came from the future could read the future on its own. Is that complicated enough for you?
It created a loop?
Or a donut.
She traced her finger in donut shapes. Or figures of eight.
So then the lawyers came.
What did they want?
To sign our rights away to whatever was on the cinnabar codes. Whatever message the future sent.
What kind of messages?
The kind that allows the doctor to ply his trade. All of those gizmos the doctor develops. Those medical devices—
They're designed for the future?
Not, they're designed in the future. The future sends the code back.
And?
They try them out on us.
She rose, finished her tea in one gulp. Picked a tiny furred animal from amongst the straw on the floor.
What do you call Cecil here?
A guinea pig?

Exactly. We're their guinea pigs.

She pulled up her cardigan. Rubbed her stomach beneath it. As if the rust-coloured code was a rash.

It gives you trouble?

Everything gives us trouble. We gave the doctor dreams, he left us with nightmares.

And that's what you told my husband?

Jan?

She nodded. Then smiled.

So you're his wife?

I was. Now his widow.

I knew it. You didn't die, did you?

No. I didn't.

And you can't work out why...

And if Isolde's recent sense of peace resembled a tranquil ocean, it had just been hit by a hurricane.

Good luck with that.

Isolde placed her cup on a mound of straw and made her way to the sagging door. Before she pulled the handle, she turned.

You know something, don't you?

Told you what I know.

About why I didn't die?

Like with most things. I know someone who does.

Who is this someone?

The first dreamer.

Where can I meet them?

When is Puck Fair?

The middle of August.

You've a long wait ahead of you. Look for the seventh daughter of the seventh daughter.

She has a name?

You know, I can't remember. And now it's time for you to go.

So she left. But she saw a footprint in the mess of mud beneath the half-open gate. Her own?

She heard a rustle in the leaves behind her and turned. A shadow rippled over the gnarled trunks.

She heard the scraping of the bucket from the cottage door and saw the clairvoyant emerge, wearing wellington boots. So the footprint must have been her own.

It was dusk, driving back. The beamed cone from the Harley headlights grew brighter as the daylight faded. She did her best to put it together, as the cold wind ruffled her hair.

Institute programs, designed in the future. Medical solutions, arrived at in the future, tested in the present. The heart valve that would outlive its owner. The skin graft that would stay fresh while the host body withered around it. Maybe even the Memorial Module was a test for an everlasting solution two hundred years from now. She thought about the Investment Module Christian had described. The future compound interest with returns approaching infinity. Commercial options that travelled time. A rapacious venture capitalist in the future investing in his own past, with the profit curve already written. In stone. Or in cinnabar codes, on a young girl's innocent flesh.

It bent her mind. She wondered, was she dreaming, had she actually died? But the wind on her face seemed real, the cone of light on grassy road seemed real, and realer still the roar of the ancient Harley.

She wondered where her anamnesis spray fitted into the scheme of things.

She wondered how she would explain it all to Christian.

But she was greeted in the cottage by the flickering light of an old Xbox.

He had something to show her.

DÉJÀ VU

Around that time, although time was becoming an oddly mutable concept in the townland, a new arrival walked into Fidelma's, the sweet shop, just across the road from Hooks, the fishing tackle shop that had once displayed a whole range of sporting goods.

Fidelma wore gloves at work, sometimes white, sometimes grey silk, which provided her with a certain elfin elegance, but the purpose of the gloves was neither sartorial nor aseptic. It was to hide the fading cinnabar codes spreading from her wrists down to her knuckles.

She had done her best to forget her nights in the clairvoyant dormitory, had indeed engaged in hours of therapy to help her banish it from her dreams and nightmares, but the sight of a fisherman's hat gliding from the open door of Hooks across the way brought a ripple of them back.

There was little demand for shotguns these days, since the last deer cull had eliminated that particular species, and game birds were as rare on the mountainsides, as – well, this particular gentleman himself. He had busied himself there with hooks and feathers, some of which now adorned the woollen bucket hat that sat comfortably above his bushy eyebrows.

And now her own small dangling doorbell pinged.

He brought an immediate sense of familiarity with him, with his gentle aura of khaki and beige. To Fidelma, in particular. She felt she knew this genial, soft-hatted gentleman who was requesting a packet of Nugent's Plug tobacco in her corner store. Fidelma had to patiently explain that pipe smoking had vanished from the peninsula years ago, along with the bittern and the marsh pipit. So, was he in the wrong era? Not at all, he just carried shards of a different past with him. His Norfolk jacket, with its complicated serried rows of pockets and zips was from another era too, just one that hadn't happened yet.

Silly me, he said, tapping those pockets. Did I bring some with me?

He had emerged through the heather, grown into a tangle of roots like witches' hair, over the mine shaft that had been first blown open by Theodorus Trebonianus Dee, how many centuries before now, he couldn't quite remember. A hand had broken through the purple and white heather flowers, dispersing flakes of them in autumn-coloured fluff, which the wind carried off towards the twisted volcanic beak of the peninsula hag, keeping watch over the thumbnail of islands in the heaving ocean beyond, and the rest of him soon followed. There was a communications tower, humming its digital music to the uncaring wind on the hill beyond. Below that, a necklace of lakes, glittering in the low autumn sunlight. So maybe he felt it was fortuitous, or serendipitous, or just plain good foresight that he had brought his fishing gear with him. He definitely wondered why his entry into eras other than his own had to always be through fissures in the earth, concave tunnels with dripping rust-coloured water from rocky overhead ceilings. In Carlsbad, it had been runnels of underground, bubbling steam. Here, it was this ferrous drip from above and he thanked his luck, or his foresight, once more that he had worn his bucket-shaped trout-fishing hat. He walked then, through mounds of heather which necessitated high, quarter-horse steps, like those of Muck Corrigan, two centuries ago.

He didn't wonder who decided these things, as he descended towards the town below, girdled by a glittering mansion on one side of the bay and a steaming fish-freezing plant on the other. He knew. Sigmund designed by way of the dreams of the clairvoyant dormitory. And if there was a flaw in this temporal arrangement, it was that the clairvoyants could still dream. So Fidelma knew this soft-hatted gentleman intimately, as she felt he knew her. Her half-buried traumas, her inner workings were as familiar to him as a lunar module would be to its astronaut. But most of all, what she felt was an immediate sense of comfort. That don't-I-know-you feeling that it would be impolite to voice. She was familiar with those bushy eyebrows, the array of hooks and flies and feathers that decorated the rim of the brim of his tweed hat.

Here for the fishing?

And although he was here for enjoyments other than fishing, he nodded, genially again.

It was only after he'd left, after his soft-hatted silhouette had vanished down the street, that she felt the certainty. She had met him before. That feeling, don't-I-know-you? That phrase, I never forget a face. That small dance we often make with passers-by, a one-step two-step, until the acquiescent one steps back. That face, half-glimpsed, tilted towards the pavement, didn't I just see you before? There was a word for it, Fidelma remembered.

Déjàvu

Or was it two words? Whatever, and she was certain now. She had dreamt of him. One of those ridiculously free-spirited dreams, running through a mound of heather, towards the small lake below, and there was the same woollen bucket hat, the cloud of pipe smoke around it like a host of midges. Or maybe they were midges – it was the summer, after all. And was she naked in the dream? No, she couldn't have been. Wearing those small cut-off jeans though, with nothing but a T-shirt to enclose her bouncing breasts. And he turned, nodded, and she asked the same redundant question.

Here for the fishing?

Which was absurd, because he obviously was. And a pike or a trout struck his lure and his reel spun and screamed, and she woke up.

Another dream: she is a deer this time, an extinct species – although still with her rear end enclosed in the same cut-off jeans – and a shot booms out and she is struck to the heart, as if by Cupid's bow, but there was nothing romantic about this projectile. It came from a smoking barrel, which is striding towards her and the same bucket hat behind. In fact, serried rows of those bucket hats, since there is a bevy of them – what is the collective noun for a group of hunters? she remembers thinking and turns her deer head to see the same bucket hat above the same bushy eyebrows, the eyes below them not genial at all, and the mouth proclaiming, Bagged us another.

How odd, Fidelma thought, to see the face from a dream, and she locked her cash register, turned the sign on the glass frontage from open to closed and followed him out. The soft winter rain blinded her eyes for a moment, but there was that smell, the smell of pipe tobacco to follow. He must have brought some with him after all, she thought, following that barely remembered odour and the sound of footsteps, of hard cowboy boots on the old cobblestones that led to the harbour. There were fishing nets hanging in the mist and she followed the sound of those boots through the muttered talk about mackerel and bream, even caught a glimpse of them as they turned left again, and it was odder still to lose them in the crush around the square because once again it was market day. Cowboy boots didn't go with the soft fishing hat, nor with the curved pipe. It was as if he'd got his periods mixed up when he dressed for the day, she thought as she made her way back, found herself outside Hooks and asked the lad who kept the tackle shop open, had there been such an oddly dressed gentleman inside?

There had been, he said, and he bought one of those cloth bucket hats. Hooks as well.

For the fishing? she asked.

Yes. For the fishing.

He was here for the fishing. He had been in Carlsbad for the architecture. And if Fidelma had the wherewithal or capability to have a chat with that blind masseuse of the Karoly Hotel, two centuries ago, she would have recognised the droplets of dew around those bushy eyebrows.

From the soft rain, on Castletown's main street.

From the steam of an immemorial hot spring, in Carlsbad.

BIRTH

And now Isolde watched the purloined disc from the Library of Traumatic Memory on her lover's old game console. She saw the pulsing red, the tiny hand grasping at the bloody cincture that seemed to lead to the heavens.
It's a womb, she said.
It's a birth, remembered, he said.
That doesn't make sense, she said.
I know, he said, which is maybe why it was harvested.
Is it mine? she asked.
It was attached to your file.
Two lost memories.
You live in one. Die in the other.
Are you sure they're mine?
I'm sure of nothing.
He thought the sentence too bare. Then added two words.
My love.
But nobody could remember that.
You remember snow?
I do.
And she hummed.
It's lovely weather for a snow ride together with you.
That's a song. You've never seen snow.

THE LIBRARY OF TRAUMATIC MEMORY

Are you sure?

The last snowfall on this peninsula was 2027.

So what happened?

Fungibility happened. The Quantum Genetic Algorithm happened. The Library of Traumatic Memory happened. And this memory is yours.

THE FISHING

Sorcha wandered through the high ferns, so wet with the morning dew that it may as well have been raining. Jeremy beat a path ahead of her, his triangular feet crushing the ferns, the nettles, and whatever blackberry thorns stood in her way. The emu knew what was expected of him, always enjoyed the early morning trek to the river, the wait, in the flowing water, on one leg, like a stork, the flash of a trout below and the whiplash stab of the darting beak. The same beak would toss the squirming trout to the bank where his mistress would stash it in her netted bag, waiting for four or five more. Six would be the maximum, the river couldn't afford more, and Sorcha would stand, make that odd clucking noise with her tongue on the roof of her mouth, and the one webbed foot would unbend itself, splash after the other through the water towards the riverbank.

Was the emu surprised to push through the last of the dripping ferns and see an interloper perched on the edge of the bank? Emus don't register surprise, but Jeremy's head did an odd back and forwards dance, from Sorcha's troubled eyes to the rod, casting it's glistening and golden thread back towards the water, and the bucket hat below it. Somebody else was fishing on this bend of the river, and although it wasn't specifically hers, it felt like an intrusion.

Out early, she said, deciding conversation was better than confrontation, at least at this juncture.

Indeed, the angler replied, with the smallest swivel of his head. The eyebrows shivered under the bucket hat, and the eyes returned to the tiny fly bobbing in the gently flowing water.

Before the bailiff gets up, she said.

There are bailiffs? he asked, and turned two surprised eyebrows towards her.

Fishing rights, she said, belong to Lord Lansdowne and his inheritors, wherever they are now. But they're rarely up before ten.

The early bird, then, catches the worm.

No worms on that hook, she said.

Fly-fishing, he said, as a splash in the water made the rod tremble, and he began to reel in.

You've got a full haul there, she said, sitting down beside the six gasping trout on the flattened grass.

And this is the seventh, he said, snapping the hook from the flapping trout's jaw.

She already knew he was from elsewhere when she led him back through the flattened ferns towards the animal shelter. Something about the hat alerted her, and his lack of questions about the large stalking bird that followed them both. She offered to gut and grill the trout and wanted to be near a serrated blade when the attack she anticipated came. And it did come, although not at all in the form that she expected.

You like trout?

I do. They tell me things.

You can chew the cud with trout?

He nodded, absurdly.

And what do they say?

They tell me someone's been talking.

Aha.

Yes. Aha indeed.

He stood in the doorway, divesting himself of his wellington boots, although the mess of straw and bird shit on the floor would have made such delicacy totally unnecessary. He was flicking the morning dew from his bucket hat when the emu came behind her, arched its beak in a stabbing motion and took out both of her eyes. Then the webbed feet began their dance, the toes arched and sharper than the serrated knife she let fall to the floor.

That's my girl, the angler said.

And as the blood poured from her emptied sockets, for the first time Sorcha realised Jeremy was female. And a hybrid at that.

REBIRTH

Isolde watched it again. Heard the beating heart first, saw the pulsing membranes of blood, the tiny fist reaching out to what she now knew was the umbilical cord, and then the spinning of the point of view, the biblical flood and the bleeding of the light.

It's impossible, she said. It can't be a memory.

It was attached to your file: iso919151245.

I didn't say mine. I said it can't be a memory. When do our eyes open?

Don't remember.

Are you trying to be funny?

No. But maybe none of us remember. What we actually experienced. Actually saw.

And the doctor's face. Why was he there?

He helped with the delivery? He was a doctor, after all.

You seem remarkably sanguine about this, Christian.

Maybe I've seen too many things. You die, you come back. I told you why and how.

You die again.

She had a secret, that Sorcha.

Sorcha?

That clairvoyant.

She was a bag of secrets.
There was one thing, she said she couldn't tell me—
Just one thing?
I have to see her again. First thing.
She slept, for some reason, like the baby she once was. If she dreamt at all, she didn't remember. She woke when the morning sun was lighting the lintel of the window.
Come with me.
This, as she slipped her bra on in one supple movement.
To the clairvoyant's. The animal rescue.
She runs an animal rescue?
With owls and foxes. Goats and emus.
Emus?
A kind of ostrich. Don't ask it to make sense.
If I miss work—
We'll be there and back within an hour.
How?
On my dead husband's Harley.
And there was a certain transgressive delight in clinging to her lithe waist as she gunned the vehicle over the Healy Gap, into the Kerry side of things, and Christian wondered why he crossed the gap so rarely. The waterfalls laced down the black faces of the hills in the early morning light. He thought of the long grey hair of an ancient woman, the hem of a wedding dress in a bridal dance. Drops fell on his face when the Harley reached the umbrella of trees, but he saw the blue sky between the dancing leaves and realised it was early morning dew. Then the rusting metal gate, the last gasp of the motorbike, and they were walking through the wet ferns towards the cottage door. A wingless swan curled its feathered neck by the rusting SUV.

And once inside, they saw the emu with its bloodied beak and between its bloodier, razor-like claws lay the body of Sorcha, the last clairvoyant.

There was an infant fox, nibbling at her exposed entrails.

Help me, Christian.

He pulled her back through the door and slammed it shut. The thing ran in two sudden steps towards the reinforced glass and began to shatter it with its reddened beak.

Can you wipe that sight from my memory?

I'm just the librarian.

Please—

She retched into the dewy ferns.

Something's happening, my love. And we don't know what it is.

They turned on her. Wild animals, after all...

No. That thing was her minder. Her protector. It was turned on her... And I think we should go now.

Before it turns its claws on us?

SEALS

The Harley brought them back. She wrapped it in a cloak of ferns and told him, whatever else he did, to act as if nothing was abnormal.

They did their best to sleep. But there was a nightmare all around them. It was as if the image of the dead clairvoyant presented them with such dreadful possibilities that they couldn't bear to dream.

Maybe the future, Isolde whispered, before she finally went under, is in the process of being cancelled.

Or the present, maybe.

But the question is, by who?

Whom, he wanted to correct her, but didn't. He had to stop this grammarian obsession.

There were seven participants in the program. Seven clairvoyants.

She counted on her fingers.

If just one of them were to meet the same fate…

There must be files—

Amongst my dead husband's things.

Go back to sleep, he murmured.

Which she did, to his surprise. And he left, in his high-viz jacket, as the sun brushed across her dreaming face.

She woke alone in the blazing daylight. She saw a scribbled note by her pillow.

Sleep on. Christian x.

She walked out naked into the brambles and heard the seaweed bulbs pop as she dove into the cold water. And as she came to the surface, she saw two bobbing heads, seals, tracing her path through the bay.
She turned with her next stroke. She saw something else moving, through the ferns.
A bucket hat, tracing her path through the greenworld.
She had been followed. Then and now. She had somehow brought that dreadful doom on Sorcha the Clairvoyant.
She heard the whip of a splash and turned to see two seal tails vanishing under.
Could death by seal be any bloodier than death by hybrid emu?
She didn't want to find out and swam in a panic to the shore.
She was naked then, and aware of each and every movement in the ferns, the heather. Was it human? Or even worse?
No, it was wind, she realised, as a gust blew the ferns into a kind of curtsey. There was nothing there.
But there had been, she thought, as she darted naked towards the cottage door.

MARCUS WILLOUGHBY

Any deviation from the norm, he reminded himself, could be a clue leading to disclosure. The world of secrets was buffeting him the way the wind did, and the wind was punishing as normal, that morning, on his cycle into town.

So he ordered a Serendipity coffee, as usual, and it struck him that no coffee shop had ever been more inappropriately named.

How is it, Christian?

Not too bad, Martin.

Although something was bad, he just wasn't sure what. He paid for his frothy, unsugared cappuccino and sat by the Gothic church wall and was surprised to see a pipe-smoking figure walking through the gravestones.

Not a bad morning.

Bad again, Christian thought.

The accent was neutral, like a glass of water awaiting its tincture.

Not bad at all.

He wore a fisherman's bucket hat, Christian observed, pierced with an array of hooks and tiny feathers.

I've read about this church.

And the accent slowly, almost imperceptibly, approached the timbres of his own.

You have?

Montagu Cartwright. Completed two designs for the Anglican Communion. One in Ireland, one in what was then called Carlsbad. In Bohemia. Now Karoly Vary, in some faraway precinct of the West Asian Soviet.

It was as if he was learning to speak, by speaking. But what was odd, Christian felt, was the completeness of the dialogue.

And the story goes, they mixed them up.

Just a story? You think?

He sat down on the blunt surface of a gravestone.

Hey, Christian thought to himself, I'm drinking my coffee. You haven't been asked.

So this church could have a Celtic double.

In faraway Karoly Vary?

It's a possibility.

Christian nodded. It was indeed a possibility. He finished his coffee and dropped his cup in the rubbish dispenser. He said his goodbyes and remounted his bike, and no vehicle passed him on his journey down the rutted path to the Institute, so he was surprised, having locked his bike in the appointed place, and made his entry into the horned hall, to find the same gentleman, unlit pipe between his teeth, descending the oak staircase with Dr Rainer Fischer.

Christian.

Doctor Fischer.

His eyebrows were behaving themselves once more. Two simple wavelets, forming a unibrow.

I want you to meet Chairman Marcus Willoughby.

Mr Willoughby. We've already met.

And Christian, for some reason unknown to even himself, made a short Austrian bow and almost clicked his heels.

Chairman of what? he wondered.

Indeed, said the Chairman. We met by the graveyard of the Montagu Cartwright church.

And did Christian imagine it, or had the accent subtly changed? It seemed to have acquired a sibilant Germanic hiss. Maybe it adopted the speech patterns of those closest to him. As if, and the same thought came back to Christian, he was learning to speak.

Chairman of what? Christian wondered again. And Dr Fischer answered for him.

He's assembling the board.

The board? Christian asked. He hadn't been aware there was one.

For a general meeting. The future is presenting us with various options.

Does the future present options? Christian wondered. It would have to, of course, if it invested in the present. Which was its own past. The profits of which were to be reinvested in its own present. Which became the future, again. And he bowed his head again, to disguise his confusion.

Chairman Willoughby.

Call me Marcus.

Although he could have called him a brace of pseudonyms. Amongst them, Magnus Wilderstein.

But for the moment, he was Marcus Willoughby.

SPYCRAFT

Christian took a walk, that lunchtime. He needed to be away from all observers, chew a sandwich as he walked along the hinterland of the Huxley mansion.

There were the scattered beginnings of bonfires by every football pitch. Hallowe'en was coming, of course. So the dead could walk once more.

He saw the full glory of what the wind could do to the ocean, as he made his way through the heathered walkway to the back door of his dead rival's cottage.

He had a brief pang of regret, seeing the banks of heather bow under the wind. They had made their bed in it, after all. He wondered had Jan been more perceptive than he seemed, spying on them through the telescope perched on the stone recess of the kitchen window?

And Dr Rainer Fischer spied on him now. He had nibbled on his son's mouldering trail mix and granola bar, while the virtual code breaker did its thing on his computer, had taken screenshots of a range of files to be decoded later, when he saw a figure outside moving with difficulty against the prevailing wind. He had swung the spyglass to his own tufted eyebrow and observed through the battening wind, Christian whorled in his own drama of ocean and heather, pushing his way up the slope. How simple it must be, to be cuckolded, he thought. And *oh, what a tangled web we weave*, he thought, as he made his way through to the larder.

He couldn't remember the next verse.

It was strange, to insert his thin form into the coffin of shelves that held his son's decaying health supplements. Spirulina, magnesium, manuka honey. Couldn't he have found a cure? Too late now.

When first we practise to deceive. That was it.

The doctor heard the door scrape open, with difficulty, given the expansion of the wood with the damp sea air. He heard the rustle of papers, round the desk. Then the whirr of a computer firing up.

You've lost something? he asked, stepping out from the larder. A file, perhaps?

I was just passing, and…

The doctor raised his eyebrows. They made an almost perfect V.

Tell the truth, Christian. You're snooping.

I am?

Your attitude is one of a snoop. Your entrance was snooplike. And your answers, dare I say it, give every indication of snoop.

I was looking for an earpiece, Christian muttered. I tried to help with his hearing problems.

And to his immense relief, it was sitting, in its small bud, in the desk drawer.

He held it up for the doctor's purview.

Here. See how it works.

The doctor placed it in his capacious ear.

Seems like a version of spycraft.

Spycraft?

Those tools that enable surveillance. Those redundant versions of the PS235 with the UHD disc drives. Games of snooping. Surveillance. And the thing about surveillance is, Christian, how to know who is surveilling who?

Christian was nonplussed. He reverted, as always, to grammar.

Whom, he said.

I beg your pardon?

The doctor's eyebrows made that inquisitive V again.

Who is surveilling whom.

Your grammatical exactitude, and obsession with tenses won't help you with this particular dilemma, my dear Christian. You were surveilled, in the bowels of the Institute, amongst the redundant Xboxes and consoles that gave my son such pleasure. You were viewing a file.

Two files, actually, Christian said, surprised at his own insouciance.

He could get good at this spycraft business.

The doctor's eyebrows went from V to W.

In one, she dies. In the other, she lives.

So maybe it's best, Dr Fischer murmured, that she's dead again.

So, you still don't know, Christian thought. That she's as alive as you and I. Secrets had their own power, he was beginning to realise.

And I'm left with this loss. This grief.

Christian's eyes misted. He was surprised how much his real emotion leant to the necessary fake.

I didn't know, he continued, that you were once a obstetrician.

I observed a birth. Not quite the same as delivering.

May I ask why?

In the early days of in-vitro gametogenesis—

Ah. It was in-vitro.

You can be surprised at that.

The creation of sperm from any piece of bodily tissue.

Yes. Rather sad really. All of those great emotions that surrounded generative behaviour – love, lust, frottage, cunnilingus, fellatio...

Do you have to be so reductive, doctor?

Become like the coccyx or the appendix, organs without purpose. In this case, habits, without any apparent end or function.

The function of love is love.

That statement, Christian, makes no logical sense.

So why did you observe her birth?

The doctor blinked. His eyebrows shivered.

Research. Why else. I was considering an even more radical version of in-vitro.

Which was?

In-vitro hereditogametogenesis.

Let me guess. The creation of sperm from dead bodily tissue.

Correct. But the Institute was prevented from populating the peninsula with mewling infant Napoleons, Churchills and dead Kennedys by those accursed Vance Wilson addendums to the Data Protection Acts. Although why the dead need data protection will always be beyond me.

So, you stuck with the living?

But the Acts provided no protection whatsoever to the unborn.

The unborn foetus?

The foetus as yet undreamt of. In romances not yet written.

I'm lost, doctor.

And you should stay lost, Christian.

Had he said too much? The doctor rubbed the stippled barley field of his hair.

As in, they haven't been written yet.

THE ALCHEMICAL GOLD STANDARD

Maybe to preserve some sense of collegiality. Or maybe to keep an eye on his librarian. Or maybe he had revealed too much. Far too much.

Or maybe it was simply to keep Christian abreast with current developments.

For whatever reason, Dr Rainer Fischer accompanied Christian Cartwright along the cliff-walk at lunchtime, where the heather and the Atlantic wind and his daughter-in-law's anamnesis spray had formed a kind of ready-made boudoir for their intimacy.

Was he conscious of this? Christian couldn't tell. The doctor was, as always, as opaque as that obsidian mirror.

But for some reason, the doctor began to talk about his ancestor, Montagu Cartwright.

Two churches, he mused.

Yes, indeed, Christian replied. I've heard the legend.

We could visit, together. The Celtic one in Karoly Vary. In whatever precinct it belongs to, of the West Asian Soviet. Although maybe it no longer exists. Along with the whole of the Czech-Magyar Democratic Republic.

After that dreadful apocalypse. Although everything does exist, in some form, as we've lately been discovering. The past, Christian, is just a catalogue of what should have been. The future, we have found, is a catalogue of what could be.

Could and should? There's a difference?

Our Investment Module, about which you expressed such scepticism.

Forgive me. I was corrected. Godel's theory of incompleteness—

I could add another clue. *Amphitheatrum Sapientiae Aeternae*—

That's the inscription on my ancestor's gravestone.

And perhaps he knew more than he ever pretended. When he designed this mansion—

It loomed before them, above the dark green pine trees, with its multiple turrets, its baroque profusion of chimneys. So many of them. Christian wondered if there was a fireplace in the mansion below that related to each, with its obedient, digital flame

—and that copper mine, do you think he was aware of the implications?

And here Dr Rainer Fischer unfolded his pocket watch, attached to his tweed waistcoat by an old-fashioned chain, although there was nothing old about the fob itself. Two small flat circular screens faced each other, of a thinness that seemed impossible. Two images danced above the heather, one a circle with a circle of words, displaying an alchemist's study. The other a mage, tangling with a serpent, with a triangle of the same words.

Can I let you in on a secret, Christian?

Was this the secret Sorcha mentioned? The horribly dead clairvoyant?

Please.

They have solved it, Christian.

Who, he asked, have solved what?

The board. What was impossible in the past became plausible, more than possible, inevitable, in the future.

What was impossible?

Alchemy. The transmission of copper into gold. A new gold standard, to reinstate the Bretton Woods Agreement, underlying all future currencies. The profits will be incalculable. Probably infinite. The board is finding its way here, as we speak.

From where?

As Chairman Willoughby told us, the future is presenting us with various options…

He closed his fob, with a digital bleep.

He strode off through the heather, towards his institute.

You want my advice, Christian?

Please.

Get in early… and stay in…

THE BOARD

It was odd, the locals agreed, to witness these unseasonal visitors to the town. Even the approach of Hallowe'en couldn't explain it. And they were male, all of them, much too old for the Billie Eilish Experience. They might have passed unnoticed in the middle of summer, on Moll's Gap, maybe, Kenmare to Killarney, but on the windswept late autumn streets of Castletown, with the fishing fleet docking for the winter, the leaves clogging the gutters, the mares' tails of waterfalls decorating the hillsides? What was odder still was the familiarity of these new arrivals.

They were already known, somehow, like the faces on photographs of distant relatives. But whose relatives were they? They knew them but didn't know how. Or why.

Those survivors of the almost forgotten Clairvoyant Program with their fading cinnabar codes knew how. But not why. They saw their dreams spreading, like a virus.

It was a common experience, after all. Don't I know you? I never forget a face. And nobody, they began to realise, ever forgets a face. But these new faces had another oddness. They seemed to morph, shapeshift with each new encounter, but still had that appealing – and eventually appalling – sense of familiarity. Like faces from a dream. But who can define a face in a dream? Who could stand before one of those sketch artists in the, by now, vanished cop shows and say, No, the forehead was a little broader, and the eyes were further apart, and by the way, why is it in black and white? Because these visitors from their dreams strode around their beloved streets in full colour. So, who could blame them if it took time, too much time in the end, to realise that their dull, but generally acceptable lives, their streets, with their Spars and their butcher's shops and their haberdashers, were being inhabited by figures that should have only populated their sleeping hours?

Fourteen members of the board. The Chairman had already arrived, so thirteen new visitors to be accommodated, settled in bed and breakfasts and whatever hotels still took in visitors. Taxis drove them to their destinations, uncertain as to where they'd picked them up. The only certainty being, as they glanced at that face in the rear-view mirror, that they had seen it somewhere before.

And they had, of course. Marge, with her meter ticking the kilometres from, where was it now? Allihies, Urhan or Eyeries…? Urhan, of course, if that's what the meter said – looked from her pale coded hands on the wheel to the genial face in the rear-view mirror and wondered, was it the face of a long-lost cousin or of an old flame from a forgotten school hop? And remembered her dream of several nights ago. The drip, drip of the metallic water from the copper gleaming roof of the old mine and the same figure walking towards her, suitcases in hand. Right or left? he had asked her, and she pointed left, with the same hand, the cinnabar code still visible.

Would the dreamt one remember the dreamer? she wondered, then shivered at the insanity of the thought.

There we are now, she said, and the meter did its charging, the ticker tape rolled out its receipt and the oddly shaped card accommodatingly beeped.

The same old-fashioned leather-embossed suitcases, she thought, helping this gentleman out with his luggage, into Gretchen's bed and breakfast by the old schoolhouse.

For they were all gentlemen, all thirteen of them.

By their suitcases, you shall know them, Gretchen realised. Their suitcases had pockets within pockets, zipped enclosures within zips. They seemed to unpeel, like onions from another dimension, to reveal spaces, scarves, shaving creams, whole three-piece suits that could never have been so enclosed. They concertinaed bigger into small, small into smaller and were never beyond the trick of revealing, as in a magician's flourish, a sou'wester tucked into a sock. Yes, she realised, they could pull anything from them, and not only that, they could stuff anything into them.

VISITORS

You've come a long way?
They were crowding her small cake shop, all searching for the same variety of honeyed donut, and Josie somehow knew.

They had come. A very, very long way.

Through time, rather than space. Sigmund's simultaneity worked wonders. Time was its métier, space its singular flaw.

So, one board member emerged from the shadows of the Interpretive Centre onto the main street in Eyeries as if trying to remember how to stop a taxi. A hand raised in puzzlement to scratch a greying head and the vehicle trundled to a halt, and he smiled, surprised at how easy that was.

Josie herself had dreamt of a flock of them emerging from the ruined engine room of the old mines, although flock was the wrong word – that was birds, wasn't it? A posse, more like it, all clutching suitcases, collars raised against the whipping wind.

And here they were now, buying her cakes.

Almost a goldrush.

Where did the thought of gold come from, she wondered, as she restacked the shelves that had been quite emptied by their rapid, futuristic fingers. Were the mines to be dug up again? Did those rare earth computer ores mix in with the copper? Did whatever intelligence they ran on find a way to turn it finally into gold? And by the way, did they pay for all those? she wondered. They did, she found when she checked the laptop, but with monetary apps and financial instruments she didn't recognise. She would have to pay a rapid visit to the bank, down the street. Cash it as soon as possible, then buy that new swimsuit in Blennerhassett's before the girl in the Chinese laid her hands on it.

She had to have a coffee morning, with other dreaming girlfriends. Thirteen and counting. They could compare notes on their fading tattoos, if tattoos they were. Notes on these déjà vu travellers, with their liking for honeyed donuts.

FIDELMA

Fidelma almost set the cat amongst the pigeons because of her growing impatience with her irritating angler, his requests for plug tobacco, advice on the best inland lakes and rivers and indeed the shore of the bay. Her annoyance was such that her recognition grew, and one night she dreamt of herself as a mermaid, would you believe, emerging happily from her home in the bay to find a hook in her mouth, which was already bleeding, attached to a line that was being pulled from the very inlet she had recommended to the visitor as best for a sea bass trawl. The hook had pierced her cheek and was ripping the side of her mouth, the blood vanishing in the white water, and her efforts to dislodge it with her tongue led to her tongue being pierced in turn. So, she was gagging blood and voiceless as she was being dragged to that V-shaped spot amongst the evergreen oaks where the sign read *SEA ANGLING* and bore pictures of bass and mackerel and flounder that could be caught there but no picture of Fidelma, the already hooked mermaid. And all she could hear in her dream, which was rapidly becoming a nightmare, was the pounding of surf and the monstrous clicking of the gleaming reel which was being wound in by none other than her angler, with his soft tweed hat and the smoke curling from his plugged pipe.

She woke with a gasp, covered in sweat, and it was one of those moments from which she knew there was no retreat. So when she saw him next in the crowded supermarket, it was hard to restrain herself from pointing a finger and calling out, he's the one from my dream, or my nightmare. It would have been lethal to do so, she realised, since the new arrivals strolled down every aisle, each of whom were surely part of another's nightmare, doing their shopping as if they were perfectly entitled members of the community. Strangers, maybe, but affable ones, and didn't they bring money to spend, like the tourists of old, and wasn't their money as good as anybody else's? Maybe we always dreamt tourists?

And a child ran past her in a Frankenstein mask, and she had to remind herself it would soon be Hallowe'en.

Maybe they had come for the party.

At which point, he turned to her and smiled. In a gesture of recognition or remembrance, he made the friendly gesture of casting an imaginary rod. Which was when she remembered a further dream. It contained a message, as in a moving, full-colour postcard.

She was at Josie's coffee morning. She was struggling to talk, to convey her fear of these recent arrivals. But she couldn't. She stared at her coffee-and-cake group, in the chintzy wallpapered room of the recently opened Petals Tea Shop, and they were all staring at her. Mouths open, at first. Then those mouths gradually reshaped themselves into ridiculous grins. They were laughing. The laughter was echoing round Fidelma's echo chamber of a brain. But no, she wanted to say, that's not the thing at all at all.

And the laughter changed into quizzical, polite and patient smiles. They could wait, until she got her voice back. So she stood, tried mutely to excuse herself, failed, made it to the bathroom. Where she saw, in the bathroom mirror, her lips sewed together with the bloodied needle that had sewed them silent, still dangling from the bloodied thread.

And she knew the message of this dream, as if it were a postcard stuck in the top pocket of her blue smock.

Keep your pretty mouth shut.

That's when she knew that face was a mask that could be pulled away like an orange peel, that said this is your mission should you choose to accept it, revealing the inhuman thing beneath.

TÊTE-À-TÊTE

But they were human. They were all too human. As Christian realised when Marcus Willoughby entered the Library of Traumatic Memory scraping his pipe of the remains of Nugent's Plug Tobacco and leaving the residue unceremoniously on the floor.

I believe you have questions, he stated bleakly.

I don't ask questions, Christian replied, trying to keep the tenor of his voice as close to untroubled water as it could be.

Asking questions, the angler replied, is not at all the same as having them. And I happen to know you have them.

Tell me then, Christian finally asked, where do you hail from?

Better ask when.

The future? I was always led to believe there wouldn't be one.

The future, the angler told him, is not the blasted apocalyptic nightmare of so many dystopian TV series, comic books and sci-fi novels. And I'm sure you've seen most of them.

Christian agreed he had. Probably all.

The future endlessly perfects itself. It interacts with the present only to perfect itself. It considers all options and chooses the one that suits its survival best.

Idiot me, said Christian. For having consumed the dystopian one so readily.

We could have written them ourselves.

Maybe you did?

And I'm actually writing one right now. As we speak.

You have a title?

From Carlsbad to Castletown. You like it?

Somewhat.

Or maybe, *Montagu Cartwright and Copper John*?

That has a ring to it.

A saga, bringing us right up to what you like to call the present day. It will end badly.

How badly?

Maybe that's down to you.

His eyes seemed to change colour. From flecked green to almond and then to green again. He dropped his eyelids as if to hide those changes, and Christian felt it safest to continue the conversation.

Your first?

No. My first published title was *The Angler's Guide to The Late Apocalypse.*

A success?

If anyone read it. I suppose it added to the dystopian delusion. Occluded the reality.

Which was?

Endless perfectibility. And the various modules of the Institute played their part in it. Even your partner's... And here the eyes narrowed, as if they wished to be party to a joke. And she is your partner, surely?

Isolde?

She's alive, isn't she?

Christian didn't know what to say.

Yes, she's alive. And I don't need your silence to confirm that fact. She survived a drowning, avoided a bath in arsenic. I know that. The board knows that. The doctor, it seems, doesn't yet. She'll even survive you, if you can bear that thought.

How? he asked. Very softly.

The Quantum Genetic Algorithm. It preserves. It ensures survival. It anticipates. It can view clearly its own, and by implication, its host's possible extinction. Its calculations are like those of Q on what used to be a Formula 1 racing tyre. You remember Formula 1?

I prefer the bicycle.

From the days of petrol. Large whining cars, like hares around a track. Q churned data by the millisecond, saw a wet slick to be avoided, a turn to be taken with greater or lesser torque. The QGA saw your beloved's tumble into that tunnel of arsenic and copper slag and saw only one outcome. Which is why she tumbled leftwards.

And that's why she survived?

So you finally admit it. She survived. The way this mansion has survived. By reason of the masonic capability built into its construction, from a handbook I gifted to your ancestor. *The Immaterialitie of Perfect Architecture.*

Isolde—

Beautiful name, by the way. Endlessly anagrammable.

You play with anagrams?

Soiled. Siloed. And others in languages that haven't been thought of yet. Her anamnesis spray, for example, will develop into a particle cyclotron that enables, strangely enough, my presence here. I and indeed the entire board are suspended somewhere in that future that is being constructed as we speak.

Christian thought of that kiss that would stretch time, beneath the midges in her husband's kitchen, themselves time-suspended. And maybe that kiss still existed, stretched itself the way the thin band of saliva between their lips had stretched. Maybe love bent time better than her spray did—

No, the Chairman muttered, as if reading his thoughts. One mimicked the other. And her anamnesis spray improved itself, the way the skin grafts the doctor had developed acquired a plasticity that he himself could never have dreamt of. Similarly, the heart valve that could survive generations grew with a momentum of its own and invaded the body's contours, much in the same way as the nervous system of an octopus spread through its eight-armed form. For example – the angler paused here and raised his left, non-pipe-holding hand to reveal an inner palm that pulsed as if the lined skin concealed an urgently beating heart – despite what you think of me, I am all heart. Cut me up like a conger eel and I will still beat. I will reassemble myself, change when necessary and then return, like a homing pigeon, to something like the original.

The original what? asked Christian.

The original me, the angler said, which is a duplicate of what I departed from, which sits with the other board members in perfect form, frozen, oddly enough, by your loved one's anamnesis spray.

Happy to be of such service, Christian said, and wished he had a secret button like the one that the aged tweed-costumed lady in those films of long ago – what were their names? Bond films, that's it, and what was her name? XYZ?

THE LIBRARY OF TRAUMATIC MEMORY

No, M, he remembered. A button to press, security to be called, and this shape-shifting fisherman to be dragged from his office, incarcerated in whatever mental hospital was closest. But there was no secret button, no more Bond films, and the nodding tweed bucket hat with its decorations of fish hooks and feathers seemed all too real.

And she herself – Siloedsoiled—

He coughed into a covered hand to disguise the gouts of brown spittle.

Forgive me – Isolde – must be congratulated for the part she has played in the Institute's development, as must you, in fairness. The very success of your efforts has led to the current unfortunate situation. So, you are to be, to use your beloved's anagram, siloed.

Siloed?

Let go. Your employment terminated. Because all of the Institute's programs, active or not, must henceforth be sublimated into one.

And let me guess, hazarded Christian. The Investment Module?

Profit, the angler continued. Which should be the goal of all of them, surely. You will still keep your stock options—

With the future compound interest reinvested in the present?

But there is a problem, the angler continued, restuffing the bowl of his pipe with Nugent's Plug Tobacco. Which is when Christian realised there was no such Nugent's Plug. Or there hadn't been for years.

A problem? Christian echoed, playing of course for time. There would be a denouement, he felt, to this encounter and it would be terrible.

Have you ever wondered how she invented it? That spray that froze living organisms in time?

She's an exceptionally brilliant chemist.

But the brilliance had to come from somewhere.

I'm confused.

And so you should be. And here I have to blame myself. You must remember those Greek and Roman myths where the god becomes a snake, a swan or a bull and impregnates a clueless human?

Vanity, you see – and he struck a match off his thumb. Did the resultant flare drain the colour from his face, or was it Christian's memory of an adipose, smiling face in a mystery whose name he couldn't quite remember? The Something Man? – undoes us all.

Third. His eyes were brown now, and shaded with a tear.

I conceived of a program. Various names were floated for it. For the process. In-vitro futurogametogenesis. Or was it futurum? But I should have recognised it as an absurdity from the outset.

He finally lit the bowl. The resultant smoke, it seemed to Christian, formed something like a question mark.

And the program turned no profit whatsoever.

No profit?

And the repetition here was to hide the horrible dawning realisation.

You see, even in our endlessly perfectible future, most people find eternity unbearable.

Most people?

There are some curious exceptions. To the rule—

The rule?

THE LIBRARY OF TRAUMATIC MEMORY

That death is not so much a design flaw as an essential feature. Life is fine, but what makes it tolerable for most is that it someday ends. So, my Eternity Program will prove stillborn, to use an uncomfortable metaphor. Apart from your beloved's anamnesis spray. Which, in a paradoxical way, enables this conversation, even now.

So you—

Yes, you've guessed it. I am her father. My genetic code travelled through the centuries, enabled by the anamnesis spray she would invent, by Doctor Rainer Fischer's Clairvoyant and In-Vitro Programs and entered her mother's womb in a unique experiment that's best forgotten.

I've already forgotten what you've just said.

But I know your library hasn't. So, I must ask for all of the codes. All of the files. All of the cross-referenced data of the Library of Traumatic Memory – in particular, its interactions with the Clairvoyant, the Anamnesis... in fact, with all other Institute programs – is to be surrendered. Before the entire board. At conference. Tomorrow night.

Tomorrow night? asked Christian.

Tomorrow night. And your stock options will be secured. With maybe even a bonus.

And Isolde?

Hers too. But on one inescapable, irreducible, ineluctable condition. That you tell no-one.

A secret, then?

From everyone. But most particularly from her.

Why would I tell her?

Why indeed? That she was born from a monster such as me?

He sucked on his pipe once more. Two threads of conical smoke streamed through his nostrils.

There will be NDAs, of course, to be signed.

Tomorrow is Hallowe'en night.

So?

Won't the board want to view our peculiar customs? Our quaint obsessions with the Celtic past? Masks, bonfires, trick or treating, to name just a few?

That evening when the dead rise? When ghosts walk?

He lit his pipe again.

We are your ghosts, Christian Cartwright. The board already walks in your dreams. One of the few pleasures we have. And the same board will want an index-linked file. Will check every memory stored on its retinal display terminal. All of your traumatic memories will be on view. Will dance for us. Like a Hallowe'en you've never seen before.

There was a threat there, without a doubt. Christian remembered the disembowelled, rust-coded body of Sorcha the Clairvoyant. Should he try to kill him here and now? But he had no emu to help him. All he had were his pale librarian's hands.

ETERNITY

So there had been a program. Designed by the Chairman himself. To be housed in the Forever Wing? How much information can the living take? Christian wondered as he cycled back. And there had been a deeper purpose for his beloved's anamnesis spray.

What could he tell her? She was perfect, that was all that he knew. That her perfection would still be there when his eyes had faded, that her unlined hand could one day be guiding his arthritic one across the town square, if there was still to be a town, or a square, was surely beside the point. There was a here and a now, a him, a her. Whatever was monstrous, and outside of time, was in that mansion.

He had a secret. Could he tell her? That while every father might be monstrous, hers was monstrosity in its Platonic, ideal form.

He could keep the secret. If he came up with a plan.

He had to weaponise her anamnesis spray. Whatever quantum variations the future had in store for it, its present iteration worked in miniature. There was no wind that evening, on the eve of All Hallows Eve, which might facilitate his plan, worthy of the alphabetic heroine of those Bond films of old, ABCQWERTY, no, M was her name.

He had two devices in his arsenal, one unknown to his adversaries. And he had no doubt now that Marcus Willoughby was as wily an adversary as any hero or heroine could ever come across. Heroics were not a humble librarian's thing, more suited to his lover's alter ego, Gaijin-Ra. But a librarian could always conjecture.

And plot.

The copper model on its bed of – what was the material again? Kryptonite? Zeolite? No, obsidian, he remembered. Montagu Cartwright's copper model, oxidised almost to a perfect verdigris green, was known to Christian and Isolde alone. And maybe one weapon could wreak havoc on the other.

He stopped by the graveyard of his ancestor's church, propped his bike against his gravestone and let himself in by the side door.

He blundered his way through the opaque interior – the moonlight provided just a wash of weak silver – to the pulpit and the lectern underneath. He pulled out the drawer and lifted the model gingerly from its resting place. He slid it into his backpack, made his way to the gravestone and read the inscription beneath the handlebars of his bike.

AMPHITHEATRUM SAPIENTIAE AETERNAE

He cycled home, through the windless moonlight.
You have your spray? he asked his lover, once inside.
Somewhere, she said, and what about my kiss?
This isn't really time for kissing, he said, but kissed her anyway. He couldn't resist it.
I want you to do your best with this.

He extracted the model carefully, oh so carefully. He remembered the damage the miniature bent copper chimney had caused.

Spray it?

No, not the mansion. Just the maze.

She burrowed amongst her things and came up with the nozzle. That he himself had designed, he remembered.

Why the maze?

You'll see why.

So she sprayed the miniature maze. A cloud of small winged insects revealed themselves, motionless in space.

What's the word for them?

Fruit flies.

No, the other word. With the silent p.

Pterygotes, she said.

They must have been there all the time. It took the spray to reveal them.

Should I be frightened?

Maybe.

Why are we doing this?

Come with me, he said.

The Harley roared through the ancient back roads. He clung to her waist like a supplicant and was blinded by the flap of her Gaijin-Ra scarf. He told her to take the old forestry route through the moonlit pines, and when they reached the circle of oaks round the ancient fort, he told her to cut the engine, so they glided on the slight downhill incline towards the maze.

The towers of the mansion were silhouetted by a bank of mackerel clouds lit by the moonlight. And they walked through the maze below it.

The barn owl, frozen in mid-flight, gave them the first inkling. The cauldron of bats, and he was proud to have remembered the collective noun, blackly frozen against the green privet gave them the second. A hare, immobile in the tangled grass, and they needed no other confirmation. The spray worked on the model like an entangled particle, a magnification in reverse.

HALLOWE'EN

She sprayed the whole mansion on Hallowe'en.
Christian entered several minutes later, the sole invitee to conference with the board.

The empty staircase his ancestor had designed was a blur of bugs, small arthropods and pterygotes frozen in something that must have been time.

The silent p, she told him, always frightened her. And he wondered, was his own terror a reflection of hers?

On the upper corridor, there were two sweet sparrows immobile in flight, one beak towards the other, as if in a suspended embrace.

Birds in an interior. Death must be on its way, he thought, and he hoped it wouldn't be his.

The door to the conference room was half open. A tangle of overhead wires, as before, spoke of mysterious intent.

And below them, immobile with an outstretched hand towards a group of board members, stood Doctor Rainer Fischer.

There was an odd stuttering effect to his immobility, however.

Christ – he began, then stopped, and tried to begin again.

Her anamnesis spray had problems with mass. With a two-hundred-pound humanoid of Dutch extraction, of a medical bent.

Christian, may I—

And his digital watch beeped, as if to remind him of something.

The same hand reached, in a stuttering, repeated gesture to the board before him.

—introduce—

Marcus Willoughby stood by a lectern, wearing an odd hat, pipe between his teeth. The cloud of tobacco around his head expanded then retracted again, as if attempting to breathe. It contorted itself into an anguished howl of silent agony, that reminded Christian of something.

An open mouth above a bridge, in an ancient painting. *The Scream.*

Marcus Willoughby's eyes flashed green and then almond-coloured and then green again.

How – he uttered, or tried to utter, the pipe shuddering by his trembling lips.

Christian wondered how long this dark magic could last.

Those eyes knew something.

So he exited, walking backwards, absurdly making excuses as he went.

Files, he muttered, I've forgotten some files.

And as he passed the Chairman, for some reason, he clicked his heels.

The eyes gave no response. But the hat seemed to tilt.

Christian recognised a Bohemian Jägermeister.

Then he shut the great metal doors and locked them once, twice and thrice with his Institute key.

He whispered into his eardrop.

Now.

Around the same time, Martin of Serendipity in an orangutan mask was throwing yet another wooden pallet onto the bonfire in the square. The effigy on top of the triangle of beer crates, rotten planks and driftwood wore a mask of a similar orange hue, topped by a plastic bouffant of yellow hair. Donald Trump had been burnt for decades on the peninsula, for reasons few could remember, the way Guy Fawkes was burnt on the larger island.

Behind the serendipitous orangutan came a figure out of an early arcade game, a ninja, to be exact, face occluded in a paisley-patterned abaya, with a bulging silk backpack which she threw into the flames.

Will it burn? The orangutan asked.

Let us hope, the ninja said. Maybe even melt.

The silk backpack burst into flame, revealing miniature verdigris chimneys and towers.

Outside the conference door, there was a faint smell of burning. Then fingers of blue flame began to flicker through the keyhole. The gap between the double doors grew into one yellow flaming pencil.

Lumps of already burning chimney came tumbling past the casement windows. Pieces of smouldering rafter came crashing through the ceiling.

Then a huge boom, which Christian could only think of as masonic, brought a rain of fire from above.

It was Sigmund, exploding in a cascade of glass and mercury vapour.

The door began to pulse, with the furies inside trying to escape whatever hell awaited them, from the melting bubble of the copper model on the bonfire in the square. Montagu Cartwright, Christian realised, was forged in older verities.

Amphitheatrum Sapientiae Aeternae, indeed. He knew his macro-micro business.

Christian thought it best to run.

Inside the conference room, the doctor was shredded into a thousand pieces by a falling chandelier. The board members proved oddly combustible, expanding like heated plastic, one of which would suddenly pop and engulf its neighbour in a molten substance not yet invented.

The burning embers of plaster added to the mayhem, gave it a ghostly, apocalyptic hue, as the invitees were decapitated by falling roofbeams, spattered like blood-engorged bugs by the weight of collapsing masonry.

Christian managed to unlock his bike, the handlebars already hot from the raging inferno.

He cycled back down the rutted avenue, the oak trees of the old Dunboy Castle gaunt against the flames behind him.

He made his way back to the town square, where his ninja lover danced a jig to a version of 'Cherish the Ladies' on Fidelma's tin whistle.

But the real inferno, Fidelma realised, was on the promontory behind them.

An apocalyptic yellow glow was licking the night sky. Strange contorted wraiths of embers soared towards the Milky Way.

Like ghosts, Martin murmured.

No, Isolde replied. Like a psychodrama in some future Ptolemaic system.

But there was one phantom cloud of something, that kept changing shape. They would have called it a murmuration of starlings, or a cauldron of bats, had there been any light left in the sky. But the only light that outlined it seemed to come from behind, or from within. It shimmered, this ellipse, stretched itself into a cigar shape, then back to an ellipse again.

Like a pheasant, Christian murmured to Martin watching the shape-shifting, or a ptarmigan. More like a pig, said Martin. All it's missing is a tail.

It was oddly appropriate, Christian thought, since the pigs of the peninsula had led to all this bother in the first place. Those organs, grafted onto porcine interiors, those sows with immaculate skin grafts, those piggeries, redesigned by the doctor as surgical experimentation stations, those algorithmic entry codes and decoy barnyards, to divert the animal rights crowd.

It was there, the next morning, on All Hallows Day, there again, that night, on the eve of All Souls, and Martin woke on the dawn of All Souls to see a thin, sausage-shaped outline in the sky over the smouldering Huxley mansion, as if drawn by a celestial pencil. It took the unseasonal blazing sun behind it to make it finally disappear.

PUCK FAIR

They used the last of their petrol to make the journey across the blasted peninsula to Killorglin, on what Isolde always referred to as the Kerry side of things.

It was some years after the Hallowe'en debacle, the bonfire of all bonfires. The coroner's report found just one charred skeleton inside, with dental work that was so immaculate in its symmetry that its source could not be traced. Maybe one day, the coroner thought, we would all be blessed with such molars. But on the peninsula, there was one missing person, so they assumed it was he.

Dr Rainer Fischer.

And it was odd, Christian thought, clinging to his beloved's back on the Harley, how rapidly the townland returned to normal. If normal meant a rather phlegmatically remembered past when things were better, when there was employment in something other than the three Fs – farming, fishing and freezing, in the refrigeration plant on Dinish Island. There were government grants to tide them over, there was the desultory summer influx of visitors, and the husk of the burnt Huxley mansion with the ruined Dunboy Castle became a feature of the Wild Atlantic Way, evidence of a peninsula history stretching back into the mists of neanderthal time.

It was easier to forget than to remember, after all.

And there were always weddings.

The wedding of Christian and Isolde took place in the deconsecrated Gothic church across the main street from what used to be the Catholic one, which now housed the Peninsula Interpretative Centre, always in need of government funding, and generally shuttered.

It was a humanist service. Almost, Christian thought, as the apple-cheeked celebrant began her recitation of vows, what Isolde had always wanted. A Quaker wedding.

It was to be a Quaker honeymoon anyway, dependent on contributions from the Society of Friends. The last of her dead husband's petrol had been siphoned from his dusty cans. A tent in a Kerry field would be their wedding bed.

Whatever she would give up, she would never give up the Harley. They wore sensible helmets now, being married, and took the back roads on the hinterland between both peninsulas, the mountain lakes flitting by them like flashes of quicksilver. The breeze in her face was like happiness, the trembling roar of the Harley between her legs like the tremble of life itself. She was alive and so was her beloved. The hillsides were smoking as she descended into Kerry. The gorse burnings had already begun.

She remembered the festival as a child, her mother lifting her tiny waist above the crowds to view the goat, far above, on his lonely, unsteady perch.

They parked the Harley, pegged the tent and headed towards the sound of distant music.

It was the sound of a banjo, on the wet August air. There was a desultory crowd around the base of the goat's perch, spilling out of the pubs. It had just rained and would soon rain again. The goat looked down, from his bales of straw and his triangle of hammered fencing, as bemused as the crowds below him. Whatever the significance of the event, it was lost on him.

Then Isolde saw, on the edge of the event, beyond the flat caps and the beanies, a rusting caravan in an adjacent field on deflated tyres.

A handwritten sign above it.

Clairvoyant, Fortunes Told

She asked Christian for silver, to cross the palm of Gypsy Rose, which was, she assumed, a pseudonym. He told her he had none. She reached her hand into her own biker's pocket and found a pebble of something better.

And why, she asked her husband, did these moments of revelation always announce themselves by the silent p? For revelation, she was certain, would be the outcome.

She entered then, and met the first member of the Clairvoyant Program, whose palm, when she placed the golden pebble across it, was marked with a pale, barely perceptible cinnabar code.

She was old, an impossibly lined face underneath a paisley headscarf, ringed with rusted medals. She took Isolde's perfect hand in her own ancient one. Isolde thought of a peninsula legend, of an ancient hag, who longed for a death that never came.

Forget about my palm, look at your own.

My own?

Your lifeline. Where does it end?

Where? Isolde had never considered the question.

It doesn't. It winds into the markings round your wrist, which lead who knows where, and emerges onto your other hand – and here, the gnarled, apparent gypsy grasped Isolde's left hand – and then goes into who knows where. Your holy of holies. You're a self-replicating system, your own eternity loop, and I know well why you've come to see me—

The program—

Yes. I was the first clairvoyant, the first to suffer the marks, the first to dream of the code, and I know what the first code led to. It led to you.

How?

Don't ask me how. In-vitro fts248 or whatever came after. Your father shot blanks, not to be polite about it, and your mother came to the doctor and asked for help. So, I dreamt of a thing that became you. A tiny speck in an ocean of nothing. But that speck hid a genetic code. That became a tattooed code. And like all of those codes, it came from the future.

She stood then, and the caravan rocked, and a parrot, sitting in a nearby cage, squawked. She pulled down her tattered paisley blouse, and Isolde saw the code, the colour of old rust, still visible on her withered breasts.

Have a look at your father.

My father?

Isolde could barely say the word.

And you won't die until you meet him. They constructed the what-you-call-it – spermy thing – out of the information on this and made that zygotey thing in your mother's womb with her eggs and the result is you. Standing here before me. They terminated the program then, don't ask me how or why. So, you were the first and the last. I saw your mother bloom with you, and it sickened me to know I was part of it.

And take back your golden pebble.

She flicked it, with her barcoded palm and it glittered in the air, under the parrot's bleak eye, and Isolde had no option but to catch it.

She pushed her way out of the caravan door and saw the goat first, way above the carousing crowds on its wooden perch. Below it, she met the concerned gaze of her husband.

One glance between them told him that she knew what he knew.

He asked her oddly, uncharacteristically, in the argot of Puck Fair.

What's the story?

The story, my love, she told him, is long life and happiness.

THE QUANTUM CONCEPTION

Was it like an illness? she wondered. No, it was the opposite of illness. But she felt she had entered a strange peninsula with a population of one.

She was born by way of the Quantum Genetic Algorithm in a way she didn't want to understand, out of a program that had been terminated because, in the future, it turned out, humans didn't want to live that much beyond their biblically allotted years. She alone would bear the burden of this aborted attempt at immortality, and it became his task, as he aged visibly before her eyes, to explain it to her.

This future, as the Chairman had told him, wasn't the blasted apocalyptic nightmare of so many dystopian TV series, films, comic books and sci-fi novels. It was endlessly perfecting itself. It considered all options and chose the one that suited its survival best. And he felt like an idiot, having consumed the dystopian one so readily.

They had proceeded from in-vitro gametogenesis, the creation of sperm from any piece of bodily tissue, to considerations of in-vitro hereditogametogenesis, the creation of sperm from dead bodily tissue, to in-vitro futurumgametogenesis, a term that would have become part of the medicinal lingua franca, outside the reach of the

Vance Wilson addendums to the Data Protection Acts, if it were not for the lack of demand for the whole enterprise. Some engineer in the future, with a nodding acquaintance to Greco-Roman mythology, was or would be lamenting his losses.

Should he have told her it was the Chairman himself? He couldn't have borne himself if he did. She was so vulnerable, stunned, tearful with the telling.

It would remain his secret.

So, the program became just one of the many the Institute had decided to abandon. Along with the clairvoyant venture, the Forever Wing and her own anamnesis spray, although she could take comfort from the fact that it gave birth to more usable patents than most.

There were ironies to this, the whole oddity of her, and, looked at in a certain way, advantages too. She could survive any cataclysm, much like the superheroes in those cinematic sagas of long ago. But there were disadvantages, the chief amongst them being that he was ageing before her. As the veins on the back of his hands began to stand out, those tiny blue clusters round the temples defined themselves as aquamarine, then purple. His eyes were losing their definition, that magic circle round the pupil was becoming blurred. She had never been pregnant and now didn't want to be, but sometimes walked as if she was, as if a hidden weight was pulling her down, towards the earth's surface. With one hand supporting her aching back.

You know what's happening? she asked, as he walked his bicycle back with her towards the cottage that would always be theirs.

Yes, he said.

We could have anticipated this?

No-one could.

Well, now that it's happening, who's the lucky one?

I am, he said.

You? she asked, and the lines around her ageless lips all creased into a smile.

Who gets to look at who? Who gets to see this aged, greying thing?

I do. And I know you're tiring. Let me cycle you home.

ALCHEMIC

She tried everything to keep pace with his ageing. Alcohol, drugs, cigarettes. Nothing helped. Nothing could mar that perfect unageing skin of hers.

How about suicide, he asked her.

You want me to kill myself?

No, both of us.

What if I survived it and you didn't? You want me to spend even longer without you?

So, she took care to document. Every one of his footfalls. That habit he had of slapping the heel of his loose sandal down before the sole. That intake of breath as he opened the wooden door to the sea. The occasional unintended sigh, when the thought of age, which would never arrive for her, would come to define him. That habit of humming an indeterminate tune to himself when melancholy took him over. She kept a diary first, then thought words were too shifting, too malleable a record, and she began to paint.

She painted him against those seascapes, always with the horizon hovering halfway above the base of the canvas.

Why halfway? he would ask her.

Because that's the way I see it.

They chose a burial place. On a small island with a rusting cable car. It was a pre-famine graveyard which for some reason seemed appropriate. Rows of sagging white crosses which led down towards the churning Atlantic.

He died on 21 September, and it happened this way. She was finishing another canvas, playing with his suggestion of raising the horizon line, ever so slightly. It was yet another version of her common theme, the white-flecked waters of the bay, and she was playing with the froth of the largest wave, a combination of cream-white and Prussian-blue to suggest the presence of a creature underneath causing the disturbance, a dolphin, a narwhal, even a whale. He had been working on the courgette drills, and she had thought of adding that detail, an aged figure in gardening clothes, an upright shadow on all of the horizontals, when she glanced up again from canvas to window and realised he was no longer there. She could see nothing but the churning white wave. She ran to the door, kicked it open and saw his prone body underneath the sagging spade.

She lifted him, hoping for one last word, one last breath, but there was neither.

And she finally understood why the program was aborted. Life was fine, but what made it tolerable was that it someday ended. The end was the thing, of course, to be managed, made acceptable, painless, even blissful. Had she managed that, for him?

The dead end for her meant that, unfortunately, she would keep on living. Maybe even long enough to meet her genetic donor in the future. Embrace him, punish him, even, quite possibly, kill him. The curious one, as Christian called him. And she herself had time to wonder, was he the bucket-hatted angler himself? Chairman of the Board? In which case, she could have killed him already.

She would have many years to contemplate it all. She could meet him in the future and finish the job. Slowly, exquisitely. Or maybe eternally. Like that Prometheus. And so, she had to find herself an eagle with a taste for liver.

But her future would be without Christian.

Unless, of course, she did manage it. Killed herself. Standing by that old pre-famine graveyard, stamping down the damp earth she had spaded over his hand-built coffin, fixing the small triangular arrangement of wood into the covering soil, the prospect seemed increasingly enticing. But perhaps her conception had already anticipated that possibility. Perhaps she had been refined with a self-replicating carapace that reconstituted its damaged self. And perhaps there was only one way to find out.

She looked out across the wild Atlantic. She had always been an indifferent swimmer and could imagine herself sinking underneath those waves, meeting him in whatever afterlife the jagged peak of the Skellig monastery had once promised. And no time like the present, she felt.

So Isolde said, I love you, Christian, one last time and filled her pockets with graveyard stones, clambered down the old broken cliff, surprised by the suddenness of the beach below when she reached it.

Sudden. How could this beach be sudden? It was the steep fall of the cutaway in the cliff, created by the beating waves, which ate into the graveyard above, storm by storm, year by year. She could see the broken wood of an ancient coffin, and the gleam of old yellowing bones exposed in the shale of the cliff face. She wondered how many souls had been sucked onto this stone beach, carried away by the foaming waves.

Well, here goes one more, she said, to the gulls, to the exposed bone, a femur, she now recognised, and to the smooth pebbles by her feet, with which she further weighted her pockets.

She walked in then, and felt the waves around her boots, the calves of her denims, eventually, her arms and chest. And then she saw it.

The curling, white-tipped peaks of a mountain range. A whole Himalaya of foam was growing before her eyes. No, not growing, it was hurtling towards her. The apocalypse at last, she thought, before it hit.

So the Chairman lied, she thought, before the maelstrom fully embraced her. She was in the whirring washing machine of time, tumbled like her own underwear and only felt sweet relief. For something like an eternity.

Then eternity ended. Something's wrong, she thought. Eternity shouldn't end.

She emerged from the brine.

Was she Aphrodite now, she wondered, rising from the foam of the immortals?

Then she fell on her face. Tried to stand again, crawling like a beetle or a scarab and realised what was weighing her down.

Stones in her pockets.

No, she wasn't Aphrodite. Maybe the peninsula hag, weighed down by substance, condemned once more to raise her face and open her eyes.

Two figures, throwing lines into the quiet tide, burnt by the morning sun.

She was on a sandy beach. Golden, perfect sand. The same sun, rising beyond it, illuminating a tranquil sea.

The apocalyptic sea had embraced her, churned her, maybe even drowned her. But she recognised this beach. She had survived.

She watched the fishermen throw their oddly shaped nets into the blazing sea. The nets billowed, as if with wings of their own, weighted with hooks at the corners that darted beneath the waves. The fishermen pulled and the nets thrashed, enclosing a horned creature that she had never seen before, in her present or her past.

She was in no-time.

Her own time.

Whether it was two minutes since her most recent death, or two centuries, it didn't matter to her.

She shook the stones out of her pockets and dropped them in the golden sand that sparkled yellow. She bent down then, took a handful of the sand, let it spill through her fingers.

And the sparkle came not from the incandescent sun, or any metaphor it suggested.

It came from flecks of gold, that once must have been copper.

She was on the beach below the mine. The beach created by the mine. The sand, created by the copper smelting. The copper, mined by the infernal machines created by Montagu Cartwright.

Au 79, she remembered from her student days. Gold. From Cu 29. Copper.

What alchemy was this, she wondered as she walked. Back through the sloping town which oddly enough seemed unchanged by the passage of years. Past a pub she remembered as Austy's. A figure with a triangular hat, smoking by the open doorway.

Looks like rain.

But it didn't. It looked like the first morning of creation, and the sun was up now, spilling over the beach, setting the gaily painted doors of the town ablaze.

She thought of asking him. Had he heard of the Amphitheatrum Sapientae Aeternae? The Philosopher's Stone? Did he know the Chairman, Marcus Willoughby? Did he know the Chairman, Marcus Willoughby? Could she find an eagle, with a taste for liver?

But all he talked about was the weather.

She ascended the slope. The colours of the housefronts were unearthly, as if the passing years had found new pigments. Or as if the morning sun had set them ablaze.

There was the crest of the hillside, and the dark skeletal finger of the old mining towers.

The sign was long gone, DANGER ARSENIC POISONING, but the pit was still there, leading down into even more unfathomable depths than the ones she remembered. She balanced at the edge of the microcyst and remembered the Jaguar's tyres skewing to a halt.

Before the roar of the exhaust-pipe and the fall.

The rock crumbled underneath her and she fell again. Somehow, she wasn't surprised. She fell weightlessly, as if borne on an eternal machine designed by Vitruvius or Tycho Brahe. In some ways she fell forever. She might be still falling. Her skirt flowering around her knees, as if kept there in an upside down tulip by the updraft, floating through glittering tunnels of copper and gold.

But it wasn't a mine-shaft. The sparkle of gilt came from something other than microcyst in the tunnelled walls.

It came from gold-embossed bindings.

Books, their ancient spines arrayed in shelves that stretched away from her into Euclidean infinities.

Of course, she thought. A library. Well, why not.

Ascending or descending, she couldn't be sure. Was she falling or flying? She was definitely doing that tulip float, her dress held down by her ageless hands.

One hand grabbed at a volume to steady herself and a blizzard of white resulted, slowing her descent.

Descent. Her dress deflated from a tulip to an orchid. So, she was falling.

Was it snow? No, she couldn't remember snow. It was an endless flutter of paper. Paper old, new, unread, maybe even unwritten.

She landed, into a bed of ancient words.

She saw a title on the broken spine.

The Immaterialitie Of Perfect Architecture.

A globule fell into her hand. What was it? A crumpled Post-it? A piece of Blu-tack, placed to mark a forgotten page?

It was an eardrop.

She placed it in her shimmering ear.

She heard a familiar voice.

Hello you.

Don't tease me, she said.

I wouldn't ever.

So are you for real? She asked.

As real as you were, when I cycled past the Silver Dollar Bar.

She could see a shadow now, moving through the vertiginous avenues of shelves.

It had the walk of her very own Christian.

But wore a three piece suit, an Edwardian hat.

Her eardrop trembled.

I've been dreaming of you, he said.

Can you dream when you're dead?

All you can do when you're dead is dream. I've been filing those dreams here.

He appeared and disappeared through the ancient bays.

In my library.

She moved past row after row of glittering book spines, to keep him in view.

Your Library of Traumatic Memory?

So long ago. They could be dreams.

Aha, she thought. So that's where we are.

Tell me one.

Under 'I' for Isolde. I dreamt we rode from Puck Fair to Moll's Gap on the Harley.

That's not a dream. It happened.

Are you sure?

I'll never forget it.

Maybe someone else's dream.

Whose?

Maybe Sigmund's. To be filed under 'S'.

He came into her bay. The dust settled as he moved towards her.

I would take any dream, she said, as long as you were in it.

Then he took her face in his hands once more and kissed her.

And her golden lips melted.

They heard a howl then, of eternal agony. It echoed through the library stacks, with the beating of wings.

What's that? She asked.

The Chairman. Chained to his own particular shelf. Filed under 'C'.

An eagle brushed through the endless bays, the glittering spines of gold-embossed books. It flexed its talons, opened its curved beak.

For eternity?

Let's find out.

Acknowledgements

To Neil Belton, without whose insights and enthusiasms this novel would not exist.

Thanks also to Karina Maduro, Katrina Harvey, Megan Harris and everyone at HOZ who was kind enough to read and improve the manuscript.

To Keith Lindsay, Dashiel, Daniel and Brenda Jordan for their early readings and responses.

My pirated copy of *The Angler's Guide to the Late Apocalypse*, (Ad Astra, 2091) by Marcus Willoughby afforded invaluable glimpses into what the future holds. His *Montagu Cartwright and Copper John*, (Ad Astra, 2092) published in the following year is remarkable for his insight into a period so far beyond his own. *The Immaterialitie of Perfect Architecture* by Magnus Wilderstein (Lazarus Zentner, 1601) offers an alternative to the prevailing aesthetic and has too long been out of print.

About the Author

Neil Jordan is an Irish film director, screenwriter and author. His first book *Night in Tunisia* won the *Guardian* Fiction Award (1979). Since then he has published nine novels, for which he was awarded the Irish PEN Achievement Award (2004) and a memoir, *Amnesiac*. In 1996 the French Ministry of Culture awarded him the title of Officier de l'Ordre des Artes et des Lettres. His films have won him world-wide recognition, including an Academy Award (*The Crying Game*) two Golden Lions at Venice (*Michael Collins*) and several BAFTAs (*Mona Lisa, The End of the Affair*). He lives in Dublin.